H
SISTER'S
CHILD

BOOKS BY ALISON JAMES

HER SISTER'S CHILD

ALISON JAMES

bookouture

Published by Bookouture in 2020

An imprint of Storyfire Ltd.
Carmelite House
50 Victoria Embankment
London EC4Y 0DZ
www.bookouture.com

ISBN: 978-1-80019-269-0
eBook ISBN: 978-1-80019-268-3

PROLOGUE

She rolls over and reaches out instinctively into the space where her baby was placed.

Her hand hits air, and flaps redundantly.

She sits up in bed and looks around her, head jerking wildly in first one direction, then the other. Perhaps someone lifted the baby off the bed and put her in the Moses basket. She squints over at the corner of the room, but where the Moses basket sat before, there's just a patch of grimy carpet.

It's dark in the room, although she has no idea what time it could be. She stumbles out of bed and switches on the light. But this only confirms it. There is no baby.

She checks her stomach but it's flattened, the skin still slightly domed, but flaccid. The sliding, shifting movement of tiny limbs has stopped. She has definitely given birth; she didn't dream it. But in that case the baby should be here next to her, lying next to her on the bed. That's how things were when she crashed out. But the baby is gone.

Someone has taken her.

PART ONE

2019

1

PAULA

Paula Donnelly's trainers dislodge the gravel as she walks along the cemetery path, sending little sprays of stones onto the grass. She's alone.

She is usually alone when she comes here, every March 15th. Occasionally at Christmas too, if the weather isn't too hostile. Small clumps of narcissi shine brightly in the sunshine; the sort of fickle spring sunshine that comes and goes constantly. Paula has no sooner put her sunglasses on than she has to take them off again, every time the sun vanishes behind a cloud.

In loving memory of Elizabeth Jane Armitage
15ᵗʰ March 1979 – 22ⁿᵈ July 2003
A much missed daughter and sister. In our hearts always

'Hello, Lizzie.'

Paula crouches down and brushes stray grass cuttings from the stone. It isn't really true, what's written there. The name and dates are true, obviously, but 'much missed' was something of an exaggeration. The same with 'in our hearts always'. Why else would Paula be the only person there today?

'You'd be forty today, eh?' she observes. 'Flipping middle-aged.'

Except that her sister wasn't middle-aged, had never even got close to that milestone. Unless you counted the way she looked when she died: twenty-four years old, but her face and body by then so ravaged by years of alcohol abuse that she looked all of forty: more.

Paula makes a clearing in the grass directly in front of the stone and sets down the small plastic pot of primulas she has brought with her. She doesn't like to leave cut flowers, because they look ghoulish when the flowers wilt and rot inside their cellophane wrapping. She hears a crunching on the gravel behind her, and the footsteps come to a halt somewhere just behind her left shoulder.

'All right, Paul?'

She turns around to see a balding, bulky man looking down at the stone. Uncle Alan, their father's twin brother, who always had a bit of a soft spot for Lizzie. He's the only other person who ever shows up here, albeit infrequently.

'Thought I'd come today seeing as how, you know… it's her fortieth.' He extends a sheaf of garage-forecourt carnations, which will turn brown with decay in the way Paula hates so much.

'They're lovely, Alan. Shall we see if we can find something to put them in?'

There's a small shed at the far north-eastern corner of the cemetery with a tap and an assortment of pots and vases gathered up by the groundsmen. Alan shambles after Paula and watches mutely as she finds a faded ceramic plant pot, fills it with water and arranges the carnations in it, tossing the cellophane into the bin.

'That looks nicer, don't you think?'

He nods. 'She'd like those.'

The truth is that Lizzie couldn't have cared less about things like flowers, but the fiction is comforting. They return to the grave and place the pot next to Paula's primulas, standing there in silence.

'Shame, you know, isn't it?' Alan observes. 'That she's got no one else to remember her.'

She should have, Paula thinks. *She should have had a sixteen year old standing here, remembering.* Except if her son or daughter had been around, maybe Lizzie wouldn't even have died. But she doesn't say anything to Alan, because he – like the rest of the family – never knew about the baby. Nobody did, apart from herself.

'Shame that she and your mum never made things right,' Alan goes on. 'Or your dad, before he passed.'

Paula nods.

'Does your mum ever come, you know… to visit her?'

She shakes her head, then – keen to change the subject from her family's failings – asks, 'Cup of tea?' There's a family-run Italian café opposite the cemetery: a North London institution that has been there forever.

Alan shakes his head. 'I better get back. The trains and that.' He and his wife Shirley now live in Chingford. 'Just wanted to… you know… pay my respects.'

'Well. Thanks for coming. I appreciate it.'

They exchange a brief, awkward hug and Paula heads back to the station to catch the overground to Palmers Green. When she lets herself into the house, all is quiet. Her children – fourteen-year-old Ben and twelve-year-old Jessica – are usually returning from school around now, hurling backpacks to the floor in the hall, loudly demanding whether there are any snacks before thundering upstairs to carry on their peer-to-peer interaction via their smartphone screens. Sometimes they linger with their friends, chatting in the street or going to the local fast-food place for a burger or fried chicken, just as she did when she was a teenager. Since it's Friday, with the heady freedom of the weekend beckoning, it's probably one of those days. Paula's part-time job takes up Monday, Tuesday and Wednesday every week, plus the occasional Thursday if the dental practice where she works is short-staffed.

Biscuit the dog paces around her, eager to get outside for some exercise.

'Just a minute,' she tells him. 'I'll take you out for a walk when I've had a cup of tea.'

It occurs to her that talking to the dog when they are alone in the house is a sign of going soft in the head, of spending too much time on her own. She has been divorced for four years now: sometimes that feels like a lifetime, and sometimes it's as though Dave only moved out yesterday. She flicks the switch on the kettle, and tosses a teabag into a mug. While she's waiting for the water to boil, she walks over to the battered bureau that used to belong to her grandparents and now sits under the kitchen window, its surface littered with unpaid bills, till receipts, letters from school. She rummages through one of the drawers and pulls out a well-thumbed photograph, its colour faded.

It's a picture of her and Lizzie taken when Paula was still at school. Lizzie was already an alcoholic by then, but she is having one of her better days. Her face is thin, but has not yet taken on the grey, sunken cast of the hopeless addict. Her straight brown hair is freshly washed, the sunlight on it making it gleam almost gold. Paula has her left arm around her older sister and is leaning her head on Lizzie's shoulder, strands of her own, wavier hair curling against her sister's neck. They are both smiling. Paula tries to remember who took the photo. Was it their father, still alive at that point? Or their brother, Steve?

Paula thinks about the child she has always believed Lizzie gave birth to, not long before her death. Had it been a boy or a girl? Was he or she still alive? As a teenager she'd been left confused about whether Lizzie had even been pregnant at all. Her attempts to settle that confusion had come to nothing. Now, with the perspective of adulthood, she is quite certain that she was.

'I'm going to find out, Lizzie,' she says out loud, speaking so firmly that Biscuit stands to attention, thinking it's time to leave. 'If it's the last bloody thing I do, I'm going to find the truth about your baby.'

2

CHARLIE

'Are you going to Nadia's party?'

Charlie's best friend, Hannah Watson, follows her out of the classroom at the end of double maths and links arms with her, swinging her backpack by one shoulder strap.

'I don't know.'

'Okay, so I've decided to wear my sparkly crop top and that black pleather skirt… what are you going to wear?'

'I said I don't know if I'm going.' Charlie is terse.

Hannah swivels her head and lets her mouth hang open in faux shock. 'Easy there, missy! Jesus, what's put you in such a bad mood?'

Before Charlie can answer her, there's a scuffling at the end of the corridor, and a whirling of male limbs as a group of the boys in Year 13 approach, thumping each other as they go. At the centre of this human Catherine wheel is Jake Palmer. He's widely acknowledged as the school's alpha male: tall, with dark blond hair cut in a fade, and brooding, slightly slanted eyes.

Instantly, Charlie drops her gaze to her feet. And Hannah, of course, notices.

'Oh Jesus, Char, please tell me you're not still obsessed with him. I thought it was all over between you guys?'

'It is,' Charlie mutters, pulling her phone out of her blazer pocket and pretending to be engrossed in something so that she can avoid eye contact. Jake's friends grunt and point at her as they pass, digging him in the ribs and making obscene gestures with their tongues and fingers. She feels her cheeks burn.

'Why don't you come over to mine now,' Hannah asks, 'and we can go through outfits, yeah? And watch some smoky eye tutorials on YouTube.'

'I can't.' Charlie pushes her phone back into her pocket and hoists her bag up on her back. 'I need to go to the shops.'

'I'll come with you, then we can go back to mine.'

'No!' Charlie snaps, and before Hannah can argue, she breaks away from her and walks off quickly down the corridor.

Once she's out of the school grounds, she heads to the nearest parade of shops. The small, family-run chemist will expose her to too much scrutiny, so she walks a bit further to the supermarket that has a pharmacy section and the anonymity of self-service checkout machines.

By the time she gets home, she has three missed calls and five WhatsApps from Hannah. She ignores them, locking herself in the bathroom and unpacking the small blue and white box, briefly scanning the instruction leaflet before peeing on the tip of the stick. Then she replaces the cap, shoves it into the pocket of her school skirt and goes into her room to wait.

And, just as she feared, there is a blue line in the second window.

She looks at the plastic stick with a shiver of shock, a lurching sense of disbelief. The instructions say it clearly, and it was even shown in the photo on the front of the pack. A second blue line means pregnant.

Her hand comes up to her mouth as she stares at the stick. Then she rocks back onto the bed, closing her eyes. She pictures his face as he thrust into her, lost in his moment of ecstasy, and quite oblivious to her. But this baby is his, so he has to know about it. He has to know what he's done.

*

The next morning, before she has even climbed out of bed, Charlie is decided. She will tell him today. After all, it's not like she's just missed a period: she hasn't had one for over two months. A small, but persistent, shelf of flesh is starting to appear above her pubic bone. Nobody has said anything yet. But they will. They will notice.

Over breakfast her mother complains that she's being moody. She suggests it's a case of PMS. If only.

'It's not bloody PMS, okay?' Charlie snarls. 'What the hell would you know about it?'

Her little brother Olly stares at her open-mouthed, pausing with his cereal spoon halfway to his mouth. Milk trickles off the corner of the spoon and drips onto the tablecloth and their mother dabs at it, irritated, as Charlie slams out of the kitchen and heads for the stairs. She shouts up them after her daughter.

'Charlie! Come on, we don't have time for this! You need to leave for school, or you're going to be late.'

Charlie wrenches open her bedroom door, shouts, 'I'm just getting ready!' then slams it again. Sitting down at her dressing table, she scrutinises her reflection in the mirror. If she's going to confront Jake, she needs to make sure she's looking her best. She sweeps foundation over her face, buffing it in with a brush in short, expert strokes. Then she contours and highlights – a routine so practised she could do it in her sleep – and creates full Insta-brows over heavily shadowed lids and two coats of mascara on her eyelashes. Finally, a matt lipstick in a natural pinky-brown. Her reflection is now glossy, her olive skin gleaming, the dark brown eyes popping in the required fashion. She takes a selfie, for good measure. For good luck. Sends it to Hannah, as a matter of habit.

Her mother thrusts the bedroom door open. 'For God's sake, Charlie, what do you need all that make-up for? You're going to school!'

Exactly, thinks Charlie. *Exactly*.

*

Jake Palmer could have his pick of the girls at Bishop Hereward School. This is one reason why Charlie won't even approach him unless she's looking her best. She knows she's pretty. Quite pretty. But not stunning. If you ranked all the girls in Year 11 according to their relative prettiness, then she would probably be around the seventieth centile. She knows how that works because they covered percentiles in their maths GCSE coursework.

And even with her Insta-ready face on, approaching Jake is difficult. He is holding court in one corner of the playing field, his faithful henchmen flanking him: other boys from Year 13 – Lewis Jeffers, Scott King and Mikey Thomas. Wherever Jake goes, they go.

As Charlie walks towards them there is nudging and snorting.

'The missus is incoming,' she hears one of them say.

'Hardly the missus,' Jake scoffs. 'Only had her once.'

Charlie feels the hot rush of shame scorch her cheeks. She meant to be bold, and brazen, but is automatically lowering her gaze. Her school bag is clutched across her midriff at an unnatural angle.

'All right, slag?' asks Mikey. He calls everyone 'slag'. She ignores him.

'Jake, I need to talk to you.'

'Ooh,' chorus the henchmen. Honestly, they're like a bunch of cackling women.

'Grow up,' she snaps at them, then addressing Jake adds, 'Alone.'

He slides off the wall he's sitting on. 'Okay.' He shrugs. The bell rings for the first lesson and the group starts gravitating in the direction of the classroom block. 'Not now. After school,' she hisses at him. 'I'll text you.' She isn't about to arrange a meeting in front of the others: it will only increase the chances of them showing up too.

*

That afternoon, Charlie waits for half an hour in Memz, the Turkish café near school that they visit occasionally, as a break from the favoured fried chicken outlets or McDonald's. She nurses a Diet Coke, desperate to eat something but not trusting the waves of queasiness being stirred by the smell of frying food.

Jake swaggers in, scuffing his shoes with an exaggerated motion. He slams his bag down on the table, spilling her Coke.

'What is it?' he asks. His deep-set blue eyes flash. He seems annoyed.

'I need to talk to you.'

'The thing is,' he says, cutting across her. 'I've been thinking about it, right, and I don't think we should hang out any more.'

She feels her stomach plunge. 'Why not?'

He shrugs. 'It's not working.'

'But…' She is genuinely confused. 'We had sex. I thought we—'

'So?'

That one, callous little word. Just the one syllable, containing a whole world of humiliation. She pushes her chair back, groping for her bag, unsteady on her feet.

'What did you want to talk about?'

But she can't tell him. Not now. Brushing tears from her eyes with the back of her hand, she shakes her head wordlessly and hurries out of the café.

Back at home, she shouts at Olly for going into her room to borrow her charger, swears at her mother and snaps at her father when he gets back from work.

'I don't remember her sister being like this,' she overhears her mother saying to her father. Charlie has an older half-sister from her mother's first marriage, who is now at university.

Her father murmurs something that sounds like assent, then: 'I wonder what's got into her.'

'Probably boy trouble. I'll try and talk to her.'

Charlie sits miserably on the edge of the bed, only half listening to her parents' conversation. Her mind is on Jake. In a sudden burst of fury, she snatches up her phone and sends a message on WhatsApp, employing capital letters to express her rage and frustration.

I'M PREGNANT. JUST SO YOU KNOW.

Trembling, she lies back against the pillows, and waits for his reply. She thinks about how much she loves this room, painted in storm grey with a huge hand-painted sunset across one wall, built-in shelves painted white and overflowing with books, photos, athletics trophies, girlish memorabilia. She tries to imagine a baby in here, but it's impossible. What will she do with a baby? Where will it go?

Ten minutes later, her phone buzzes with a text. She snatches it up, but it's from Hannah. As ever, the message has no punctuation, very much like Hannah when she talks.

What's going on with you you're being weird

There are now two blue ticks visible on the message she sent Jake, so she knows he has read it. An hour later, there is still no response. She bursts into tears, burying her face in the pillow to try and disguise the noise of her sobs.

There's a light tap on the door and her mother walks in. She sits down carefully on the edge of Charlie's bed, resting a hand between her daughter's shoulder blades. She says nothing, just waits for the sobs to subside. Eventually Charlie rolls over onto her elbows and hauls herself into a half-sitting position. Her mother is holding something in her hand.

Charlie squints at it, at first not quite recognising it, then realising with a jolt what it is. The packaging from the pregnancy test. She left it in the bathroom bin, meaning to go and dispose of it more discreetly later. Her eyes flick up to her mother's face and she bursts into noisy tears all over again. Her mother holds her, patting her until the gulping and sniffing quieten.

'I don't know what to do,' Charlie gulps. 'It's not like I want to have a baby. But after everything that… I can't not have it. You know I could never give a baby away. Not like *she* did.'

Her mother strokes her hair and Charlie looks up at her, defiant. 'Surely you can see there's no way I'm ever going to put my own child through what happened to me?'

'I know, darling.' Her mother pulls her in for a hug. 'But don't worry, this doesn't have to be the end of the world. We'll sort it out.'

3

PAULA

'So, you're coming with me to the pub quiz tonight, Paula?'

'Whoa, give me a minute, Jode!' Paula has only just arrived at the dental clinic where she works as receptionist and practice manager. She takes off her coat and hangs it on the peg on the back of the door, positions her bag underneath the reception desk and boots up her computer terminal. 'What quiz, where?'

'The Dog and Gun in Finsbury Park. Remember – I told you about it last week.'

Jody, the practice nurse, picks up a stainless steel tray of probes, mirrors and plaque removers and loads them into the autoclave in the sluice to sterilise them. She's nearly a decade younger than Paula; a tall, slender girl with her auburn hair scraped up into a high ponytail.

Calum Whittaker, the senior dentist in the practice, arrives and goes straight into the staffroom to change into his white tunic, calling, 'Any coffee going?' over his shoulder.

Paula switches on the coffee machine in the little kitchenette behind reception and follows Jody into the sluice room.

'So who's going?' she asks, watching as Jody pulls on latex gloves to sort the sterile equipment.

'There'll be loads of people there. It's always really good fun. A couple of mates of mine are going, and we need a fourth to make up a team.'

'I don't know… the kids—'

'—are old enough to take care of themselves for a couple of hours,' Jody cuts in, briskly. 'Come on, Paul, you said yourself you need to get out more! How long have you been single now?'

'Four years.'

'Exactly. Time you made a bit of an effort, girl.'

Paula opens her mouth to speak but Jody brandishes a drill bit at her. 'No more lame excuses: you're coming.'

'Will you be gone long?' Jessica asks as Paula comes down the stairs. There's a hint of a whine in her voice.

'I shouldn't think so,' says Paula. 'It's only a pub quiz. It'll be an hour tops, and then maybe a drink afterwards.'

'What are we going to eat?' Jessica pouts, winding her skinny little body around the newel post of the staircase.

'There's a pizza in the fridge – Ben will put the oven on and cook it for you.'

'But, Mum—'

'It's a pizza – not rocket science! I think the two of you can manage that. And there's ice cream in the freezer for afterwards.'

'But I don't get why you have to go at all! You never go out on school nights.'

Which is exactly the point, Paula thinks, but she's not about to tell her daughter that. She's not going to explain that Jody thinks it's high time she got herself out there and started meeting people. That having become a mother at only nineteen she's never really had an adult social life, and she wants to try and make a start now. She appraises herself in the hall mirror before she grabs her coat, trying to see what the other people in the pub will see. A woman of average height, her build athletic rather than curvy. Wide-set, hazel eyes, fringed with the lash extensions which are her monthly splurge at a local beauty salon. She's put on a pretty top and some red lipstick, and the mid-brown hair that used to be so unruly when she was young is now a glossy shoulder-length bob, thanks to the miracle of GHD straighteners. She looks all right. More than all right.

'Don't forget one of you needs to take Biscuit out for a wee,' she instructs her daughter, then heads out into the night.

The Dog and Gun in Finsbury Park is busy, and noisy. Paula and Jody weave their way through the gaggle of demob-happy office workers to the area at the back of the saloon bar where the quiz is being held. Paula is introduced to Andy and Bhopal, friends of Jody's who are making up their team, and someone fetches a round of drinks. Answer sheets and pens are passed around and discreet glances thrown at the other teams to try and gauge their own chances of success.

As Paula sips her Jack Daniel's and Coke, she notices a man on one of the other teams who keeps looking in her direction. She tries to concentrate on the questions – 'What is Ginger Spice's real name?', 'What is the capital city of Lithuania?' – but every time she looks up, his gaze is on her. Jody has noticed and nudges her, whispering that she's made a conquest. There's something vaguely familiar about him, but Paula can't place it. Uncomfortable, she avoids eye contact.

'It's Paula Armitage, isn't it?'

After the quiz is over, and they're leaving the pub, he appears in front of her, blocking her path.

'Paula Donnelly now,' she says, nodding.

'You don't remember me, do you?' He smiles down at her, and it all floods back. The older brother of Jason Shepherd, who was in her class at school. How could she have forgotten that smile, and those eyes, the colour of washed-out denim, that used to make her heart flip when she was a teenager?

Johnny Shepherd.

'Oh my God! It's you!'

Paula is grateful that in the dim light of the pub Johnny can't see her blushing as she says this. *What a moron I must sound*, she thinks.

'Well, well, well… little Paula Armitage.'

'Donnelly,' Paula repeats.

'You're married, then.'

'Divorced.'

Johnny grins ruefully. 'Snap.'

Paula remembered hearing that he'd eventually married his glamorous long-term girlfriend, Karen, but that it hadn't worked out. They were a couple for so long that she's having trouble getting her head around the idea of a single Johnny Shepherd.

'Stay and have a drink with me?'

'I should get back to the kids really.' She hesitates.

'Just a quick one. Then I'll run you home: I've got the car here.'

Paula glances over at Jody, who is engrossed in conversation with one of the women from a rival team. 'Okay, why not?'

'How are the family?' he asks easily, once he's bought drinks and they've found a table. It's as though they last spoke mere months ago.

'My dad's dead, my mum's in sheltered accommodation, and Steve's still working in the Middle East, on and off.' Johnny's looking at her intently, which makes her feel awkward. 'So, where are you working these days?' *Stick to neutral topics*, she decides. *Nothing heavy*.

Johnny tells her that he owns and runs an event staging contractor's, and she tells him about her job running the dental practice. Then they talk about Ben and Jessica, and the fact that Johnny and Karen never got around to having children.

'I would have bet my mortgage you and Karen would have a bunch of kids by now,' Paula says. 'You always seemed like such a solid couple. And Karen was so gorgeous. When I was at school, I wanted to look just like her.'

'Karen's great.' Johnny smiles to indicate that he's not harbouring a broken heart. 'We're still on good terms. We just grew apart.'

'And you were never tempted to marry again?'

'There've been a couple of relationships that both lasted around three years. But I was never tempted to tie the knot again. Once bitten, twice shy and all that. How about you?'

Paula swirls the ice cubes in her gin and tonic. 'With Dave, it was just a case of me being far too young. We started going out when I was sixteen, married at eighteen, a mum by nineteen. I had no idea what I really wanted. No idea who I was. Dave was a bit older, had a secure, well-paid job in software sales, foot on the career ladder and all that. My parents approved. And I suppose I just wanted to do the sensible thing after…'

She allows her voice to trail off. Jody appears at her elbow. 'Taxi's waiting outside, Paul, we ought to get going.'

Paula stands up, gives Johnny a little wave and turns to go.

'Wait!' He's following her out of the pub. 'Just a minute, Paula, there's something I want to talk to you about.'

Jody raises an eyebrow, but Johnny waves her on. 'It's okay, love, you get your taxi. I'll give Paula a lift.'

'No, wait, Jode, I'll only be a second.' She turns to face him, frowning, arms crossed against the chill of the air outside, after the warmth of the pub.

'Paula, now I've bumped into you, I do really need to talk to you. I need to talk to you about Lizzie.'

For a few seconds, everything goes in and out of focus. Paula moves back towards the side of the pub, leaning against the wall to give her support. Her legs are shaking. A pool of light spills out of the front door every time someone pushes it open to leave, the shadows coming and going, coming and going, along with the inebriated chatter from inside. She gathers herself.

'Lizzie died. Sixteen years ago now.'

Johnny nods as he lights a cigarette. 'I know.'

Paula reaches for Johnny's cigarette instinctively, taking a puff to calm her nerves, even though she doesn't smoke.

'Then what is there to talk about?'

'Have dinner with me, and I'll tell you.' He hands her his phone. 'Give me your number so I can contact you to set it up.'

Paula obeys dumbly, then stumbles towards the waiting taxi.

4

CHARLIE

'It's for the best.'

Charlie's older sister places a freshly brewed cup of tea on the night stand, then stands there, next to the bed. Her tone is encouraging and she manages a smile, but Charlie knows that she thinks this whole situation is a disaster. A shit-show. She would never have ended up in a mess like this herself. Not the oldest child, the perfect golden girl.

'I'll come with you, if you like?'

Charlie shakes her head, biting her lip.

'Okay, well the offer's there if you change your mind. Drink your tea, and then try and get some sleep.'

But Charlie doesn't sleep, not at all. Tomorrow she is booked in to have a termination at a private clinic. A couple of weeks ago, her parents came together to her room to talk to her. She knew straight away that this was not good. Her father rarely comes into her room, and a joint visitation is unheard of. He lowered himself awkwardly on her desk chair, and her mother positioned herself on a corner of the bed.

'You've always done so well at school, Lottie,' her father began. 'Always been so bright, such a strong student. It would be a terrible shame to disrupt your education now.'

'And at sixteen you're really far too young to have to deal with the responsibility of parenthood,' her mother said, picking at the silver-grey throw on the bed to avoid looking her daughter in the eye. 'It's not all smiley, chubby little limbs and adorable baby clothes. It's dealing with all-night crying jags, and exploding nappies and toddler tantrums. It's not something that's always going to be... fun.'

'I'm almost seventeen.' Charlie had jutted her chin. 'And I'm going to make it fun,' she had said with more conviction than she felt. 'I'm going to be a chill kind of parent.'

Her parents had exchanged glances.

'Look, it would be one thing if you had any support from the baby's dad,' her father had continued. 'If he was prepared to share the responsibility—'

'He might. You don't know that he won't. He just needs some time to get used to the idea.'

'Sweetheart...' Her mother reached out and tried to squeeze her hand, but Charlie pulled it away. 'We went and talked to Michelle Palmer, and it was pretty obvious to us that the family doesn't want anything to do with the baby.'

Charlie already knew about this confrontation, which had achieved nothing other than to ramp up the giggling and the sniggering at school. Because of course Jake had made sure to report the visit to his mates. It was so shaming.

'It's a very minor procedure at this stage,' her mother was saying. 'Over very quickly, and there should be no adverse effects. But it needs to be done soon. Obviously.'

'It'll be for the best, darling,' her father urged.

'Okay, okay,' Charlie agreed, simply to get the pair of them off her back, to make them leave her alone. 'I'll do it.'

Her mother drives her to the clinic, which is in a broad, leafy street in Hampstead.

'All set?' she asks. Her smile looks forced, and she's acting as though they are on some sort of girly day out. A treat: shopping or a trip to a spa.

'I want to go in on my own,' says Charlie fiercely, gripping the overnight bag she has packed. She almost certainly won't need to stay in overnight, but was told to bring things just in case there's a complication and she can't be discharged.

'I need to sign the paperwork, since you're under eighteen,' says her mother, patiently. 'And to settle the bill.'

'Okay, but I don't want you to stay.'

'All right.' Her mother sighs. 'If you're sure. I'll be on the other end of the phone if you need me.'

Once her mother has left, a nurse leads Charlie from reception and through to an area not unlike the women's changing rooms at the local swimming pool. There is a strong smell of floral air freshener, underpinned with antiseptic. Somewhere on the other side of the door, Charlie hears a sound like surgical instruments clattering onto a metal tray. She flinches. The nurse hands her two blue cotton gowns and a pair of turquoise slipper socks.

'Get undressed – everything off including your undies – and put these on. The second one goes round you like a dressing gown. There are lockers in there for your stuff. Keep the key with you, then come through to the day room and wait until you're called.' She gives Charlie an encouraging pat on the arm. 'It'll all be over with soon.'

Charlie does as she's told and shuffles into the day room in her stockinged feet. There's a low table with out-of-date magazines on it, a water cooler with plastic cups and some rubber plants. Two women sit in the armchairs. One flicks through a magazine, glancing nervously at the clock. The second, who has a cannula in her hand and has clearly been through her procedure, has her knees hunched up under a cotton blanket, her face pale and pinched.

Charlie stares at her for a few seconds, then turns around abruptly and hurries back to the changing area. She dresses quickly, bundles the gowns and socks into the laundry basket and walks back through reception with her bag over her arm.

'Charlotte?' the receptionist calls after her, but Charlie does not turn around, ducking her head as she swings through the revolving door and quickly onto the street. She rounds the corner and leans on a brick wall, catching her breath. In a nearby garden, two cats are fighting. A passing police siren drowns out the sound. Life is carrying on all around her. And there is life inside her. Charlie reaches down and touches her slightly rounded abdomen reverently. Her parents keep telling her that it's just a few cells, but she knows that's a convenient lie.

It's not cells, it's a baby. Her baby.

Four hours later and she has twenty-three missed calls from her mother, six from her father and two from her sister. Her sister has also sent a text.

> Mum said you walked out… I understand you're scared, and you panicked, but I'm here if you want to talk xx

Charlie does not want to talk. She hadn't panicked either. Deep down, she knows she never intended to get as far as the operating theatre. She only went along to the clinic to get her parents off her back. With her mobile switched off, she wanders around for a while, buys herself a muffin and a hot chocolate, then when it starts to rain, takes a bus up the Finchley Road and then on to Brent Cross, where she can at least wander around without getting wet. She finds an ATM and withdraws some cash, then roams the shops for another three hours as she waits for the thin, damp-streaked spring daylight to completely fade.

Once it's completely dark, she does the only thing that makes any sense to her. She goes to find Jake.

*

The Palmer family live in a drab flat in a concrete block in Lower Holloway. He has frequently referred to Charlie as 'posh' or 'snobby' because her family lives in a pretty detached villa in the much more salubrious Dartmouth Park. She rings the bell at the street entrance to the block. Nothing happens. She tries again, then tries phoning Jake's mobile. The call is cut after three rings.

A young man in Lycra cycling gear emerges from the flats, wheeling his bike. He looks up at Charlie, smiles, then props the door open for her to go in.

At the front door of Jake's flat, she rings the bell, then raps lightly with her knuckles. After a few seconds there's a scuffling sound, and voices. The door is yanked open by Jake's mother, Michelle Palmer. Her highlighted blonde hair is scraped back and she's wearing a tracksuit with pink slippers so fluffy they completely engulf her feet.

'Oh,' she says, irritated. Her eyes dart to Charlie's stomach. 'It's you. What do *you* want?' She's holding an e-cigarette, and breathes out a cloud of mint vapour.

'Is Jake in?'

Without a word, Michelle retreats into the flat. She's speaking to someone, and Charlie recognises Jake's voice instantly. That's what infatuation does to you.

'He's not in,' says Michelle, reappearing a few seconds later.

'But I just—'

'Like I say, he's not in.'

The door is closed in her face.

Charlie walks slowly down Archway Road, tears rolling down her face. She has a further five missed calls from her mother and three from her sister, along with several voicemails, and as usual there's a series of WhatsApps from Hannah. Instead of listening to the voicemails she dials Jake's number, over and over. Every time it rings out.

She phones Hannah.

'What's going on?' Hannah demands. Without waiting for an answer she continues her customary rapid-fire delivery; Hundred-Miles-An-Hour Hannah is not her nickname for nothing. 'Where are you? Why weren't you in school today? You haven't been reading my messages. There's a ton of rumours going round about you and Jake Palmer.'

Charlie bursts into tears.

'Christ, Char, what's wrong?'

'Can I come over?'

Charlie uses some of her cash to take a black cab to the Watsons' house in Noel Park. 'Han, I need to stay the night,' she says, as soon as the front door is opened to her.

'Mum, okay if Charlie sleeps over?' Hannah yells over her shoulder, into the house. Hannah's father, a paramedic, is out on a late shift and her mother, a beautician, is threading eyebrows in the small back room that serves as her treatment room. There's no reply. 'It'll be fine,' Hannah reassures her. The two girls frequently stay at one another's houses and Charlie still has her overnight bag with her. She composes a quick text to her mother before switching off her phone.

> *Am at Hannah's but don't come over here or I'll just leave.*
> *Need time to get my head together.*

Loud sounds of gunshots erupt from the living room, where Hannah's brother Ethan is playing a computer game. 'Come upstairs…' she commands, darting into the kitchen to grab a large packet of tortilla chips, 'and tell me *everything*.'

Charlie waits until they're positioned side by side on Hannah's double bed, for all the world like an old married couple. 'I went to get an abortion,' she says, bleakly. No point dressing it up for her best friend.

Hannah's lower jaw drops. 'Shut the front door!' she hisses. 'So it's true… you were pregnant? Only there was *so* much gossip. About you and Jake Palmer… What was it like? Was it horrible?'

'I didn't have it.'

'Oh my God!' Hannah's eyes widen and she fans her face with overdramatic hand gestures. 'So you're still pregnant?'

Charlie nods. 'I just couldn't do it.'

'Does that mean you're keeping it?' Hannah's eyes widen still further. 'And… hold on… do your parents know? That you didn't go through with it?'

'They must do by now. I haven't spoken to them, though. I don't want to go home. Not now. I can't.'

'So, what are you going to do?' Hannah's voice is practically a squeak. 'I mean, it's cool for you to stay here for now, obviously, but like, not forever.'

'I don't know.' Charlie leans her head on Hannah's shoulder. 'But I'll have to think of something, won't I?'

The next morning, Charlie sits at the Watson family breakfast table and eats a bowl of cereal and three slices of toast, allowing Hannah's mother to believe that she's going to go to school.

'You've not got your uniform,' Mrs Watson observes, raising an eyebrow in query.

'I'll pop home and change on the way,' Charlie tells her. She wonders if the others can hear, or even see, her heart pounding in her chest. Because she has no intention of going to school. 'First period is independent study.'

She says goodbye to Hannah at the bus stop, then catches the 29 bus in the direction of Dartmouth Park. It's Thursday morning. She knows her father is at a site meeting and it's her mother's day to go to her office. Ollie will have been dropped at school and her sister has just returned to uni and won't be back until the summer holidays start. The cleaner only comes on a Tuesday. So the coast will be clear.

Before she's even had a chance to put her key in the front door, her phone rings.

Mum calling.

This time she answers it.

'Lottie, thank God! Are you okay?'

'Yeah, I told you, I stayed over at Hannah's.' This, at least, is true.

'Only the clinic phoned yesterday and said you didn't go ahead with the… procedure. They wondered if you wanted to book another appointment.'

'No,' Charlie mutters. 'I don't. I'm keeping it.' She unlocks the front door and walks into the kitchen, helping herself to a banana from the fruit bowl. Pregnancy makes her starving all the time.

'But, sweetheart…'

'I've got to go. I'm supposed to be at school.'

This is also true, if misleading. Charlie slings the banana skin into the bin and goes into the small room off the hallway that acts as a home office. She opens the drawers in the filing cabinets that her highly organised mother has labelled with things like 'Passports', 'Birth Certificates' and 'Utility Bills'. She pockets her own passport because she has a feeling that what she has planned will require formal ID, then after flicking through two drawers she finds what she's looking for: a file labelled, 'Savings – kids'.

Charlie knows – because her parents have shown her – that it contains a building society passbook in her name. Her maternal grandmother opened savings accounts for her and her siblings with a deposit of £15,000, and every Christmas and birthday sends a very generous cheque to top up the total. She also knows, because her sister talked about it, that after the age of fifteen the account was switched from a Child's Saver to a Young Adults account, with a debit card. The debit card has not been handed over to Charlie because the account is intended to be for her university expenses. But she knows it exists.

She opens the file and flicks through the contents. The passbook is identified easily enough, and fastened to it with a paperclip is a manila envelope. Charlie knows from just touching it that it contains a bank card and a paper statement for the new account. She takes it out and strokes the embossed letters of her name reverentially. She has a Monzo account for her pocket money and occasional earnings from babysitting, but this is different. This gives her access to – she checks the balance – just under £30,000, including interest.

Charlie smiles. This changes everything, she tells herself. For herself and for the baby. And the first thing she's got to do is tell Jake. He won't be able to ignore her now.

5

PAULA

Johnny Shepherd phones Paula a few days after the pub quiz night and suggests they meet that evening. She agrees.

'Great, it's a date.'

'Um… is it? Not a proper one, surely? I thought you just wanted to talk.'

'Relax, it's just a figure of speech.' He laughs that easy laugh of his. 'But it can be if you want.'

'It's a bit soon for that, I'd say.'

Of course she is attracted to Johnny. How could she not be? She's had the biggest crush on him since adolescence. But that crush was based on him being a distant, unattainable figure. She doesn't know how she feels about him suddenly being around, and apparently available. It feels ever so slightly wrong.

'Don't worry, Paul, this isn't going to be anything heavy. Call it two old mates meeting up for a bit of a chinwag. Like I said, I've been wanting to talk to you. About Lizzie.'

That clinches it. Over the years, no one – not her husband or her close friends – had been the slightest bit interested in what happened to Lizzie Armitage. Dave had actively avoided any mention of her. And here, out of the blue, is someone who *is* interested. Someone she already knows and likes. If all they are going to do is talk, where's the harm?

'Okay then. Where?'

'At Giovanni's. Where else?'

Giovanni's Trattoria in Green Lanes has been around for fifty years and is something of an institution for people like Johnny and Paula, who have grown up in the area. It was the venue for special family occasions, birthdays and anniversaries.

'I can't believe this place is still going,' Paula says, sitting in the chair that Johnny has pulled out for her. 'I remember coming here when my cousin got a place at university.'

Johnny grins. 'It was where my dad had his fiftieth. We reckoned it was posh.' He looks around at the white tablecloths with their red napkins and faux Tiffany lamps, the fixtures in heavy, dark wood. 'That was nearly twenty years ago, and it looks exactly the same. Even the waiters haven't changed.' He glances at a stooped and grey-haired man who is bringing them a bread basket.

Paula smothers a giggle. 'Everyone knew Giovanni's back in the day.'

'Which is why I thought it would be fun to meet here. Hope it wasn't too far to come from Palmers Green.'

She shakes her head. 'I got a minicab. Only took about ten minutes. How about you? Did you have to come far?'

'About the same. I've got a place in Hornsey now, since the divorce.'

Paula gives him a long look, taking him in. He's wearing a plain, pale grey T-shirt under a blue blazer, with well-cut jeans. His blue eyes are bright in his slightly tanned face, and he's smiling that ready smile. He still has that swagger, that innate chutzpah.

'You look really nice tonight, Paul,' he observes.

She has deliberately not dressed up too much, and kept the make-up subtle so as not to give the impression of trying hard.

'This is not a date, remember,' she tells him, with mock sternness.

'I know, I know, I'm just saying.' He pours her some red wine from the carafe the ancient waiter has brought them. 'I'll be honest, I've not stopped thinking about Lizzie since we were in the Dog and Gun. Her death was alcohol-related, wasn't it?'

Paula nods, takes a mouthful of the red wine and pauses with the glass in front of her face, saying nothing.

'So… what happened exactly?'

'Abdominal aortic aneurysm. It's when a blood vessel ruptures in your stomach. Happens very quickly. She was on her own. A couple of days later a neighbour got worried about the curtains staying drawn and got the caretaker to let her in. The first Mum and I knew about it was a visit from the police. We were away on holiday when it happened.'

'I'm sorry.' He touches her hand briefly and she sees that he still has beautiful forearms. He must be nearer forty than thirty now, but he's in great shape. 'Is that, like, an inherited thing?'

Paula shakes her head. 'If you're an alcoholic you're at higher risk of it happening. And her liver was shot to pieces, anyway.'

'Such a waste.' Johnny looks genuinely sad.

The waiter brings them a plate of antipasti. Paula spears a piece of prosciutto with her fork. Johnny waits, fork poised, until the waiter is out of earshot. 'This is going to sound weird,' he says, 'but didn't Lizzie have a baby?'

The shock is so profound that Paula can only stare.

Eventually she recovers herself. 'Who the hell told you that?' she demands. She's vaguely aware she sounds rude, but doesn't care.

Johnny takes a large gulp of wine and offers the bottle to Paula, but she shakes her head. 'I used to work for the police part-time as special constable, and I'm sure I remember there being a house-to-house enquiry a few months after her death. It was talked

about around the Tottenham station where I was working, and
when I saw the name Elizabeth Armitage on the paperwork, of
course I recognised it straight away. As I recall, the door-to-door
was to ask people about a baby that she'd given birth to. A baby
that disappeared.'

He waits for Paula to speak, his expression kindly, concerned.
'Hey, are you okay? You've gone really pale.'

She nods, but still feels shaky, blindsided by this unexpected
revelation. 'I went round to her flat a few days before she died. She
was passed out, alone, and I just thought… well, I didn't know
what to think. I assumed that if she'd had the baby, it had been
taken by someone.' The words tumble out of Paula's mouth in
a rush. She hesitates. She has never talked to anyone about this,
not since it happened. 'But before I had a chance to check on her
again, Mum and I went to visit my great-aunt, like we did every
summer. And then she died. But it would make sense that she'd
given birth, because another risk factor for aneurysms is pregnancy.
So it would add up.'

'So what did happen to her baby? Did you ever find out?'

'That's the thing,' Paula says. 'The police never said anything
about it when they came to tell us Lizzie had died. Afterwards, I
even went to the police station and checked. They said she was
definitely on her own when she was found dead.' She pauses,
remembering. 'It's a weird coincidence, but that was the day you
gave me a lift, when I left Wood Green police station. I remember deciding not to say anything to you about it, though. I felt
uncomfortable talking about it.'

'Wood Green nick wouldn't have been much help to you.'
Johnny raises his wine glass to his lips, his expression intently
focussed. 'It was Tottenham that handled the enquiry, so I doubt
your statement ever got tied up with Lizzie's file. That was the early
days of computer records, and separate police stations couldn't
automatically cross-reference cases, I'm afraid. And as I remember

it, the police never found any evidence of the baby's existence, despite the investigation.'

'She was pregnant before she died,' Paula says firmly. 'I saw it.'

'Did you tell anyone about this? Your parents?'

Paula nods. 'I told Mum after Lizzie died, but she just said that heavy drinkers often get very swollen stomachs. That her pains were probably just cold turkey or something. Afterwards I went to see the social worker and *she* implied the same thing – that the baby never existed – or else that it had died and Lizzie had covered up the evidence. But I didn't believe it. I never believed that Lizzie was capable of doing something as calculated as that. She said she'd go and check on Lizzie, but it was just to get rid of me, I'm sure. Her visit was supposed to be on the Monday, but the very next day Lizzie was dead.'

'Odd that she was so keen to shut the matter down…' Johnny takes another swallow of wine. 'Could your mum be right, though, with the liver disease theory? It would explain the absence of a baby.'

'But I felt the baby kick: I wasn't imagining it. Her stomach was huge.'

Johnny thinks about this for a few seconds, sipping his wine again. 'The social worker must have been right, then: that the baby died. Otherwise she and her colleagues would have arranged for it to be taken into care pretty smartish. They're not going to leave the baby with – no offence – a drunk.'

Paula shakes her head. 'But if that was the case, wouldn't the police have come to the same conclusion?'

He shrugs. 'I expect they did. But back then violent crime in that part of London was at an all-time high. I know it sounds harsh, but there simply weren't the resources to devote to finding the probably deceased kid of an addict.'

Paula feels herself growing agitated. She takes a few slow breaths to calm herself. 'Listen, Johnny, I was only a kid myself at the time, and I didn't know how to go about finding anything out. Official stuff. My parents didn't want to know; just shut the whole subject down after Lizzie's funeral. Mum sank into clinical depression and I was constantly scared of making her worse. When I was a bit older I tried phoning social services about it, but they said you only have a right to access child protection information if it regards yourself or your own children. I've tried searching the register of births, but there's nothing.'

The waiter brings their main courses, and once again they fall silent until they're left alone.

'Maybe the baby survived, and Lizzie gave it away; you know, realised she couldn't cope and dumped it somewhere? Or gave it to someone she knew?' Johnny talks through his mouthful of *melanzane parmigiana.* 'You hear of these things happening. Perhaps you could look up records of abandoned babies in London for that period?'

'I suppose I could.'

Johnny's eyes are bright; he is clearly warming to the challenge of an unsolved mystery. 'I'll bet we can find something if we get a bit of outside help. Like I said, I worked as a PCSO for a bit: I've still got contacts in the police.'

But Paula is shaking her head. None of this is making any sense to her.

'Why would you do that?' she asks, taking a forkful of risotto. Her tone is wary. 'Why would you care?'

Johnny sets his own fork down on the table. 'Lizzie would be forty if she was alive, right?'

Paula nods.

'And I'm forty-one. We were at Turnbull Comp together; she was in the year below me.'

Because Lizzie and Paula's secondary schooling hadn't over-lapped, this hadn't occurred to her before. When she had been at Turnbull Comprehensive herself, she knew of Johnny only as

Jason Shepherd's older brother. But of course it made perfect sense that Johnny and Lizzie had been school friends.

'She was quite something, your big sister.' Johnny's face softens. 'Such a larger-than-life character. Always up for fun. If there was a party of any sort, she was always the one instigating it.'

That must have been when the drinking started, Paula thinks sadly. Out loud, she says, 'I wish I had known her then. Known what sort of a person she was, outside our home. Well, I mean, I did, but I was only little, so she wouldn't have confided in me about her social life. She was great when it came to playing with me, mucking about, but we were never confidantes, not even when I was older. By the time I left primary school, she already had an alcohol problem and had moved out.'

'Lizzie was a real pistol. So full of energy. And bright, too. She should really have gone to university.'

'So you and she were good friends?'

Johnny looks right back at her, and she sees the start of tears in his eyes. 'We were more than that. She was my girlfriend. My first real love.'

Paula is shaking her head slowly. 'I'm sorry, I had no idea. Or maybe she mentioned you, but I don't remember it. If I had, of course I would have said something to you sooner.'

'It was only a short-lived thing; maybe that's why she never thought to tell you about it. When she got heavily into the drink I never really saw her any more anyway. But I used to keep an eye out for you, because I knew it was what she would have wanted.'

'Again, I just wish I'd known.'

Johnny pushes his plate away from him. 'Well, you do now. And you know I meant it when I said I'd like to try and help you. There must be a way of confirming that there really was a baby.'

Paula sighs. 'There *definitely* was. At the time I suppose I found it easier to pretend to swallow the line I'd been fed by Mum – that Lizzie had looked pregnant because of liver disease. I mean, my gut instinct told me otherwise, but I started to tell myself that my eyes must have been playing tricks on me.'

Johnny pours himself more wine. 'But you don't think that now?'

She shakes her head, firmly. 'Definitely not. And especially after what you've just told me about the police investigation. And because since 2003 I've been pregnant twice myself. I know exactly how it feels. And when I touched Lizzie's stomach, I felt a limb moving under my hand. It couldn't have been anything else. From what I understand of cirrhosis of the liver, it takes quite a long time to show, and affects the upper abdomen. Lizzie got really big really quickly, but the shape was the shape of a pregnant belly. She was so skinny that it was obvious.' She flushes slightly, made self-conscious by the way Johnny is focussing on her face. 'Again, having kids myself clinched that for me.'

'And Lizzie only told you what was going on – have I got that right?'

'Me and her social worker. Mary, I think her name was. No – Miriam? I remember her face, but not her name... the one who said the baby might have died. Like I said, I went round to her house to confront her in person.'

'Wow – you actually went to her home?' Johnny looks impressed.

'By complete chance I knew where she lived. Lizzie told me herself. She used to like to drink with her mates at this pub in Muswell Hill called the Half Moon. But she said that she'd found out her social worker lived on the same road as the pub, so she didn't like going there any more in case she bumped into her. So I just looked up the address of the pub.'

'But you didn't know the house number?'

'No, but I knew what car the woman – Mary, Miriam – drove, and I spotted it. So it was easy enough to pick out the house.'

Johnny beckons the waiter over and asks for coffee. 'So what did Lizzie think happened to her baby?'

Paula sighs heavily. 'The last time I saw her was when I went back to her flat a few hours after it would have been born, but she'd been drinking and passed out. So obviously I couldn't ask her, and I never got another chance to go back there and speak to her before she died. Even at the best of times it wasn't easy to find the chance to visit, and that week Mum and I were on our annual trip to the seaside.'

'What about the baby's father? Did you ask him what happened?'

'He was a druggie called Macca. Most of the time he was too out of it to know what was going on. He went to prison for robbery around the time we lost Lizzie.'

'Could his family have intervened? Taken the baby?'

Paula puts down her fork and wipes her mouth slowly with her napkin. 'That's what the police suggested when I went to ask about it. I suppose it has to be a possibility. God knows how we'd find them, though. I've no idea what his real name was.'

'And nobody else knew? Not even your family?'

She shakes her head. 'I tried to tell Dad but he didn't want to know. Mum and Dad had washed their hands of Lizzie by then.'

'If you want my opinion, the social worker's as good a starting point as any. She has to be, surely?' Johnny tops up her wine glass. 'I mean, she might have been right about it being a stillbirth or neonatal death. But why not put that on the record? Why didn't she speak to the police straight away?'

'Exactly. That's what I've always thought.'

'Well, the good news is, you know where she lives.' Johnny pours out the dregs of the bottle, raises his glass and clinks it against Paula's. 'So we know where we need to start. We're going to pay a visit to that house in Muswell Hill.'

6

CHARLIE

At least she knows exactly where, and when, to find him.

Her long-standing obsession with Jake Palmer has given Charlie a comprehensive knowledge of his habits and usual haunts. True, he is leaving school this summer, so his timetable is less regimented, but she knows where he and his friends usually congregate at lunchtime – the Chicken Cottage on Junction Road – and later that morning she is ready to waylay him when he arrives. While she waits, she checks her phone. About twenty WhatsApps from Hannah, and a text from her mother.

> *Mr Pollard has just phoned to say you're not in school. Please tell me what is going on. Daddy and I are worried about you M xx*

Charlie composes a reply. It's important to keep her parents happy for the time being.

> *I'm fine, going in later. Will probably stay at Hannah's again tonight xxx*

As she looks up from her phone, Jake and his entourage are approaching, just as she had anticipated.

'Hey,' she says, making an awkward salute with one hand.

His initial reaction is surprise, then his face darkens. 'See you in a bit, bro,' he tells Lewis Jeffers, moving away from the group.

'Have you got rid of it?' he asks. 'Only your mum told my mum you were going to.'

Charlie shakes her head. Jake mutters something under his breath, then turns to go back to his friends.

'No, wait, Jake! Things are different. I need to talk to you about something.'

She's thought about this constantly for the past twenty-four hours, rehearsed what she's going to say. While she and Jake don't exactly know one another intimately, she knows a fair bit about his home life. That he and his mother argue constantly. That he hates his stepfather. That all the household attention and resources are directed to his younger half-siblings. With no school to go to in a few weeks' time, and no work lined up, Jake will be trapped in the flat, in the family environment he claims to despise. She can offer him a way out.

'I was thinking,' Charlie falters, worried she's going to sound like a complete moron. 'We could get a place. Live together.'

'Oh, yeah, right. With what money? Your parents going to pay, are they? Like fuck they are!'

He turns to go again, but Charlie thrusts the statement in his face. 'Look! £28,978. It's mine.'

'You're winding me up!' is his first reaction. 'This is some bullshit you and that Hannah have cooked up. You don't have that money!'

'I'm not.' She reaches into her purse and shows him the debit card.

Ask about how I am. Ask about the baby.

'Nearly thirty grand? For real?' She can sense the metaphorical cogs beginning to grind in his brain. 'What about your mum and dad, though?' he asks, warily. 'Won't they be able to stop you?

Charlie shakes her head. 'The money's in my name. Only I can withdraw it.'

The truth is, she hasn't yet worked out how she's going to handle her parents' fury. The obvious answer is to make sure they don't find out until it's too late. She looks down at the grimy pavement, studded with cigarette butts. A takeaway wrapper snakes around her ankles. 'Look, we can't talk properly here. Let's go to Memz.'

'Okay.' Jake still seems sceptical but also intrigued. 'Catch you later, yeah?' he shouts at his friends and follows Charlie down the street.

He doesn't make any move to hold her hand, instead thrusting his hands deep into the pockets of his jacket.

'So, you want to spend this cash on renting a place?' he asks, once they have ordered tea for her and a can of Coke for him. 'I guess thirty Gs is more than enough. We could get somewhere banging with that.'

'I don't want to spend all of it on housing,' Charlie says, quickly. 'But most of it, I guess, yeah.'

'So you don't want, like, to stay at your parents' place and spend the cash on holidays and clothes and shit?' Jake looks confused. Compared to his own living situation, Charlie's family home in Dartmouth Park is idyllic.

She shakes her head. 'Not now I'm having the baby. I want my own place. And that's where you come in.'

Jake takes a swig of Coke and chews his top lip.

'The thing is…' Charlie is suddenly acutely nervous, and crosses her legs under the table to stop them shaking. 'I'm not old enough to sign a tenancy agreement. You have to be at least eighteen.'

She lets this last sentence hang in the air. Jake is eighteen and a half.

'So you for real want me to move into a place with you? You're not messing around?'

Charlie half expects him to scoff or sneer, but he looks serious. Recently he and his stepfather have been fighting, and he's talked openly about how he'll move out as soon as he can. His impatience to leave home is the biggest weapon she has in her armoury.

'Yes.' She inhales sharply, nervous. She imagines this must be how people feel when they propose marriage. 'We'll be able to rent somewhere decent. And there'll be a bit of cash left over to live on. You know, just until you've managed to find a job.'

Charlie has just completed her AS levels, and Jake will be sitting two A levels and leaving school for good in the next fortnight. He has never spoken about what he would or could do next. 'All mouth, no ambition' was her father's description of Jake on the one occasion they met.

'Can we get a car?' he asks. 'We could get something pretty cool with that sort of money.'

A car would be useful when they become parents, Charlie reasons. And Jake, who has a licence, will be able to help her learn to drive. 'Maybe. The flat is the most important thing, though.'

'We'd have to have a bank account in both our names.' Jake twists the Coke can round and round, not meeting her eye. 'I don't want to be kept by my baby-mother. It would have to be fifty-fifty.'

'Of course.' Charlie smiles uncertainly. 'I wouldn't want you to feel like you're being kept. We'd be a family.'

'Okay then.' Jake finally looks up, and grins. 'Cool. Let's do it.'

'So shall we…?'

'Laters, okay.' He stands up and turns away, dismissing her.

'Okay.' Charlie feels instantly deflated. She'd hoped they would hang out for a while. 'So I'll text you about seeing some places, right?'

He still hasn't mentioned the baby.

7

PAULA

'Wow,' exclaims Johnny, gazing along the street. 'You surely can't buy much round here on a social worker's salary…?'

Ranmoor Road in Muswell Hill is lined with substantial Edwardian semis, all featuring generous bay fronts with pavilioned gables, and tiled front paths.

Paula climbs out of his car and puts on sunglasses to keep the bright, early summer sunlight from her eyes. 'I suppose it's possible if your other half has a well-paid job.'

At the far end of the street, at the junction with Alexandra Park Road, the Half Moon pub is still there, only now its rendered brick façade has been painted a deep blue-grey and there are well-tended window boxes and a front awning.

'The local's changed, that's for sure,' she observes. 'In the days when Lizzie and her mates drank there it was just your typical run-down North London boozer.'

'Which number are we looking for? Johnny asks, putting on his own sunglasses. He's wearing a plain white T-shirt and a dark Harrington jacket, and with the aviator shades he looks like a glamorous secret agent.

'Twenty-one.' Paula points.

'You're quite sure? It's a while since you were here.'

She nods slowly. 'Marian. Now I think about it, I'm pretty sure that was her name. I think I'd recognise her, too. Though I'm not sure she'd recognise me. I was just a kid.'

'Still are.' Johnny grins.

She gives him a sidelong glance. 'And if she's in, who do I say you are? A friend? A colleague? A partner?'

'Say what you like; I don't mind. You can even say I'm your boyfriend.'

Paula flushes. 'Don't be daft.' She juts out her chin and strides up the path to number twenty-one. 'Come on then.'

'I'm terribly sorry.' The woman who answers the door to them sounds as though she really means this. She's tall and lean with greying hair and long dangly earrings. She wears an apron over a faded cotton sundress, her bare arms freckled from the first really warm spell of weather that year. 'But I'm afraid I don't know where Marian moved to.'

Paula's disappointment registers and she adds quickly, 'I'm Alice Evershott. Why don't you come in for a minute?'

'I'm Paula. Paula Armitage. And this is my… friend, Johnny Shepherd. Marian was my late sister's social worker, and I had some questions I wanted to ask her. About the time when my sister was her client.'

Alice leads them into a rustic-feeling kitchen that looks out over a large lawn bordered with shrubs.

'You bought this place from Marian?' Johnny asks.

'From the Glynns? Yes, that's right.' Alice indicates they should sit at the large scrubbed pine table. 'Can I offer you tea or anything?'

They both shake their heads.

'Adrian and I… that's my husband… bought the place from Tom and Marian back in 2003.'

'So she was married?'

'Yes, well…' Alice pauses. 'If I remember rightly, he dealt mostly with the paperwork and both names were on the deeds, but he was never at the house, only her. Marian. The agents did the viewings, but we went round there after we'd exchanged contracts to measure a few things and talk about the fixtures they were leaving. We met her then. We didn't want to pry, but we got the impression that they were recently separated. Certainly I remember he – Tom Glynn – wanted to push the sale through quickly. We paid what they were asking, but they'd marketed it at what agents call a "realistic" price, to get it sold.'

'Did they have kids?' Johnny asks.

'No, they didn't.' Alice fetches a jug of water and some glasses, pouring herself some. There is flour on her forearms and under her fingernails, and the half-completed batter for a cake on the worktop. 'We bought this as a family home: our two were quite little back then. They're both at uni now, but they still come and go. This is still home.'

She smiles warmly in the direction of a cluster of family photos on the bookcase.

'And the Glynns didn't leave you a forwarding address?' Paula asks.

Alice looks perplexed. 'Not that I was aware. They would have provided our solicitor with an address, I expect. We used Hooper and Chilton in Muswell Hill for the conveyancing. I don't know if they'd be able to help you.'

'What about the neighbours?' Johnny asks. 'Are there any still in the street that were around when the Glynns were here? That might know where they moved to.'

'Next door on both sides are fairly new, I'm afraid. Number nineteen – Nick and Tamsin – moved in this year. Number twenty-three have only lived here four or five years so they wouldn't have known them. Mrs Pinker at number twenty-five might know, though. She's elderly; been here donkeys' years, so she must have overlapped with the Glynns.'

Johnny and Paula exchange glances and Paula makes a note on her phone. 'Look, thanks, Alice; you've been really helpful,' Johnny says, pushing his chair back and extending a hand to her. 'We shouldn't hold you up any longer. And looks like you've got a cake to finish.' He gives her his most charming smile.

'I'm just sorry I didn't know more,' Alice says, as she leads them back through the hall to the front door. Then, as they head back down the tiled path, she holds up a floury hand and beckons them back. 'Wait!'

Paul and Johnny retrace their steps.

'There is one thing. I've only just thought of it. Wait here a second…'

She scurries upstairs to the first floor and comes down a minute or so later with something in her hand.

'We found this behind the kitchen dresser soon after we moved in. The dresser was left behind as a fixture, but we ended up refitting the kitchen and getting rid of it. I assumed this must have belonged to the Glynns, because it looked new. I hung on to it in case it had sentimental value and they came back for it. But they never did.'

She holds out the object towards them.

Paula exhales sharply as she realises what it is. 'Oh my God.'

'May I?'

Paula takes the folded fabric and turns it over between her fingers. It's pale pink, a bit discoloured in places, but very obviously a baby's blanket. In one corner, a large 'S' has been appliquéd.

'You said the Glynns didn't have children of their own?' she asks.

'As far as I know,' Alice Evershott replies quietly. 'I mean, one supposes it's possible they lost a baby at some point. Or that could have been left here by someone visiting. Although…'

'Go on,' Johnny prompts. He takes the blanket from Paula and examines it.

'It was wedged in there out of sight behind the dresser back, as though it had been put there deliberately. It hadn't just been dropped on the floor.'

'So either Marian or Tom Glynn put it there?'

Alice frowns. 'Well, not necessarily. The dresser was an ancient, battered thing that looked like it had been there forever. It's possible it was in situ when the Glynns themselves moved in. They were only here three or four years.'

'Is it okay if we keep this?' Paula asks.

'I suppose you might as well, if you're planning on speaking to her at some point,' sighs Alice. 'Though if you don't find her, then I don't suppose you'll ever know the true story.'

'Oh, we will.' Johnny puts his sunglasses back on. 'We fully intend to find out.'

8

PAULA

Johnny phones Paula a few days later.

'I've been thinking.'

'Careful,' she teases. 'You'll do yourself a mischief.'

She's folding and putting away a pile of laundry, phone tucked under her chin. The last item in the pile is the pink blanket, which she has very carefully hand-washed to get rid of the musty smell. She strokes it absently, tracing the contours of the letter S with one finger.

'What that lady – Alice – said about the blanket makes sense. It might not have belonged to the Glynns.'

'I know. We agreed on that.'

'But what I've been thinking is, maybe we're barking up the wrong tree.'

'In what way?'

'Instead of getting sidetracked by things we can't prove, we should be concentrating on what we *can* prove.'

Paula presses the blanket against her cheek, before putting it on a shelf in the airing cupboard and closing the door. 'Go on.'

'Given how your sister died, right, there must have been a post-mortem. There always is when a dead body is found, and the circumstances are unexplained.'

Paula frowns. 'But they *were* explained. She haemorrhaged to death after drinking herself stupid.'

'Yes, but what I'm saying, Paul, is that for them to know the aneurysm was the cause of death, there must have been a post-mortem done first.'

'So? I still don't follow. There was never any doubt about how Lizzie died.'

'Ah, but what else might they have found? They examine absolutely everything. If she had just had a baby, they would have been able to tell. And it would have been in the report.'

Paula leans against the landing wall, taking this in. Biscuit presses against her legs, wagging his tail, and she reaches down and fondles his ears absently.

'So what happens to the report?'

'I've just looked this up. The coroner's office has to report the pathologist's findings to the deceased's family, if they're known. Then a full copy of the written report is sent to the deceased's GP.'

'I'm pretty sure Lizzie never had a GP.'

'Well, in that case, it probably would have been sent to the next of kin. Your mother?'

'I suppose it must have been.' Paula's hand starts to shake and she grips the phone. Her mother has never said a word. Had she known all along, but decided for some reason not to say anything?

Johnny eventually breaks the silence. 'You okay, Paul?'

'Yes… yes… it's just a lot to think about.' She's quiet for a few seconds. 'What I'm trying to get my head around is… if it did say in the report that she'd had a baby, why didn't anyone in my family say anything?'

Johnny's tone is gentle. 'You said your family had disowned Lizzie a long time before she died. Maybe they couldn't face reading the coroner's report. Or simply didn't want to. That would make sense. You know, like they were unwilling to reopen that can of worms. They must have been feeling guilty, right?'

Paula opens the door of the airing cupboard, touches the blanket. 'I suppose they were. But why didn't anyone else do something? Surely the coroner would have raised the question of what happened to the baby at Lizzie's inquest?'

'Yes, exactly. So that must have been why there was a police investigation when I was a Special. I'll ask around if you like, see if anyone can find a file from… when was it?'

'2003. The twenty-second of July 2003 was when she died.'

'And you probably need to speak to your mum.'

'Yes,' Paula agrees without enthusiasm. 'I probably do.'

'I want to come with you to see Granny Wendy.'

'You can't,' Paula tells her daughter, firmly.

The following weekend, she's in the car with both children, dropping them off with her ex-husband before driving on to her mother's flat in Edgware.

'But we always go with you to Granny Wendy's,' Jessica complains. 'She has the special sweetie tin ready.'

Ben, who has his headphones plugged in, rolls his eyes.

'Not this time. I need to go on my own.'

'But why?'

'Because, okay?' Paula doesn't hide her irritation, jumping out of the car in the driveway of Dave's house and yanking the rear door open. 'Come on, out you get!'

Dave appears on the driveway and takes Jessica's overnight bag from his ex-wife. 'All right, Paul?'

She nods curtly, already getting back into the car.

'When am I bringing them back? Only Natalie and I—'

'I'll ring you,' Paula says through the open window, before backing the car off the drive again. 'Got to go.'

Disraeli Court is a red-brick development of thirty-eight flats, built in the 1980s and surrounded by well-tended gardens. There's a residents' lounge, a laundry and on-site support staff. Wendy Armitage is lucky to live there, as she never tires of telling anyone who'll listen.

'Shame you didn't bring the kids with you,' she sniffs, kissing her daughter on the cheek. 'Not like they're at school today.' She still has the slight, wiry frame she's always had, only now she doesn't bother to dye her hair, which is completely white.

'It's Dave's weekend,' Paula says, shortly. 'And, anyway, I need to talk to you.'

'Oh, yes?' Wendy's tone is wary. She goes into the kitchenette and switches on the kettle, arranging tea things on a tray.

'It's about Lizzie,' Paula says, when her mother comes back into the living room with the tea.

Wendy raises her eyes heavenwards and sighs. 'Why now, Paula? It's all done with, long ago. Can't we just let her rest in peace?'

'Mum, please, this is important.' Paula takes a deep breath, trying to control her rising frustration. 'When she died, there must have been a post-mortem done.'

'I expect there would have been. The police got involved… when she… you know.'

Even now, her mother can't bring herself to speak about the pitifully sad circumstances of her eldest daughter's death: the discovery of her unattended dead body by a total stranger. And then there was the travesty of a funeral. One single sheaf of wilting carnations, and Wendy staring at the coffin throughout with a stony expression. Steve had not been able to get back to the UK, so there had only been Paula, her parents, Great-Aunt Cissie, Uncle Alan and Aunt Shirley and her two oldest cousins. A short, bleak service at the crematorium, with no wake afterwards.

'Have you ever even visited the cemetery? Where her ashes are buried?'

Paula knows the answer to this question, yet still feels the need to prod her mother, to try and understand.

'What's the point? She's not there.' Wendy pours milk into the tea cups, but her hand is shaking. She draws in her breath sharply before holding one out to her daughter. 'Biscuit?'

'But she's your *daughter*, that's the point! Christ, if anything ever happened to Jessie' – Paula crosses herself to ward off the possibility – 'you wouldn't be able to drag me away from her grave. I'd practically camp there.'

'That's different,' says Wendy, stirring sugar into her tea. 'You haven't been lied to, and abused and stolen from by your daughter.'

Ah, yes, Paula thinks, *the business of Great-Aunt Winifred's ring*. Wendy Armitage had two childless aunts, Winifred and Cissie. Winifred had married a well-to-do solicitor, and when she died, she left her jewellery to her nieces. Wendy's bequest had been an Edwardian ring that featured an octagonal emerald flanked by diamonds. Paula had never seen her mother wear it, but occasionally she took it out to clean it, turning it this way and that, admiring it. It was valuable to her not just because of its monetary worth but because of what it represented: a link to a better, more gracious world.

When Paula was ten, she heard her parents having a heated argument one night, and lurked at the door of her bedroom to listen.

'Maybe we should give her one last chance?' she heard Colin Armitage saying.

'But how many times have we been here?' her mother protested. Her voice sounded strangely distorted, and Paula realised it was because she was crying. She had never heard her mother cry before. 'How many promises has she made to sort herself out? How many disappointments has she put us through?'

'It's not really her, though, is it? This isn't our Lizzie. It's the drinking.'

'I told her I couldn't take it any longer, and I mean it. Oh, yes, sure, she's full of good intentions. She's going to do this or stop doing that, and before you know it she's drinking again. And *this*… this is the final bloody straw, Colin!'

The next morning Paula had discovered that the final straw had been Lizzie taking Aunt Winifred's emerald ring and selling it to buy vodka and cannabis. She was ordered to leave the family home, packing her bags and moving into a squat. Soon afterwards Colin and Wendy's marriage collapsed. Paula met Dave some years later while she was in the sixth form, and married as soon as she had left school. Her parents both approved of the solid, steady Dave and she had been desperate to please them, to prove that they still had one 'good' daughter. A daughter they could be proud of.

She sets her tea cup back on its saucer. 'She did that because she was an alcoholic,' she says now. 'She was an addict. It's an illness. And what about forgiveness, eh? What the hell happened to that?' Her voice rises, as does the colour in her cheeks.

Wendy looks away. 'We all have different ways of dealing with things. It wasn't that I didn't love her. You mustn't think that.' There's sorrow in her voice, despite her attempts to mask it, and her hand shakes again as she lifts her tea cup.

'In that case, will you come to the cemetery one day then?'

'I don't know about that.'

'We could take the kids, too. I've been meaning to take them; now they're old enough to understand. About Lizzie.'

'Maybe. I'll think about it.'

Paula wonders if she should tell her mother about the search that she and Johnny Shepherd have embarked on, but decides now is not the time. Perhaps when they have some definite proof of what happened. Or if her mother ever does make the visit to Lizzie's resting place.

'The post-mortem,' her mother says suddenly, looking at Paula directly. 'I never saw it, but now I think about it, I'm pretty sure the report was sent to your dad.'

9

CHARLIE

It's another four days before Jake bothers to return her text about flat hunting.

Charlie spends one more night with Hannah, but Faye Watson is preparing for relatives to visit. She drops hints about her daughter's friend out-staying her welcome, so Charlie is forced, reluctantly, to return to her own family home.

And it's awkward. She's committed to the pregnancy, but her parents are not – not really. They keep raising the question of how her education will be able to continue. How will she manage at university with a three year old? People do, Charlie tells them, but still they carp. She mustn't think that she can just leave the baby with them while she goes out clubbing and to festivals with her mates, her parents insist. That's not how this is going to work. She's going to have to miss out.

Charlie sends a series of text updates to Hannah.

Mum's googling unis with childcare facilities
Now she's telling me where all her friends kids are having their gap years
Dad and Mum are arguing about whether I should defer school for a year. Grim

During this time, Charlie also keeps a close eye on the filing cabinet in the office, but as far as she can tell, nobody has had reason to look in the savings file and in doing so, discover the missing debit card. She plays along with her mother's micro-managing, keeping a constant eye on her phone until finally Jake sends a message.

Tomorrow morning good for me

She forces herself to wait at least ten minutes before replying.

Cool. See you then

Charlie avoids the elite estate agencies, which she is sure will refuse to deal with her once they know her age. Instead, she and Jake visit a high street agent that claims to welcome students as renters.

'This is sick.' Jake immediately seizes on the details for a newbuild flat with floor-to-ceiling windows and a roof terrace. 'Party central.'

'The price, though. There's no way we can afford that.'

Jake pulls a face. 'I don't want to wind up in some shithole.' He continues to scowl as the agent pulls out details for more affordable properties, then drives them to see a dilapidated two-bedroom flat in an ex-local authority block in Tufnell Park. If they can overlook the peeling paintwork and stained carpets, then – the agent assures them – it's a steal at £1,095 per month.

'It's been empty for a while; I could probably get the landlord to accept £1,050.'

'Great,' says Charlie. 'We'll take it, won't we, Jake?'

He merely grunts. 'Whatever.'

The estate agent says their credit scores will have to be checked, and they will both need to provide a reference and the name of a guarantor. Neither of them has a credit score, or can think of a suitable referee.

'How about something from your employers?' the woman suggests.

Charlie and Jake exchange glances. 'Jake's about to start looking for employment,' Charlie mutters.

'How about you?' the woman asks.

Charlie doesn't want to have to tell her that she's still at school. Her father works with the construction and property industries, and she's often heard him bargaining with agents on the phone. 'How about this?' she says, quickly. 'I've got the money in my account now; we're in a position to pay the full twelve months' rent up front. Then the issue of our credit scores and income is irrelevant.'

The agent taps her long, shellacked nails on her cheek. 'It's not what we usually do,' she prevaricates. 'But I know the landlord is keen to get someone in the property as soon possible. Let me give him a call and explain the situation, and I'll get back to you.'

While they're killing time, Jake wants to visit a car dealership. 'There's one just up the road,' he wheedles. 'Just to look.'

But of course once he's looked, the looking alone is not enough. And a salesman with pound signs in his eyes is only too happy to let Jake test drive an Audi TT.

'We should get it,' he tells Charlie, his eyes shining.

'Surely something a bit cheaper,' she suggests, trying to keep her tone light. 'A bit more practical.' *Something compatible with a child seat.*

'It's only £250 a month to lease it,' Jake scoffs. 'Two hundred and fifty poxy quid. What's that – a couple of grand a year? That's nothing when you've got thirty K.'

'But we've already spent a third of it on the flat,' Charlie protests. 'We need the rest to live on. Surely you realise that.'

Jake's lip curls. 'And surely *you* realise that I'm not going to let any chick dictate what I do. You said the money would be joint, yeah?'

'No, I didn't, I said I'd put *some* of it in a joint account. That money will be half yours, half mine.'

'Not what you said earlier, babe.'

'Maybe I wasn't clear,' Charlie says desperately, thinking of her grandmother's university fund evaporating.

Jake shrugs. 'Whatever. No car, no moving in together. The whole thing's off.'

He strides out of the dealership, with the salesman and receptionist staring curiously after him. Charlie's cheeks flush crimson with shame, and she can feel tears welling up.

She smiles helplessly at the dealer, who takes pity on her and asks the receptionist to make her some coffee. She doesn't want any, but accepts it anyway as it gives her a chance to sit down and text Jake.

Fine, we'll get a car

There is no response, so five minutes later she swallows her pride.

Please come back

Twenty minutes later, he lopes back in, hands in his pockets, thrusting his jeans down so far that the Calvin Klein logo on his boxers is exposed.

'You're right,' she says, trying to soothe his bruised ego. 'It's not a huge amount of money. And we could use a car.'

Just after Jake has signed the lease paperwork and they're walking out of the dealership with the promise of a comparable Audi being available within forty-eight hours, the lettings agent phones Charlie's mobile. She relays the news that the landlord will be only too happy to have the £12,600 transferred into his bank account. As soon as the funds are received and the contract cleaners have been in, they can collect the keys. The next morning should work fine.

'Sweet.' Jake gives a genuine grin, and Charlie feels her stomach flip to see him happy. 'I guess I'll go back to Mum's and pack my shit. Her and that wanker she married are going to be so happy. How about yours?'

'Um, I don't know. I guess they'll be cool.'

But Charlie knows full well that her parents won't be cool. They'll be horrified. And doubly so when they find out how she's funded the whole endeavour.

So when she gets home that evening she says nothing about it, sitting down to a Chinese takeaway with her parents, younger brother and her sister, recently returned home after the end of her university term.

After supper she sits on her bed for hours, waiting for the rest of the household to go to bed. She texts Hannah.

Can you keep a secret. You've got to promise not to tell ANYBODY

Omigod girl WTF you have GOT to tell me!!! shiiitttt what's happening

I'm moving in with Jake

SHIT DO YOUR PARENTS KNOW

Not yet. Don't tell yours okay? Promise?

I won't but why the hell would you want to do that boys are pigs

And Hannah adds a stream of pig emojis to reinforce the point.

Once she's sure everyone is asleep, Charlie takes a suitcase from the cupboard on the landing and packs, indiscriminately, as much as she can cram into it before eventually falling asleep for a few hours.

She's woken by her mother shouting up the stairs: 'Lottie, can you mind Olly for a bit? Thanks.'

Charlie's stomach lurches, and it's not just morning sickness. This wasn't part of the plan. She shouts back, 'Why? Why isn't he at school?'

'Because he broke up for the summer on Friday! Goodness, those hormones are making you scatty.'

'But I'm going out,' Charlie protests. *To pick up the keys to the new home you don't know anything about.*

'It's only for an hour or so. Then Lucy will be back.'

As soon as she hears the door slam, Charlie grabs her purse and hurries to her brother's room, still in her pyjamas. She waves a twenty pound note in his face. 'Oll, I'll give you this if you can find a mate to go and hang out with till Lucy comes back.'

His eyes widen. 'Why, where are you going?'

'Away for a bit.'

'Do Mum and Dad know?'

'They will.'

As soon as Olly has cycled off to his friend Josh's house, Charlie scribbles a note, which she leaves propped against the toast rack.

I'm moving out to live with Jake. Please don't try and stop me and DON'T call the police, because I've checked and I'm old enough to live independently of my parents if I'm with another adult (Jake). I'll be in touch soon. C xx

She drags her suitcase downstairs, switches off her phone, and pulls the case out onto the front step, slamming the door firmly behind her.

10

PAULA

Estelle Armitage still lives in the house she shared with her late husband.

After he divorced Wendy, Colin Armitage and his then-girlfriend Estelle pooled their financial resources and bought a run-down semi-detached house in the affluent suburb of Totteridge, pouring time and money into it over the years until they had created an attractive, and now quite valuable, home. They had eventually got around to marrying when Paula was nineteen.

Paula has always got on well with her stepmother, without ever feeling close to her. Estelle has a family of her own, and while she was always pleasant to Steve and Paula, she was never particularly invested in them either, instead engrossing herself in her two grown-up daughters and handful of grandchildren.

'Come in, love,' Estelle says, kissing Paula warmly. She's a well-preserved sixty-something who highlights her hair blonde and would never dream of being seen without a full face of make-up. 'Coffee? Or would you prefer a G and T?'

'Coffee, please. I'm driving.' Paula follows her into the ostentatiously tidy sitting room, with its faux marble fireplace, gilt-trimmed lamp tables and heavy brocade sofas.

'How are the kids doing?' Estelle enquires. 'Goodness… how long is it since I've seen them? Ages.'

Paula reaches for her phone to pull up the most recent pictures, but Estelle holds up a hand. 'You can show me in a minute, when I've fetched the coffee.'

She returns with two mugs of coffee, plates, paper napkins and a large cake tin on a tray. Estelle has always loved to bake, and makes even more cakes and biscuits now she lives alone. 'It fills the time,' she confessed to Paula in the months after Colin died of a stroke. 'So much time, and I've no idea what to do with it.'

'So…' She hands Paula a large slice of lemon drizzle cake. 'To what do I owe this pleasure? Any special reason?'

Paula visits with the children for Sunday lunch every few months, but hasn't been to Totteridge on her own since before she was married to Dave.

'It's… well, it's about Lizzie.'

Estelle's expression is one of puzzlement. Thanks to Colin's long estrangement from his oldest daughter, she never met Lizzie. 'Oh?'

'When she died, I know it was Dad who organised the funeral, and took care of any arrangements.'

Estelle looks down at her hands, neatly folded on her lap. 'Yes, that's right. He didn't like talking about it, but I know he was very cut up about it… about what happened.'

'Did he ever mention the post-mortem?'

Estelle blinks. 'No, I don't think so. In what sense, love?'

'There would have been a copy of the pathologist's report sent to Lizzie's next of kin. I've asked Mum, and she says it was sent to Dad.'

'Let me see now…' Estelle half closes her eyes. 'I do vaguely remember something about that. I tell you what; any family papers on Colin's side are all filed together. I can fetch them, and then we can take a look.'

She disappears into the small back reception room which acted as a study when Colin Armitage was alive, and brings back a large lever arch box file. 'Here…' She starts flicking through the contents.

Paula recognises some sepia photos of her grandparents, a couple of death certificates, her father's old passport. Near the bottom is a large manila envelope, printed with 'Coroner's Office, Borough of Haringey'.

Estelle hands it to Paula. 'I think this must be it.'

Paula wipes the cake crumbs from her fingers then takes the envelope and turns it over, puzzled. The envelope is still sealed. 'It hasn't been opened?'

Estelle shakes her head. 'Your dad couldn't face reading it. It just upset him too much.'

'Is it okay if I take it away with me?' Paula asks.

'Of course, darling. Though I can't think what you'd want with it now. It's been, what, fifteen years or more?'

'Let's just say that something's come up.'

Paula texts Johnny when she gets home.

Kids with their dad. Want to come over? X

He shows up at seven with a bottle of Prosecco, a bottle of Merlot and a six-pack of Mexican beer. 'Wasn't sure what you'd be cooking, so I thought I'd better cover all bases.'

Paula reddens slightly. 'Actually, I wasn't planning on making anything.'

Despite – or perhaps because of – her mother always drafting her into preparing the evening meal when she was a teenager, she's not much of a cook. And during her marriage, the kitchen was always Dave's domain.

'If you're hungry, I've got snacks,' she says, hurriedly, reaching in the cupboard for bags of crisps and taking cheese, tomatoes, cold meats and a melon from the fridge. 'When you've got teenagers, you always have to have plenty of food in.'

Johnny shrugs. 'Or we could order a pizza?'

She hands him a takeaway menu. 'Maybe later. Let's just have a drink first.'

They take the beers and some crisps onto the rear patio. It's a warm evening, and the air is filled with the drone of a neighbour's lawnmower and the sound of someone kicking a ball against a fence.

'The reason I asked you round is because I've found something out,' Paula tells Johnny, as he flips the tops of their beer bottles. 'I've read the coroner's report on Lizzie.'

He looks up. 'Really?'

'It was sent to my dad. He never opened it, apparently, but my stepmum still had it at the house.'

'And?' Johnny hands her a beer.

'You were right.'

He grins. 'I'll let you into a secret: I always am.'

She raises her eyebrows in exasperation, and his sober expression returns. 'There was a paragraph in the description of the findings that said there was evidence that Lizzie had been pregnant and given birth recently, probably within the last few days before she died. They used a lot of medical terminology, but that was the gist of it.'

Johnny gives a long exhalation. 'I know.'

She looks at him sharply. 'What do you mean?'

'I asked my mate at the cop shop to look into it a couple of days ago and he just texted me back today. The police were just at the start of keeping digital records back in 2003, so he managed to find the case on the system. At the inquest, the coroner passed his findings on to the police, and requested they urgently try and find what happened to the baby. This would have been some weeks after you went to the Wood Green nick and asked about it yourself. Hence the house-to-house enquiries I remembered.'

'And?'

'Apparently they turned up the boyfriend: he was in Wormwood Scrubs serving time for armed robbery. They spoke to some neighbours, and to your mum. Everyone denied knowledge of a baby.'

Paula feels a strange sinking in her stomach. 'Mum never said a word about it to me.'

She tries to picture the officers calling at the flat and breaking the news to her mother that she had a grandchild that had mysteriously gone missing. Was that what her mother had meant when she said 'the police got involved'? Was it a guilty conscience that prevented her ever sharing this news with Paula?

Johnny reaches out and squeezes her hand. 'Maybe she decided it was best not to discuss it when the police failed to get to the bottom of it and closed the case. Like I said before, there was so much gang and drug stuff going on in Tottenham at the time, they were over-stretched. They concluded that given her drink problem, the baby was probably born dead or died soon after birth, and she got rid of the body somehow.'

Got rid of the body. Is that what had happened? That was certainly what Marian Glynn had wanted her to believe, when she had spoken to her at the time.

'The thing is, Paul, you were right all along. There *was* a baby. You definitely didn't imagine it, and now we have hard proof.' Johnny reaches down and strokes Biscuit, who has followed them outside and is waiting patiently to hoover up any pieces of crisp that are dropped.

Paula sits up and drains the beer in her bottle. 'Thanks, Johnny. I can't tell you how much I appreciate your help. You've been so fantastic.'

He leans forward, and she realises that he's going to kiss her. She closes her eyes and lets it happen. He smells of musk and fabric conditioner, and tastes like the beer she's just drunk. The kiss goes on for a while. The lawnmower continues to drone somewhere behind them.

'Listen, Paul, I'd love to help you some more, but I'm going to be working away for the next few months.' Johnny squeezes her fingers, then straightens up again. He hasn't talked much about his work, so all she knows is that his company acts as a contractor for the event management industry: setting up and taking down tents, providing sound and lighting and security services.

'It's the festival season from now till the end of September, and that's the core of our business. I'm going to be up in Suffolk, then Derbyshire, then down in Wiltshire, then Cornwall.'

'Shame,' says Paula, lightly. 'I've got used to having you around.'

'We've still got tonight…' He fixes those clear, blue eyes on her face, tipping his head in the direction of the house. 'We could go upstairs.'

Does she want to sleep with Johnny Shepherd? Paula asks herself. The question is redundant. Of course she does. But does she want to do it now, when he's about to disappear for three months and hang out with a load of young, flower-crowned festival groupies? No, she does not.

She stands up. 'Let's order that pizza,' she says, firmly, gathering up the drinks and crisps. Johnny shrugs ruefully and follows her inside.

'There was something else,' he says, half an hour later, when they are sitting at the kitchen table, washing down their American Hot with glasses of the Merlot. 'I almost forgot.'

'What's that?'

'When the police were investigating Lizzie's baby, they interviewed the social worker. Marian Glynn.'

Paula sets down her pizza on her plate and looks at him. 'They did? Can you remember what she said?'

He nods. 'I read her statement. She said the last time she'd been to visit your sister was Thursday, the third of July. She showed the official record of the visit she'd made in her paperwork, apparently.'

'No,' says Paula, firmly. 'That doesn't sound right. When I called round to her house, she made it sound like she'd just seen Lizzie. Like, very recently. And that she would definitely go round and see her a couple of days later.'

Johnny pours more wine. 'In her statement, she's adamant that she never saw Lizzie or had any contact after the third.'

'Well, there we are then!' Paula says triumphantly. 'What she says definitely can't be trusted.'

Johnny nods. 'I reckon she knows something about what happened to that baby.'

11

CHARLIE

She takes a deep breath and rings the doorbell.

The wisteria finished flowering many weeks ago, and now that summer is almost over, its carpet of pale purple petals has turned to a brownish mush that sticks to the soles of her trainers. She tries to remember how long it has been since she was last there. A couple of months at least. She's celebrated a birthday since. The thought prompts her to touch her abdomen. She's well into the second trimester of her pregnancy now, almost in the third. Her family will find that strange, she decides. Awkward. The whole thing is going to be awkward. But it has to be done, to get them off her back.

It's not as if there has been no contact since she walked out and left that note. She has been in touch with her parents fairly regularly by text. Mostly with her mother. Reassuring them that she's fine, but that – for now – she doesn't intend to give them her address. But this time they have asked – no, demanded – to see her, and told her it's nothing to do with Jake Palmer. Whatever it is, it's bound to be awkward. *Awkward AF.*

The door is flung wide, and her father embraces her, but it's a cursory embrace, and when he straightens up, his jaw is clenched. He forces a smile. 'Why didn't you use your key, you noodle?'

'I think I lost it,' she says, vaguely. The truth is it didn't occur to her. She doesn't live here in Dartmouth Park any more.

'Come through, come through. Mum's in the kitchen.'

She expects her mother to be emotional, but instead she just looks pissed off.

'So you haven't forgotten where we live,' she says drily, giving her daughter a half-embrace with one arm, stirring a pan of chilli with the other. Her eyes automatically dart to the now prominent curve of Charlie's belly, visible under a baggy shirt.

'Want some tea? Coffee? Or are you not allowed coffee now?' Her father nods in the direction of her midriff.

'It's fine, I don't want anything. I'm not going to stay long.'

Charlie plonks herself down at the large kitchen table, dented and scratched from years of family life, and for a moment it feels as though she never left.

'Where are the others?' she asks.

'Olly's at football practice; your sister's got a summer job at a café in Highgate.'

'Oh, okay.' Charlie bites her lower lip. She had been hoping to see her siblings, and the fact that they are not here seems ominous. Keen to keep the visit as short as possible, she launches into her rehearsed speech: 'You do realise there's really no point involving the police, or the authorities, don't you? I'm seventeen now, so you can't make me live at home.'

'Legally you're still a child. Until you're eighteen.' Her mother is clenching her jaw as she speaks. Charlie recognises that expression. 'But that's not why we asked you round.'

Her father disappears into the office for a few minutes and returns with the building society passbook for her original savings account. 'There should be a debit card in the file with this. Only, it's mysteriously gone missing.'

Charlie feels the colour blaze in her cheeks. Her palms feel clammy. 'I've got it.'

'Funnily enough, we worked that out for ourselves. We might not have been any the wiser if a statement hadn't arrived for that account, and when we went to file it with the rest of the paperwork we saw that nearly all the money Granny Nancy put away for you has gone.'

Charlie picks at her fingernails. 'I know. I used it to pay the rent.'

'What – all of it?' Her mother's face is thunderous. 'But, Charlotte, you know full well that that money was set aside to pay for your university education.'

'Some of it went on rent. We used the rest on other stuff. Stuff for the baby.'

This isn't strictly true, but she decided her parents don't need to know exactly how it's been spent. It's not like she can get the money back now.

'"We" used it?' Her father frowns. 'You mean this Jake lad is living off you? You're keeping him?'

Charlie shakes her head miserably. 'Look, it's only while he's trying to get a job. Then we'll both be spending his earnings.'

'Presumably he didn't have the guts to tell his mother about this arrangement. We've been in touch with Michelle Palmer, and she's denied all knowledge of where you're living. She did give me Jake's mobile number but, of course, I've not been able to get any response.'

'He's got a new phone,' Charlie says.

'Presumably one you paid for?' her father spits. 'And from the sound of it, he's still unemployed. And you can't exactly look for work, can you? You're due back at school in a couple of weeks, not to mention the whole pregnancy business.'

Charlie rolls her eyes. As if she needs reminding. But that's what parents do. Constantly tell you stuff you already know.

'Look, I'm really sorry about the money. About taking the card without telling you. But it *is* in my name. And as soon as Jake has got a job, he's going to start paying it back. So by the time I'm ready to go to uni, it'll all be fine, okay?'

Her parents exchange a look of pure disbelief.

'Anyway,' Charlie stands up. 'I want to go and fetch some of my things from my room, if that's okay with you.' She fishes in the handbag slung across her body and pulls out two large supermarket carriers.

Her father raises a hand. 'Hold on a minute, young lady. Is that it? Aren't you going to tell us where this amazing love nest of yours is? The one you've deceived us to pay for? I take it it's local? Can't see that boy wanting to be too far from his gang of mates.'

Gang of mates, thinks Charlie. *Jesus.*

'No,' she says, 'I'm not going to tell you.'

They would only come round, and her father would undoubtedly lay into Jake.

'Charlotte, for heaven's sake. Seriously?' Her mother only calls her by her full name when she's deeply pissed off. 'You're still officially a minor. And you are still having our grandchild.' She waves a wooden spoon in the direction of Charlie's bump. 'Surely we have a right to know where you are?'

'Look, we won't come round and make trouble, if that's what you're worried about.' Her father, as always, tries to lighten the tone. 'We just need to be sure you're safe.'

She sighs. 'Maybe. Eventually. Just give it a bit of time, yeah?'

Her father relents and pulls her into a hug. 'As long as you're all right? As long as he's looking after you. That's what really matters at the end of the day, not the money.'

'Yeah, everything's great,' Charlie says. She forces the corners of her mouth to lift into a smile. 'Me and Jake are really, really happy.'

As soon as she gets out of the lift Charlie hears it, and her heart sinks.

Voices audible through the front door of the flat. Male voices, and several of them. Charlie knows before she even inserts her key into the lock that it will be Scott, Lewis and Mikey. They have always been Jake's acolytes, but now that he lives in his own flat, they hang round him more than ever.

Just as she knows who will be in the flat, she knows exactly what state it will be in: overflowing ashtrays, a forest of empty lager cans on the coffee table, empty takeaway packaging all over the floor. The air is thick with the smell of marijuana, and Charlie – still prone to pregnancy sickness – gags.

Jake and Mikey are playing Phantasmagoria on the PlayStation, which is hooked up to the huge wall-mounted TV he insisted on buying. On the 65-inch, high-definition plasma screen, a male figure with a machete is decapitating a screaming female. Digital blood splashes in all directions. Jake grunts in Charlie's direction, but doesn't tear his eyes from the screen.

She sets down the bags of clothes and make-up she has taken from her old bedroom in Dartmouth Park. 'Are you guys going to be here long? Only I really need to take a nap.'

She's referring just to Mikey, Scott and Lewis, but Jake replies: 'We're heading out soon.'

'Where are you going?' Charlie's aware she sounds plaintive, needy. 'We're supposed to be going to the supermarket.'

'Going to drive out to the dog track in Essex in J's new wheels,' says Scott, cheerfully.

Charlie frowns. 'What for?'

'Have a few drinks, place a few bets, get some food.'

'We'll probably spend the night up there,' Jake says, airily. 'I'll be too pissed to drive us back.' He seems quite oblivious to the fact that four large adults can barely fit into his Audi in the first place.

'Spend the night… how?'

'I'll get us all hotel rooms.' He grins at Charlie, powering down the game but leaving the TV switched on as he gropes in his pocket for his car keys. 'Not like we can't afford it.'

'Thirty fucking K!' crows Lewis in a fake American accent, miming flicking bank notes in a 'make it rain' gesture.

Charlie watches them go, dumb with misery, then fetches a black bin bag and starts slowly cleaning up the place that she now calls home.

12

PAULA

'How can I help you? Mrs…?'

The woman on the other end of the phone is neutral, professional.

'Evershott,' says Paula. 'My name's Alice Evershott.'

She breathes in and out to steady her voice, then trots out the rehearsed spiel. 'The person we sold our house to has left some things here, and I wondered if you could give me their address? Our solicitor says that you were the agent who dealt with her next purchase.'

There's a silence as the estate agent tries to take in this request. She had no doubt been expecting a run-of-the-mill viewing or valuation. 'And when was this, exactly?'

'October 2003.'

'Oh, goodness. Quite a long time ago then. I was assuming this was a recent property purchase.'

'I know, sorry.' Paula puts on a 'silly old me' voice. 'The thing is, we've only just got round to clearing out the loft when we found her stuff. Mrs Glynn's.'

'I'm not sure if we'll still have the file, but even if we do, we can't give out the address. Not without Mrs…?'

'Glynn.'

'Not without Mrs Glynn's permission.'

'Oh, that's a shame. Only we think she'll probably want these things back.'

'Hold the line a second, let me go and have a word with my colleague.'

The line goes silence for several minutes, and when it's unmuted, it's an older woman's voice.

'Mrs Evershott? Hi, I'm Sheila Whittaker. Jo's passed this over to me because I've worked here the longest, so she thought I might know. The transaction file will have been archived by now, but I remember Mrs Glynn, because I handled the sale. You've got something of hers that she left in her old place?'

'Yes, that's right.' Paula prepares to play her trump card. 'Some baby things. Though I suppose the baby must be all grown up by now.'

'Baby things?' The woman sounds mystified. 'But Mrs Glynn was a single lady, in the process of getting divorced. And she didn't have any children.'

'Are you sure? She may just not have mentioned it.'

'She bought a one-bedroom flat. A lovely large flat, but it only had the one bedroom and a small study. And I was the one who met her at the property to hand over the keys on the day of completion. She had the removal van with her, with her furniture being unloaded. I remember thinking she had some nice pieces. But there was definitely no baby moving in. I'd have seen if there was a cot. And I imagine she would have bought a two-bedroom property if there'd been a child to accommodate.'

'I see.' Paula tries to order her thoughts. 'I must be mistaken then. Perhaps this stuff belongs to the people who lived here before the Glynns.'

'I expect that will be it.'

Paula thanks her and hangs up. Beyond the bedroom door, footsteps thunder down the stairs.

'Mum!' Ben yells. 'I'm going over to Connor's for a bit, okay?'

'Make sure you take your bike lights,' she shouts from the landing. 'It'll be dark soon.'

Jessica is at a sleepover with her best friend Chloe, so once the front door has slammed, the house falls silent. Paula does a circuit of the top floor, closing all the curtains against the early November gloom, then goes downstairs and lights the gas fire in the living room before pouring herself a glass of red wine.

A text arrives on her phone. Her heartbeat speeds up when she sees it's from Johnny Shepherd. She hasn't seen him for several months, since the day they kissed in the garden.

You in? xx

She wants to play it cool, but can hang on barely thirty seconds before replying.

Yes. Does this mean you're back in London?

Open your front door.

She does, and he's standing there in a camel overcoat with a brown velvet collar. It makes him look like a gangland boss.

'So, are you back for good now?' She gives him a side hug, but doesn't want to seem too eager. 'Thought the festival season ended in September? That was over a month ago.'

'I know, I know, I'm crap.' He grins, and his eyes crinkle at the corners in that way she finds so irresistible. 'We took on a big conference job up in Newcastle in October. I got back about ten days ago, but since then I've been completely snowed with paperwork. Sorry.'

He follows her into the kitchen, tugging off his coat. After tossing it over the back of the chair, he pulls her into a proper hug. 'Good to see you. I've missed you, Paul.'

'Yes, well…' She allows the broad smile she'd been repressing to light up her face. 'You're back now. Hungry?'

She makes them omelettes and garlic bread and they sit at the kitchen table and catch up. At some point Ben returns, thundering upstairs again with a quick yelled, 'Hi.'

'So…' Johnny leans back in his chair. 'You ready to resume the investigation into Lizzie's kid? Or have you been beavering away without me?'

'I'll be honest, I've taken a bit of a break from it too. It was all getting a bit much. The kids and I went to the Algarve for a couple of weeks after you left.'

'Nice.'

'Yeah, it was. Really nice. And then when they were with their dad I went away with a girlfriend for a few days. After that I did think about sitting down with Mum again and trying to make her talk about it, but I've been worrying about triggering her depression… and then there was the usual manic rush to get them ready to go back to school, and things have been extra stressful at work because we've had the builders in doing a refit at the surgery, so…'

'It's okay, you don't need to explain. It's heavy stuff. Not surprising you needed some time out.'

'Not a total time out, as it happens. Actually, I found out something interesting today.' Paula twirls the stem of her wine glass.

'Tell me.'

'You remember Alice Evershott told us the name of the solicitors' firm she used?'

'Yeah, it was a local one, wasn't it?'

'Hooper and Chilton. It stuck in my mind because my cousin's sister-in-law, Leanne, works there as a clerk. I mentioned it to Leanne back in the summer and she finally got a chance to take a look into the Evershotts' conveyancing file. I'd asked her to see if she could find out where Marian Glynn moved to.'

Johnny raises his eyebrows. 'Wow, nice work. And?'

'There wasn't an address, but she did find a note of the lawyers and estate agents dealing with both the Glynns' new property purchases. The husband, Tom Glynn, was buying another house in North London, but his wife's new place was in the Brighton area.'

She relays the conversation she had with Marian Glynn's estate agent that afternoon.

Johnny rubs his chin. 'Blimey. That's odd.'

'I know. I'm not sure what to think. I mean, Alice Evershott seemed to think that pink baby blanket might have belonged to the Glynns. But the agent was adamant no baby arrived in Brighton with her.'

'Sounds that way.'

'If she did have something to do with the disappearance of Lizzie's baby, then perhaps the Glynns were in it together somehow. Perhaps he kept it – or her, we're assuming a girl from that pink blanket, right? – when they split?'

'If that's the case I suppose we could easily check.' Johnny reaches for his wine glass and swallows a mouthful. 'But… listen, I've had plenty of time to think about all this over the past three months, and I've got another theory.'

Paula gives him a questioning look.

'Leave it with me for a bit. I need to call in a couple of favours.'

13

CHARLIE

'Won't be long now.'

The midwife smiles as she wipes the gel from Charlie's swollen midriff and puts the Doppler away. 'Baby seems fine – nice strong heartbeat. Do you know what you're having?'

She shakes her head. 'No. We wanted the surprise.'

This isn't exactly true. Jake has made it clear that he's only interested in having a boy. So to keep that possibility alive in his mind, Charlie elected not to be told the baby's sex when she went to her twenty-week scan. She went alone, of course. Jake has failed to attend any of her antenatal appointments and classes, and although he's told her he'll be there for the birth, he has shown very little interest in this event.

The midwife places her hands low down on the bump. 'Head's nice and low… are you experiencing any Braxton Hicks? Those are the practice contractions.'

Charlie nods. 'A bit.'

'Well, if they get a lot stronger and close together – five minutes or less – make sure you phone the maternity unit, okay?'

As she walks slowly back from the bus stop to the flat, Charlie is hoping that Jake won't be in.

They've not been getting on well lately. Not that they ever have, if she's honest with herself, but it's become worse. Now that she's nearing the end of pregnancy, and more tired than usual, she's placed a ban on Lewis and the others spending their whole time at the flat. To begin with, he continued to invite his 'crew' over anyway, but they seemed intimidated by the tense atmosphere and repelled by Charlie's hugely swollen body, and have stayed away; taking Jake with them, nine times out of ten, to play pool or video games and spend her money. It's not how she imagined living with a boyfriend would be. Not at all.

'Hello?'

She lumbers into the flat and slams her bag of shopping onto the kitchen worktop, now scratched and stained. The kitchen forms one corner of an open plan living area, and something in the room seems different. After staring for a few seconds, she realises what it is. The huge plasma screen has been taken off the wall, leaving behind ugly metal brackets and scuffed paintwork. The PlayStation and controllers are gone too.

Her heart pounding, Charlie hurries into the bedroom. Drawers have been pulled out, wardrobe doors left open. She reaches for her phone to ring the police and tell them they have been burgled. But then she stops. This is not a burglary.

Even so, something bad has happened, she can feel it in her bones. Something very bad.

The empty drawers are the ones that Jake used for his clothes. Hers have all been left undisturbed. The only things missing from the wardrobe are Jake's jeans and trainers. The small second bedroom, which now houses a cot and a changing table, is also untouched. She tries phoning Jake's mobile.

'The number you have dialled is no longer in service,' the robotic voice tells her.

What does that mean? She tries Mikey's number, but it rings out. And then, with a horrible, chill sense of foreboding, she opens her banking app. After paying for the flat rental and the car deposit, Charlie had transferred most of what remained of the £29,000 to a joint account that Jake could also access, as she had agreed to. The money was supposed to be for household expenses, but he only ever withdrew cash to spend on gambling and going out.

She checks the balance. £0.37. There should have been the best part of £10,000 in the account. Frantic, her heart racing and the baby twisting inside her, she tries Jake's phone again.

'The number you have dialled is no longer in service.'

She sinks to the floor as the truth hits home. He's taken all her money, and he's left her.

14

PAULA

'GPR.'

Paula looks at Johnny and blinks. 'I'm sorry – what?'

The two of them are on a trip to Westfield, Stratford, eating coffee and cake before they wander the shops together. In her case, trying to find a winter party dress for Jessica; in his, seeking trainers that don't make him either look old or as though he's trying too hard to seem young.

'Stands for ground penetrating radar.'

Paula scoops whipped cream from her coffee and licks the spoon. 'And we need this thing because…'

'Okay, here's my thinking. From the baby blanket Marian Glynn left behind in Muswell Hill, we have reason to believe she might have had Lizzie's baby there at some point. We also have reason to believe she misled the police about contact with Lizzie around the time of the birth.'

'So?'

'We also know that she arrived at her next home in Brighton with no sign of a child in tow. So, it's fair to assume that something happened to that baby while it was in her care.'

'Yes, but I still don't see why ground thingy radar… *oh*.' Paula feels her stomach lurch. 'Oh, God. You mean…?'

'That...' He hesitates. 'I know it's awful, but that a baby might be buried somewhere at the property. Or, put it this way, it's something that definitely needs to be ruled out. That's the first thing the police would do in the circumstances.'

'So why don't we just tell the police about it? Get them to check.'

'Time, really. We don't want to wait months and months for answers, do we? It could take the plod ages to get to the point of actually doing it. Anyway, I'm not sure they'd see the existence of a baby's blanket as strong enough evidence on its own. The blanket could be anyone's at the end of the day.'

Paula hugs her arms around her chest, suddenly chilly. She pictures Lizzie's baby dead, and it makes her shudder. 'I don't know, Johnny...'

He reaches out and squeezes her hand. 'Look, it's actually quite quick to do and relatively easy to organise. Only needs one bit of equipment. This guy I know, Roddy Davidson, works for a specialist geophysical surveyor. Sometimes festival sites have to be surveyed before they can be set up, if they think there could be something of archaeological significance there. The GPR scanners work a bit like metal detectors, except they scan for all sorts. Including human remains. Anyway, Roddy says he can get a guy over to the Evershotts' house with the equipment, no problem. With a garden that size it wouldn't take them long.'

'But even if we did set it up, it's not our house. It would be up to the Evershotts. They'd have to give permission.'

'You could talk to them. To her. Or we both could, but I think it would be better coming from you.'

Paula stares down at her fingernails for some time. 'Okay, I'll try,' she agrees. 'I guess it would be a good idea to check. On one condition.'

'Go on.'

'If they do find... something, we involve the police right away.'

'No problem,' Johnny agrees. He reaches over and ruffles her hair. 'Come on, I need you to help me find age-appropriate footwear.'

'That sounds like girlfriend territory.'

He gives her a searching look, then breaks into a grin, before grabbing her hand. 'You can call it whatever you like.'

Three days later, Paula is back in Ranmoor Road, alone this time.

She calls at number twenty-one, but there's no one in. For a second or two she wonders whether she should wait outside or come back later in the evening, but then she remembers something Alice Evershott told them when she and Johnny met her. She mentioned someone at number twenty-five, who had been living in the street a long time. Paula doesn't remember the name, just that the lady in question was elderly. *She'll probably be in then*, Paula decides. *Old people are always at home around tea time.*

Sure enough, she catches a glimpse of a flickering TV screen through the living room window. A late afternoon quiz show. It takes a few attempts for the doorbell to penetrate the noise of the TV. Eventually the front door is pulled open by a tiny, stooped woman with white hair and a hearing aid.

'You been standing here long, love?' she asks. 'Only I don't hear so well these days.'

'My name's Paula Donnelly.' Paula extends a hand. 'I'm sorry, I don't know your name?..

'Pinker. Maud Pinker. Are you from the broadband people?'

'No—'

'Pity,' Maud huffs. 'I can't figure out what's wrong with my what-d'you-call-it. Wretched thing.'

'Your router?'

'Yes, that's the one.'

'I could take a look for you if you like,' Paula offers. She set up the broadband in her house on her own, so she can't be that useless, she decides.

Maud Pinker is delighted by this suggestion. 'Ooh, if you wouldn't mind, dear.'

'I was calling in to see Alice Evershott.' Paula kneels down on the sitting room carpet and tries to untangle a nest of USB cables. 'But she's not at home.'

'Oh, yes? You a friend of hers?'

'Actually, I'm more a friend of the lady who lived there before Alice did. Marian Glynn.'

Maud's mouth twists into a grimace of disapproval.

'You knew her?'

'Strange fish she was.'

'In what way?' Paula switches off the router at the wall, then on again, before scrambling to her feet. 'There you are, it should be working now.'

'Always seemed an unhappy soul. She and her husband were a real mismatch. You'd never in a million years put them together. And then there was all that business with the baby.'

Paula freezes. 'They had a baby?'

'Well, whether it was his or not was anyone's guess. I never saw her in the family way, but after he left her… people said he'd got a bit on the side, you know… she – Mrs Glynn – shows up one day with a baby. I suppose she could have been minding it for someone else, but I tell you, it was pretty odd.'

'Really?' Paula manages to keep her tone mildly interested.

'Of course, there's no one round here that would remember it now, but I recall Mrs Fletcher – she used to live between me and the Glynns – saying how she kept hearing a baby crying. And then one night I saw her.'

'Saw…?'

'I couldn't sleep so I got out of bed to make a cocoa, and I heard a car door slam. I looked out of the window and I saw Marian Glynn lifting a baby out of the back of her car and carrying it into her house. A tiny baby.'

'I'm afraid that's out of the question.'

Adrian Evershott is a tall, portly man with thinning hair and a patrician manner. He's wearing corduroys and a pair of leather slippers. Paula can picture him smoking a pipe.

'The GPR scanner is relatively small, and doesn't do any damage,' she says, sounding more confident than she feels. She's sitting at the kitchen table with both Evershotts, drinking a glass of home-made lemonade. 'They're a reputable firm, professionals, and they wouldn't take very long. We'd be prepared to pay some compensation, you know, for your inconvenience.'

'It's really not a question of money,' Adrian says, stiffly, 'but the whole idea of having someone turn up and start searching for a body in one's garden on the strength of some amateur sleuthing nonsense that amounts to nothing more than a theory… Frankly, it's beyond the pale.'

'There is some compelling evidence that Marian Glynn had a baby here, in this house, though.' Paula has just told them Mrs Pinker's account of what she saw. 'A baby that subsequently completely vanished.'

'No, I'm sorry, but if that genuinely is the case and not just neighbourhood gossip, then it's a matter for the authorities. Now if you'll excuse me, I've got an appointment with a stiff Scotch and the six o'clock news.' Adrian picks up his paper and heads out of the kitchen.

'I'm really sorry,' his wife says, frowning at his retreating back.

Her only chance now is to appeal to Alice's maternal instincts, Paula realises. She reaches across the table for her hand. 'This could be my sister's child,' she explains, and she doesn't need to force the tears that well up in her eyes. 'I've spent the last sixteen years wondering what happened to her. If we don't find anything then fair enough, we've reached a dead end. But if there is a baby buried in your back garden, wouldn't you want to know? I know I would.'

Alice squeezes Paula's hand back, but shakes her head sadly. 'I do understand how you feel, honestly I do. And I dare say I'd feel the same. But you heard what Adrian said. He's not going to change his mind, and I don't entirely blame him. The idea of searching the garden for a dead body, it's just…' She shudders. 'I'm really sorry, but it's out of the question.'

15

CHARLIE

'We really ought to report this to the police.'

Her parents stand in the living room of the flat in Tufnell Park, taking in the place where their daughter has been living for the past six months. They've never been able to visit before, because she stubbornly refused to divulge the address. But now that Jake has gone and taken her money, she has been forced to capitulate and call them. She didn't know what else to do.

Her father points at the spot on the wall where the TV used to be. 'I'm not so much concerned about the vicious little sod nicking the TV, but taking the money. Ten grand – that's a *lot* of cash.'

'But the account was in our joint names,' Charlie points out. Her face is puffy and the baggy T-shirt she's wearing to cover her bump is stained and crumpled. 'It's not a crime to take money from your own account.'

'He still had no right to it, if you ask me.'

'Especially since it was supposed to be your university funding. What possessed you to let him near it, I'll never know.' Her mother's tone is devoid of sympathy, and Charlie bursts into tears.

'I'm sorry, darling, I know this probably isn't the right time to be having a go.' Her mother draws her into a hug. 'But you can see why we're angry about the situation. Even with a joint account, half of that money was technically yours, and all of it was yours, morally. We ought to at least try and find out where Jake's got to.'

'His phone's switched off.' Charlie drags her sleeve across her eyes. 'And before you say it, he's not at his mum's place. I've checked. I just don't know what I'm supposed to do now.'

'Okay, well, let's forget about Jake, for now at least.' Her father sighs. 'At least until after the baby's here.'

'Exactly,' her mother agrees. 'That needs to be your priority. So why don't you go and pack your things, and we'll get going.'

Charlie shakes her head. 'I'm staying here. This is where we live, and it's where the baby's going to live.'

She doesn't say it out loud, but if Jake comes back and she's moved out, that will mark the end for them. She won't see him again, baby or no baby. Their relationship may have been hanging by the thinnest of threads, but she still doesn't want it to end. Part of her hates him, but she still wants him. Or the idea of him, at least.

'But, sweetheart, don't be silly, you're going to need help. You can't manage a new baby all on your own, with no support. Come on, let's get your stuff. Is your case in the bedroom?'

'No,' says Charlie, firmly. 'I've left home, remember? It doesn't actually make any difference that Jake's not here; he wouldn't have helped anyway.'

'Come on, be sensible!' Her father goes into the hall and starts rummaging through the cupboard looking for a suitcase. 'You're a seventeen year old about to give birth for the first time,' he calls over his shoulder. 'What if the baby arrives in a hurry? You should have someone with you.'

'I'll text Hannah and get her to come over,' Charlie says quickly.

'All right then.' Her mother is still guarded. 'But I still want you to think about coming home, all right?'

Her father sighs, pulling his daughter into his arms. 'Oh, Lott-pott.' He uses the diminutive he gave her when she was tiny. 'Stubborn as ever. Okay, well, we'll get going. But you know we're just at the end of the phone if you need us. Promise me you'll call us at least, any time, day or night.'

Charlie feels a contraction surge through her lower abdomen. She clutches the edge of the worktop, blinks hard until it's gone. *Probably only another practice one*, she tells herself, and the last thing she wants is her mother getting hysterical and boiling kettles.

'Okay, okay, I promise.'

Six hours later, just as she has climbed into bed with a bowl of ice cream and Netflix on her iPad, it happens.

There's a strange pinging sensation between her legs, then a gush of liquid soaks her pyjama trousers. Her waters have broken.

Immediately a strong contraction surges over her body, making her back hurt and her thighs tremble. She feels it in her brain too, as though she can no longer think with any clarity. Panic engulfs her just as viciously as the pain does.

After what feels like forever, the pain recedes, leaving Charlie on her knees on the damp mattress. A temporary stillness follows. She edges cautiously off the bed. Grabbing her phone, she tries dialling Hannah, who hasn't yet replied to her earlier texts. There's no reply. The panic builds again as she tries her mother's phone. No reply from her either. It's 11.30 p.m., and her parents will be in bed and probably asleep, or at least with their mobiles on silent. She texts her sister, Lucy.

You awake Lu?

The phone buzzes just as another contraction starts to build.

Yep why?

I'm in labour

Her sister phones her immediately, but already Charlie is unable to speak as the wave of pain crashes over her. 'Get Mum,' she manages to gasp. 'I need Mum.'

Charlie's daughter is born seven hours later, just as a pale November dawn is breaking. Her mother is in the delivery room, and the rest of her family are waiting outside.

At lunchtime her father goes out and buys them all a picnic and they sit around Charlie's bed on the ward, eating Scotch eggs and KitKats. Her mother is cradling her newborn granddaughter, her expression beatific, if a little stunned.

'She's got a real look of you about her,' she says to Charlie, pulling back the corner of the white blanket. 'Of course, we didn't have you when you were this small, but your foster mother gave us some pictures from when you were tiny.' She sighs with unadulterated pleasure. 'She's really bonny.'

'That's what I'm going to call her,' says Charlie, reaching out for the white bundle and cradling her with surprising confidence. 'Bonnie.'

'Aw, that's so pretty, Char.' Her sister snaps away with her phone. 'Bonnie Lucy.'

Charlie shakes her head. 'Bonnie Lucy doesn't work. Sounds dead wrong.'

'No worse than Bonnie Charlotte,' her sister retorts waspishly.

Charlie strokes the downy head. 'Her middle name's Isadora,' she tells her family. 'I've always loved that name, but it's a bit grand for every day. So she's Bonnie Isadora.'

16

PAULA

Paula climbs into her car, but before she switches on the ignition she makes a phone call.

'Mum, it's me. What are you up to?'

It's been a few days since Johnny's plan came to nothing, and the search for Lizzie's baby has once again lost momentum. But now that she knows about the police investigation in the wake of the inquest, there is still one person who might have relevant information, however sketchy. Her mother.

'Just been out to the shops,' Wendy tells her. 'About to put a wash on.' Her tone sharpens. 'Why, is there something wrong?'

'I'm going to the cemetery to visit Lizzie. I thought you might want to come with me.'

'No, thank you,' her mother says, stiffly. 'It's not really convenient just now. I need some notice.'

Paula sighs, and slides the key into the ignition. 'Mum, I know this is hard for you, but can I at least just ask you something? I know the police spoke to you after the inquest.'

'I imagine they spoke to plenty of people, not just me.'

'But they asked you if you knew what might have happened to Lizzie's baby. Because they had evidence from the post-mortem that she'd given birth just before she died.'

There's a long silence.

'Mum?'

'I would have told them the truth: that I hadn't seen Lizzie in years, so knew nothing about it.'

Paula grips the steering wheel. 'When I tried asking you about it back then, when I was at school, you told me I was just imagining that Lizzie was pregnant.'

'Well, how do we know you weren't? The police never found any baby, so it was safest to assume there was no baby in the first place.' There's a forced bravado in Wendy's voice, making her sound harsh. It's as though she is trying to convince herself – as much as her daughter – that she believes this.

'But, Mum—'

'Sorry, love, I've got to go, there's someone at the door.'

There's only silence at the end of the line.

Paula looks down at Lizzie's grave, before placing the potted poinsettia on the ground in front of it.

In our hearts always

She always reads the headstone when she comes. She could never forget what it says, but it's part of the ritual, part of communing with her sister's spirit. Not that Lizzie would have approved of the carved message. She would have preferred it to say something along the lines of: *She was great fun, for an alkie*

It's a bitterly cold Saturday afternoon, but the glow of the autumn foliage has not quite given way to winter. Dry leaves cover the cemetery paths, but the trees are still partially clothed in crimson and amber. Paula felt a strong urge to come today, to try and spur herself on. Find some inspiration to carry on with the search even though they've hit a dead end. Predictably her mother had been no help.

Safest to assume there was no baby…

She looks at the surrounding graves, studies the size and proportions of the burial plots. Some of them, she knows, have more than one person buried in them. Would Lizzie's baby be permitted burial here, with her mother's ashes, if it were to turn out that she had died? The possibility that this small human, all that is left of her sister, could also be gone fills her with sorrow. Even worse is the idea that they will never know for sure either way.

However things turn out, she's going to move heaven and earth to bring her mother here eventually. She knows that, deep down, Wendy did love Lizzie, and that she needs, finally, to mourn. And Paula loved her sister too, even though at times she was hard to love. She has happy memories from before the drinking started: Lizzie playing dress-up with her, reading to her, teaching her to roller skate.

'If only you could have stayed sober, Lizzie,' she tells the empty air. 'You would have made a great mum.'

As she turns and walks back to her car, her phones rings.

'Is that Paula Donnelly?'

'Speaking.' She recognises the voice, but can't place it.

'It's Alice. Alice Evershott.'

'Hi.'

'Since you were here, I've been thinking and thinking about… what might be in the garden and I just can't get it out of my head. I don't think I'll be able to rest until I know. So, I was going to ask…' She trails off.

'It's okay, go on.'

'Do you think there's any chance you could get the people with that equipment here at short notice? Only Adrian's away this weekend, so I thought it might be a good time to have a go… at looking. And if there's nothing there, well, he doesn't ever need to know, does he?'

*

Three hours later, Paula and Johnny are in the back garden at number twenty-one, Ranmoor Road.

As soon as Alice Evershott had hung up, Paula phoned Johnny, and within a couple of hours, his friend arranged to send one of his employees to the site. The technician, Lee, has just arrived with the GPR equipment and Alice joins Paula to watch from the kitchen window as he sets it up. Like Paula, she is probably feeling a little underwhelmed both by Lee, who looks about fifteen, and his scanner. It resembles a small yellow lawnmower with a digital screen fixed to the handle.

His breath forming clouds in the frosty air, Lee trundles the scanner in a grid pattern across the lawn, first moving longitudinally, then turning the scanner through ninety degrees and going across it. He pushes the equipment over the patio, into the corners and under the foliage that fringes the lawn.

'To be honest, I was expecting something a bit more dramatic,' Paula whispers to Alice. 'You know, some bleeps or flashes, or an alarm going off.' The radar remains eerily quiet.

Eventually Lee brings the GPR to a halt. 'Right, all done,' he tells Johnny.

'Is that it?' asks Paula, who has left Alice in the house and headed outside. Her heart sinks like a stone.

'Not quite.' Lee starts pressing icons on the digital screen. 'That's the scanning done. Now we look at the data. Everything the radar's picked up is recorded on here.'

The screen displays what looks like an incomprehensible jumble of lines and numbers. Lee studies it intently for a moment, then points to a large ceanothus bush at the far end of the garden. 'It looks like there's something buried there.'

Johnny and Paula exchange a look.

'From the time taken for the signal to bounce back from the object to the receiver, it suggests that whatever's there is about eighteen inches from the surface.'

Lee checks the grid on his screen, then strides down to the bush and points to the soil slightly to the right of it. 'Here.'

'Oh my God, have you found something?' Alice comes out into the garden, her face pale, her hands clutched to her chest in panic. 'Oh my goodness, I really didn't expect them to find anything. What will happen now?'

'Lee here says there's definitely something.' Johnny says. 'Got a spade? The obvious thing is to start digging, surely?'

But Alice is shaking her head. 'Adrian would never forgive me. If they've found… what you suspect might be there… then I'm afraid I'm going to have to call the police.'

17

CHARLIE

After two nights in hospital, Charlie and Bonnie return to the family home in Dartmouth Park.

'It's only temporary,' Charlie tells her parents, firmly. 'Then we're going back to the flat.'

They exchange an anxious glance. 'Give it a while,' her mother urges. 'Don't make a decision yet. At least not until you've done a few more nights of three a.m. feeds.'

She glances down at Bonnie, tucking the blanket around her and rearranging Charlie's faded yellow duckling at the end of her crib. The stuffed creature is a little battered after seventeen years of being fiercely loved by its owner, but it was her oldest and best-loved toy when she was young, the only possession she still has that pre-dates her adoption.

'Mum, I'll be fine. I've got to manage on my own some time.' Charlie employs more bravado than she's actually feeling. Already, she's exhausted. But within a few days, Bonnie – who everyone agrees is a very good baby – has settled into a rudimentary routine. Charlie is adamant that she's going to return to the flat. She doesn't want to admit it to her family, but she's still hopeful that Jake might return. There's been no word from him, but surely now he will have seen on social media that his daughter has arrived. Surely that will make him want to give things another try?

'How hard can it be?' she asks, with the optimism of youth.

'Hard,' her mother replies, drily.

'That's a load of crap. Look at her now, sleeping peacefully. All I have to do is feed her every few hours, and nap when she naps. It'll be fine.'

But it's not fine.

Bonnie continues to be the dream baby, even back at the flat, but what no one could have anticipated was the thirty-something professional couple in the flat below moving out and a group of students moving in. Any and all hours of the day and night are filled with baying laughter, booze-fuelled arguments and thumping drum and bass.

'Shut up, you wankers!' Charlie screams, thumping the floor, when they've woken her for the fourth or fifth time in one night. Unable to get back to sleep, she pulls up Jake's number and tries calling it, just as she has done over and over since he disappeared.

'The number you have dialled is no longer in service.'

In desperation, she calls Hannah.

'What?' she screeches at the other end of the line. In the background are the unmistakable sounds of partying. 'I'm out. In a bar. You'll have to speak up.'

'Can you come over?' Charlie pleads. 'I can't sleep, and I don't want to be on my own.'

The connection is lost, but Hannah WhatsApps her later.

In uber on way over

Good old Hannah, thinks Charlie, as she settles Bonnie in her crib and boils the kettle to make herself a herbal tea. The neighbours downstairs start up the thumping dance music again.

'Jesus Christ!' says Hannah when she arrives. 'Noisy bastards round here, aren't they? Never mind, babe, I'm here now.'

But Hannah has been drinking all evening, and within fifteen minutes she's fast asleep on the sofa, and snoring, and Bonnie is awake again for a feed. Her mother was right, Charlie thinks miserably, as her tears drip slowly onto her daughter's fuzzy head, she can't do this on her own. She needs another adult human being, if only to have someone to talk to. She presses 'Dial' once more, even though she knows the outcome.

'The number you have dialled is no longer in service.'

She sticks it out for two nights, three nights, four nights, still convinced that the door will open and Jake will walk in as though nothing has happened. But eventually the toll on her nerves becomes unsustainable.

'You win,' Charlie concedes wearily to her mother after a week of disrupted sleep. 'Not because of the baby, because of the selfish arseholes downstairs. As soon as I can get myself organised, I'll move home. For good.'

18

PAULA

'We will need to take a DNA sample from you, Mrs Donnelly, but I imagine you'll be okay with that?'

'Of course.' Paula is sitting in an interview room at Wood Green police station. It's two days since the officers arrived in Ranmoor Road, followed by a specialist crime scene team. Two days since Paula and Johnny watched helplessly from the Evershotts' kitchen as Adrian Evershott, his weekend away disrupted, paced angrily behind them. Two days since the officers in Tyvek suits and protective booties erected a white cover tent before starting to dig at the end of the garden, while a videographer recorded the process. Two days since a small wooden box was carried out to the back of the forensics van.

The CID officer, DI Kevin Stratton, pushes a glass of water towards Paula, offers a tissue. He's a short, stocky man with thinning ginger hair and horn-rimmed glasses. In Paula's opinion he looks more like an accountant than a policeman. 'You all right to continue?'

She nods. She wishes Johnny could have stayed with her, but she understands that their statements have to be taken separately.

'So, you've made your statement outlining how and why you came to be looking in the garden of number twenty-one Ranmoor Road for the remains of your late sister's child.'

Paula nods again.

'Okay.' He looks at her over the rims of his glasses. 'I'm afraid I can now confirm that the skeletal remains of a small male infant were found buried in the garden. Obviously the pathologists are conducting further tests.'

She takes a sip of water and hugs her arms tightly around herself, feeling suddenly cold. So it was true. She had so wanted it not to be. But a boy. She hadn't been expecting that. Neither had Lizzie.

'Now, I'm going to show you some pictures…'

DI Stratton pushes a tablet across the table towards her, displaying a photograph. 'And I want you to tell me if you recognise this as having belonged to your sister.'

Paula stares uncomprehendingly at the first picture of what looks like a dirty, bluish-grey rag. The second picture he flicks to is a close-up of one corner of the rag. A clear capital 'N'. She bends her head so that her face is nearer the image, letting her eyes scan over all of it: top to bottom, side to side. And only then does she realise what she's looking at. An embroidered letter, exactly like the 'S' on the pink blanket she has at home. A blue baby blanket. Blue for a boy.

'No,' she says, 'that wasn't my sister's.'

'You said your sister had some baby things at her flat. But this wasn't among them?'

'No. Definitely not.'

'So you haven't seen it before?'

Paula hesitates. 'No.' She wonders whether she should now mention the pink blanket. Perhaps Alice Evershott has already done so, when she gave her own statement. 'It must have belonged to Marian Glynn.'

DI Stratton gives a grim little smile. 'We will certainly be speaking to Mrs Glynn as a matter of urgency. Sussex Police are sending officers to her home to bring her in for questioning.'

'Well, there you are then,' says Paula. She feels suddenly overwhelmed, unwilling to talk. 'You'll soon have her side of the story. Can I go now?'

Johnny is waiting for her in reception.

He opens his mouth to speak but she cuts him off. 'Let's get out of here. I need a bloody drink.'

They go to the Prince on Finsbury Road. Johnny fetches a pint for himself and a glass of red wine for Paula, who finds a table in a corner.

'They told me the baby they found at the bottom of the garden is a little boy. And here's the thing that will blow your mind: he was buried with an initialled blanket identical to the one Alice Evershott gave us. Only it was blue. And it had the letter "N" on it.'

Johnny's eyes widen over the rim of his pint glass. He sets it down slowly on the table. 'So if the baby we've found is "N", then who is "S"? And more to the point… where is she?'

PART TWO

2003

19

MARIAN

'They're going to have to run some tests.'

'Uh huh.' Her husband's voice is muted slightly by a poor phone connection, but Marian Glynn can tell that he's subdued. 'What kind of tests?'

'On both of us. It's standard procedure; I'm sure it's nothing to worry about. I'm sure they'll all be fine. And if the results are okay, they'll accept us for treatment.'

There's a beat of silence. 'Okay, well… let's talk about it this evening when I get home.'

'What time will you be back?'

'Normal sort of time. About seven.'

'I'll make dinner for us, shall I?'

'Sure, if you can be bothered. Otherwise, we can grab takeout.'

'Okay… bye, darling.'

But Marian is speaking into dead air. Tom has already hung up.

She goes back to her desk in the always busy, always over-stretched social services department in the North London borough where she lives and works. After making a cup of instant coffee and grabbing a biscuit from the tin on the filing cabinet, she fields a call about a child that a neighbour suspects is being abused, and another from a school where a pupil hasn't attended for several weeks.

'Any news on the Taylor court case?' she calls over to her colleague and friend, Angela Dixon. A hearing is due for a couple whose three children have been taken away and put into care because of the couple's inability to care for them adequately. The same old story: family breakdown due to drink, drugs, petty crime, poverty.

'Not yet. We'll be able to hear Darren Taylor kicking off from here when it happens.' Angela grins. She's a sturdy woman, both physically and emotionally; her cheerful mood is rarely knocked off course. 'Christ knows why he's so keen to get the kids back.'

'Probably so he can spend the benefits on cannabis,' Marian says with a sigh. She thinks of her job as a leaky boat. All she can do is bail out water as fast as possible to stop it from sinking, but the thing will never be an invincible whole. The excessive caseload, fuelled by a slashed budget and increasing social need, means doing several things at once and rarely doing anything well. It's simply a matter of trying to stay afloat.

'It's Terry's birthday,' Angela observes now. 'I think there's going to be cake in the meeting room in a bit.'

'I've got to go out on a call,' Marian says, standing up and shouldering her bag. 'Lizzie Armitage.'

'Ah.' Angela raises her eyebrows to indicate that no further explanation is needed. 'Good luck.'

As soon as she sees Lizzie's eyes, Marian knows that she's drinking again.

It's no big surprise. Lizzie Armitage is her longest-standing client, an alcoholic who has been in and out of prison for theft and fraud a few times, and occasionally sober for brief periods. She's not as thin and gaunt as she usually is, having gained some weight during a recent stint in rehab. But as soon as Marian sees the flushed face and dazed expression, she knows. She knows that when she gets closer, she'll be able to smell the booze. She's seen it enough times before.

Lizzie is beyond speech, staring blankly at her social worker with an unfocussed gaze, wiping her nose with the cuff of her long-sleeved T-shirt. Marian picks her way through the empty takeaway boxes, discarded clothes, empty lager cans and plastic bags and sits on the edge of the grimy sofa, on a brown patch that looks suspiciously like excrement. An underfed cat darts from beneath the sofa and leaps onto the windowsill. Marian makes a note on her clipboard to alert the local RSPCA.

'How are you doing, Lizzie?' The question is redundant; she already has her answer just by looking at her. 'Shall I make us a cuppa?'

She doesn't really want one herself, and dreads entering Lizzie's kitchen. But at least this way she will know that Lizzie has taken in some fluid. Like many drinkers, her self-neglect means failing to drink sufficient amounts of water, putting her kidneys at risk, in addition to her liver. She switches on the limescale-crusted kettle, and finds mugs and teabags. There's a milk carton in the fridge, but it's out of date by over a month. Black tea it is, then.

If Lizzie will admit she's drinking again, then Marian can try and find her a place on one of the many oversubscribed local rehab programmes. But Lizzie, as usual, is in denial.

'I don't even know why you would say that,' she whines. 'I'm fucking sober, and that's the God's honest truth.'

Marian gives her client a long look. Lizzie could be an attractive young woman, she thinks. Should be. She's still only in her twenties. But years of alcohol addiction and smoking marijuana have taken the shine from her hair, left her complexion sallow and spotty and mottled her limbs with rashes. Marian points silently to the empty vodka bottle on the floor.

'That wasn't me,' Lizzie protests. 'That was Macca. My fella. He brought his booze round here.'

Marian sighs and takes a printed flyer out of her bag. 'There's a new alcohol dependency programme opening up, run by a charity, quite near here. They've even got some residential places, which I think would be good for you. So if you're interested, give me a call and I'll see if I can get them to take you. But don't leave it too long – it's bound to fill up fast.'

Lizzie puts the flyer on the sofa without even looking at it, her eyes a blank.

'Maybe discuss it with your sister?'

Paula Armitage is a bright and sensible girl who has been doggedly looking out for her older sister since she was a child.

There's no reply. Marian stands up, glancing at the back of her skirt as she does so. 'Well, you've got my number. Give me a call if you want to talk, and I'll call round to check up on you soon, okay?'

In her house in Muswell Hill, Marian strips off her skirt and shirt and throws them straight into the washing machine. Not for the first time after a day at work, her primary need is to feel clean again. Only then can she begin to unwind and organise her thoughts. She takes a shower, puts on jeans and a T-shirt and goes back down to the kitchen, where she makes herself a cup of proper tea: Earl Grey in a china pot, with milk.

Once she's seated at the table with her tea, she fishes in her handbag for the leaflet she was given at the fertility clinic earlier that day, reading through it carefully.

While our clinic prides itself on an IFV success rate of over 30%, maternal age is a factor, and in women over 40 the live birth rate drops to under 10%.

Marian reads this sentence several times as she sips her tea. *Under 10%.* She is forty now, almost forty-one. So her chances of success are less than one in ten. Even if their initial test results are favourable, they still have a 90 per cent likelihood of failure. But then again, they could be among the lucky ones. One thing is certain: there is no point in embarking on such an expensive and stressful course of treatment unless they believe it could work. They have to remain optimistic. Because Marian wants to have a baby of her own. She wants it more than anything.

As she clears the tea things into the dishwasher, Marian reflects – and not for the first time – that they should have started to try and conceive sooner. It's a painful thought process, because nearly a decade ago she had wanted to press on with starting a family and Tom, who is two years her junior, had wanted to wait a while. They were thirty-three and thirty-one when they met at a conference where Tom, an architect, had been giving a talk on public sector housing. They married two years later when Marian was thirty-five. She was keen to abandon contraception straight away, but at Tom's insistence, she delayed throwing her diaphragm into the bin until they had moved from a flat to a house. But by then she was thirty-seven, and entering the realm of reduced fertility. When they tried having scheduled, unprotected sex, nothing happened.

'We'll just keep trying,' Tom had told her. 'No need to get doctors involved; it will happen eventually.'

But it didn't.

By the time they were referred to an infertility specialist, Marian was several months past her fortieth birthday. She was, in theory, still eligible for a single NHS-funded cycle of IVF, but with a six-month waiting list for the treatment, the Glynns were advised to cut their losses and pursue private treatment rather than delay further. And even with a choice of private clinics in North London, a wait of several weeks to be seen was still the norm. A large number of middle-class women were leaving child-rearing until later life, and many of them were paying the price for that delay.

Marian puts the leaflet back in her bag and makes a start on peeling potatoes and setting them to boil. They'll have cottage pie, she has decided; it's easy to make and one of Tom's favourites, especially if he can wash it down with a glass of full-bodied red. Once the potatoes are cooking, she calls Tom's mobile, but there's no reply. She chops celery and carrot, then tries calling again, but once more her call goes to voicemail. A few seconds later, a text arrives.

Sorry, work emergency. Should be back in an hour x

What sort of emergency can an architect experience outside office hours? Marian wonders, irritably. A building collapsing? A disastrous choice of window material? She wants to text and ask him exactly that, but she knows that she won't. It's not in her nature to rock the boat. It never has been. She's never really done anything egregious in her life. In contrast to the disordered and chaotic home lives of her clients, her own upbringing was conventional and deeply dull. There was no abuse and no broken home. No excitement either. No dramatic highs or desperate lows. Her father was a provincial bank manager and her mother a housewife, and she and her younger sister were raised in a comfortable semi-detached in Esher.

At her girls' grammar school, Marian had been bright but unambitious. She liked to produce good work and please her teachers, but there was little originality, or spark. She enjoyed art, but knew she was not sufficiently gifted to go to art school, so assumed she would end up working in an office somewhere, until such time as marriage and motherhood released her. It was the school careers officer who suggested she consider social work, and she took hold of the suggestion even though she didn't really know what social work entailed. It sounded like something worthwhile, worthy even, but the early idealism acquired while taking her degree at York University and during her subsequent training quickly evaporated when she started work.

Marian likes doing things well and, as she began her career, she hoped to be efficient in her job, even if she lacked genuine passion. But her working days are about constantly letting people down and never fully meeting the needs of her clients. A good day is simply one where no overt disaster occurs.

It's not forever, she tells herself frequently. Tom has said it too. The unspoken assumption has remained that when they become parents she will give up work, exchanging tramping around council estates and municipal buildings for the cosy world of NCT coffee mornings and play dates. But here they are on the cusp of middle age, and that day has still not arrived. They can afford to live on Tom's salary whether she becomes pregnant or not, but if she gave up her job now, what would she do all day? For Marian there is no alternative calling apart from motherhood. That is what she wants; what she has always assumed she'll have.

A search of the weekly veg box turns out a single, wizened onion, which Marian starts to chop, punctuating the task with swigs from the large glass of red wine she has poured. She sautés the vegetables and meat, mashes the potatoes and assembles the pie, and as she is sliding it under the grill, Tom's key clicks in the lock.

'All right?' he says, coming into the room and slapping a copy of the *Evening Standard* down on the kitchen island. His overcoat is streaked with rain, and he pushes his damp hair back off his forehead. It's still as dark as it ever was, and apart from a few lines in the corners of his eyes, and a slight softening of his jawline, he hasn't aged. He's still a handsome man. Whereas she *has* aged, Marian knows. Her hips have spread, her brown hair has become frizzy and streaked with grey, and her eyelids droop a little at the corners.

She pours Tom a glass of wine and hands it to him. 'What happened at work?'

'Oh… something and nothing.' He rubs a hand through his hair again. 'Not my job actually; one of Vanessa Rowley's… her client was freaking out about the poured concrete in their skyscraper not being up to standard. It's an engineering problem really, but we got dragged into it.' He smiles at his wife, touching her arm briefly. 'How about you? How did you get on at the clinic?'

Marian passes him the leaflet and he reads it, his face betraying no emotion other than mild exasperation. 'Bloody hell – look at the prices!'

'We need to get ourselves booked in for the preliminary tests,' Marian says, taking knives and forks from a drawer. 'What's your diary looking like for the next few days?'

'Not now, okay? I haven't even got my coat off. Let me go and change out of this wet shirt, too.'

Before Marian can speak, he's headed back into the hall. 'We can talk about it later,' he says, without turning to look at her.

20

PAULA

Paula Armitage jumps down from the bus platform and starts the fifteen-minute trudge along Green Lanes to the block of flats where she lives.

Other pupils from Turnbull Comprehensive take the same route, and there's usually a gaggle of boys from her own year. They're a pain, and Paula ignores them, or tries to.

'Oi, Paul!' Jason Shepherd shouts. 'Paul!'

He's not shortening her name as a sign of affection or familiarity. It's because the Year 11 in-joke is that she looks like a boy. Her light brown, stubbornly wavy hair is cut short and stands up in wayward fronds. She has freckles, and a gap in her front teeth, and her body is strong and stocky and devoid of curves. She shrugs her backpack higher on her shoulders, dips her head and ignores the taunts, but this seems to annoy them. They don't like being ignored. They want her to show how upset she is, or how angry, or to come up with a smart remark.

'Here, Paul, I've got something for you!'

Instinctively, Paula glances behind her, to see a fat, ginger boy called Shane Creswell hurl an empty drink can in her direction.

'What the fuck do you lot think you're doing?' A car pulls up at the kerb, and a window is rolled down. Paula already knows whose car it is. It belongs to Johnny Shepherd: Jason's older brother. 'Pack it in, you lot. Leave her alone.'

'Or what?' sneers Adil Kumar. He's the brains in the group, although that bar is set low.

'Or you'll have me to deal with. All right?'

When there's no response, Johnny repeats, 'I said – all right?'

One of them mumbles something, then Adil says, 'Fuck this, I'm going to the chippy,' and the group slinks off in the opposite direction.

Johnny rests his right forearm on the sill of the open window as he lights a cigarette. 'You okay, kiddo?' he asks Paula, through a little cloud of smoke.

'Fine,' she mumbles. She can't look him in the eye, but she does look at his broad, muscled forearm resting on the car door frame. It's tanned, even though it's only April, and lightly dusted with golden hair.

'Good stuff.' He throws the car into gear and pulls out into the traffic, but not before turning his head and winking at her.

Johnny Shepherd winked at me. Paula embraces this little nugget of joy in what has otherwise been a drab day. Johnny left school ages ago, so he must be well over twenty. He looks like someone you'd see on TV, and has a glamorous girlfriend called Karen who works on one of the make-up counters in Selfridges. Paula sees her at the bus stop sometimes, and envies her porcelain-smooth skin and glossy, dark curls. She envies Karen being able to kiss Johnny Shepherd. And sleep with him. Imagine that. Her cheeks grow warm at the thought.

She'll think about that later, but first she has stuff to do. She puts her key in the door to the flat – it turns reluctantly. Her mother won't be back from her job as a supermarket supervisor for around three hours, so there's plenty of time for Paula to make a start on supper, as she's expected to do. But if she's to go out and come back again without her mother knowing about it, she needs to get to work quickly. She sits on a tall stool in the flat's tiny kitchen and sets about peeling and chopping onions and peppers.

It's been five years since her parents separated, and she's used to it just being her and Mum at home now. Her father lives in Totteridge with his new partner, and she sees him every few weeks or so, along with other relatives from that side of the family: her paternal grandmother, her Uncle Alan and Aunt Shirley and sundry cousins. Her older brother, Steve, works in Dubai and Lizzie… well, Lizzie hasn't lived at home for many years. Because of the age gap between them, she barely remembers a time when they were both under the same roof.

Paula works swiftly and efficiently, piling up the prepared vegetables on the chopping board and rinsing rice through a sieve to cook later. Her mother has worked full-time since her parents separated, and Paula has been fending for herself after school for years. It's made her self-sufficient and a competent cook, even if she is sometimes a little lonely. Her mother texts her to ask if everything is okay, and she replies that it is.

She doesn't mention that she's going out to see her sister. She's not supposed to see her any more. The Armitage family have decided, unanimously, that Lizzie can only be a bad influence on her younger sister. Nobody visits Lizzie. Nobody even talks about Lizzie. It's been that way for several years now.

Once she has changed out of her school uniform and into jeans and a sweatshirt, Paula stuffs supplies into her bag – cat food, a few teabags and some biscuits: nothing that will be missed – and trudges back to the main road. The traffic is so heavy that it will be quicker to walk rather than sit on a slow-moving bus, so she continues on foot, up Westbury Avenue and towards Tottenham, where Lizzie lives in a run-down housing association flat.

Her sister seems pleased to see her, which Paula knows from experience means she can't be all that drunk. If she's hammered,

she's barely aware of her surroundings, let alone able to acknowledge a visitor.

And Lizzie's out of bed and dressed, which isn't always the case.
In fact, there's something different about her today: something
intense and yet calm. She hugs her younger sister, then sits down
again on the grimy couch while Paula feeds the cat and puts away
the tea and biscuits she has brought. Outside, a blue-grey sky is
studded with clouds, fast-moving in the April breeze, but the dark
brown living room curtains are drawn, making the flat seem even
pokier than it already is.

'You need to get some fresh air in here,' Paula says briskly,
yanking at the tatty curtains and forcing the window open a crack.
'It's a lovely day outside.' She switches on the kettle and pulls out
the rubber gloves she has brought with her, setting about cleaning
up the worst of the mess in the kitchen. Then she makes tea and
puts biscuits on one of the plates she has just washed.

'Here,' she says, holding them out in Lizzie's direction. 'Take
these and I'll grab the mugs.'

Lizzie stands and reaches across the coffee table to take the
plate, and the stretching motion makes her loose T-shirt ride up.
Paula stares, her lower jaw dropping in a silent 'Oh' of surprise
and shock.

'Lizzie!' she breathes. 'Is that…?'

Lizzie takes the biscuits and sits down again abruptly as though
nothing has happened. But Paula, whose mother says she has a
stubborn streak a mile wide, won't be deterred. She pulls her older
sister to her feet and yanks up her top, confirming that she didn't
just imagine the change in her shape.

'You mustn't tell anyone, Paul.' Lizzie's hands instinctively fall
to her swollen abdomen. 'And I mean fucking *anyone*. If they
know I'm pregnant, social services'll take the baby away as soon
as it's born.'

'But Lizzie—'

'You've got to promise me!'

'Okay,' Paula says calmly. Lizzie is getting agitated, and the more agitated she is, the more likely she is to turn to drink. 'I won't say anything. Who would I tell anyway, apart from Mum? But what are you going to do? If you go to the hospital to have it, people will know.'

'I'll have a home birth,' says Lizzie, breaking off a corner of a biscuit. 'It's much more natural that way, anyway. And then I'll just look after it. Having a baby will keep me off the booze, you'll see.'

Paula doubts this. And while she doesn't know much about pregnancy, she can tell that Lizzie must be quite far along for it to show so much on her tiny, thin frame. She wonders why she never noticed before, but then realises that the last couple of times she visited Lizzie was in bed, her body covered with her grubby duvet, and before that it had been winter and Lizzie, who is always cold, was shrouded in thick layers.

Lizzie sips her tea, then setting her mug down carefully, asks: 'She's awake now… want to feel her?'

She reaches for Paula's hand and lays it flat against the tight mound of flesh, its skin stretched taut. Paula feels a strange shifting sensation under her fingers, then the prod of something hard, something alive. Her eyes widen in amazement.

'It's kicking!'

'She's kicking,' Lizzie corrects her.

'How do you know it's a girl if you haven't been for a scan?'

'I just know,' Lizzie says dreamily, an intense expression lighting up her thin face and returning some of the beauty that the drink has eroded. 'I just know she's a girl. But you mustn't tell anyone about her: she's our secret.'

21

MARIAN

'Is this all right?' Marian is looking at herself in the full length mirror. She has squeezed herself into a flowing muslin dress, one that's a little too summery for the showery, early May evening, but which at least she can still fasten. Most of her formal dresses and cocktail wear were purchased years ago, and are now a couple of sizes too small. She pinches the roll of flesh just above her hip fretfully, and twists through ninety degrees to survey her back fat.

'You look fine,' Tom assures her, threading blue enamelled links through his shirt cuffs. Then, clearly realising he has just damned with faint praise, he adds: 'I've always liked you in that dress.'

Marian manages a smile, twisting her dull and unruly hair into a sparkly clip and applying blusher and lipstick. She has had a long day in court at a child custody hearing, and the make-up only serves to make her look more tired.

She and Tom are having dinner with his university friend Gareth Coker, and Gareth's Iranian wife, Farzeen. All Marian really wants to do is to slip into a pair of trousers with an elasticated waist and curl up on the sofa with a large glass of Chardonnay to watch *Have I Got News For You*. But Tom frequently complains that they never go out in the evening, and she knows that he really enjoys Gareth's company, so she feigns an enthusiasm that she's not really feeling.

'Are you ready?' she asks, shrugging a pashmina over her shoulders and trying to forget how bulky she looks. She dreads the imminent side-by-side comparison with Farzeen, who is whippet-thin and would look stylish in a bin bag.

'As I'll ever be,' says Tom, straightening his cuffs and picking up his jacket. 'We can grab a bottle of wine en route.'

Gareth and Farzeen live in Highgate, in a converted flat on a road of large, prosperous-looking red-brick villas. The interior is all pale-coloured minimalism, and as elegant as Farzeen herself. Tom and Marian walk into a cloud of scented ambergris candles and a spiced Persian lamb dish, to be embraced by Farzeen, slender and cat-like in black leggings and a striped grey and white man's shirt. Marian feels like an over-stuffed sofa in the fussy floral dress.

'What's your poison, M?' asks Gareth, as Farzeen goes back to the kitchen island to prepare a pomegranate salad. He's as stocky as Farzeen is slight, slicks his hair back with gel and wears a heavy gold signet ring. Marian has never felt comfortable around her husband's friend. After twenty years of friendship, the two men have a long history of shared secrets and misdemeanours, and he barely bothers to hide that he thinks Tom could have done better.

'I'll have a gin and tonic, please,' Marian says with as much grace as she can muster, adding desperately, 'Farzeen, do let me know if I can help.'

'All under control, darling,' Farzeen says easily, tossing her long hair off her face while she makes a salad dressing. Sensing that Marian would rather hover near her than be a third wheel in the men's conversation, she adds, 'Maybe just put some knives and forks out for us.'

Half an hour later, the four of them sit on two benches at the scrubbed oak table, and Farzeen passes round bowls of fragrant couscous and lamb stew. Gareth asks Tom about the latest projects at his practice and then they discuss Gareth's work as an analyst for a right-wing think tank. Almost as an after-thought, Gareth asks Marian, 'Still doing the government's dirty work down at social services?'

'Yes.' Marian nods, but doesn't elaborate.

Farzeen shudders slightly, and Gareth says, 'I don't know how you stand it. To be honest I thought you'd have moved onto something a bit more salubrious by now.'

So did I, thinks Marian, merely giving a rueful smile.

Tom uncorks the bottle of Shiraz they brought with them, and waves it over their glasses. Instantly Farzeen places a hand over the top of hers, and Marian notices that she only has water in it. Farzeen sees her noticing, and colours prettily.

'You might as well know...' she says, with a coy smile. 'We have some news.'

Marian's heart sinks.

'You're not...?' Tom's eyes widen, and he gestures towards Gareth. 'You're finally going to make this old reprobate a dad?'

Farzeen nods. 'I'm due in November.'

'Congratulations! Seriously, that's fantastic!' Tom claps his friend on the back.

Marian puts her fork down, glancing at her husband. 'We've got some news too, haven't we?'

'You're pregnant too?' Farzeen looks confused, taking in Marian's empty gin and tonic glass and the wine in front of her.

'No, not yet.' Marian feels herself blushing. 'But I hope to be soon. That's the news. We're about to start IVF treatment.'

'Why did you tell them that?' Tom demands irritably, as they sit in the back of a taxi two hours later.

'I thought it seemed like a good moment. Anyway, I assumed you'd already spoken to Gareth about... our issues.'

'Of course I haven't,' Tom scoffs. 'We're blokes. We don't talk about stuff like that.'

'But…' Marian suppresses a vague sense of unease. 'Why shouldn't we tell people? We've got our tests at the clinic tomorrow. And if it works, they'll know soon enough.'

Tom turns his head to look out of the window of the taxi.

'Don't you want a baby?' Marian demands.

'Of course – it's not that. It's just that some stuff… the fertility problems… it's our personal business, that's all.'

Once they're home, Marian retreats to the bedroom in hurt silence. She hears Tom come in while she's showering, and when she emerges she finds an olive branch in the form of a cup of peppermint tea on her night stand.

'Sorry,' Tom mumbles. 'It's just not an easy thing to talk about. Not when Gareth has managed to get Farzeen up the duff just like that.'

'You don't know it was just like that,' Marian points out, stiffly. 'They might have been trying for ages. The point is, unless people talk openly about this stuff, you never know.'

Tom leans his head on her shoulder. 'Tell you what,' he says, and she knows from his tone he's trying to make amends for his earlier gruffness. 'Why don't we get ahead of the game and pick out a few baby names?'

Marian softens slightly, taking a sip of her tea. 'You go first.'

'Well…' Tom smiles. 'I've always really liked solid, traditional names. William, Alexander, Henry. And for girls, things like Victoria or Charlotte.'

Marian raises an eyebrow. 'Really?' She's amazed that she's only just finding out this fact about her husband. Her own tastes are far more bohemian; more along the lines of Otto and Willow. But she doesn't say so now, because she wants to keep Tom engaged in the process. 'Charlotte's pretty,' she says, cautiously. 'And I've always quite liked Alexander.'

'Percy?' suggests Tom.

'Oh, no,' Marian says with a shudder. 'Not Percy!'

They continue this game after they've switched off the light, saying names out loud into the darkness until eventually there's silence, followed by the sound of Tom's snores.

The following morning, when they drive to the fertility clinic, Tom has gone silent again. His moods have been erratic over the past few months, swinging from monosyllabic to affectionate and back again.

'Are you okay?' Marian asks quietly, looking at the road ahead.

'Fine. Bit hungover, that's all.'

'Are you sure? Only—'

'Look, I'm making time to come to the bloody clinic and wank into a paper cup, aren't I? Can't you just be glad about that? Jesus, Marian. You'd try the patience of a bloody saint!'

Once they're in the clinic reception area, Tom helps himself to free coffee and biscuits and his mood stabilises sufficiently for him to give her a wan smile as she's led off first for her scan and blood tests. After he's donated his sample and they've filled in reams of paperwork, Marian prepares to set off on foot to her office, leaving Tom to go and retrieve the car.

She gives him a dry kiss on the cheek. 'See you for supper?'

Tom shakes his head. 'We're being wined and dined by a big new corporate client.'

'We?'

'Me and Vanessa.'

Ah yes, Vanessa Rowley. That name again.

'Fine,' says Marian, forcing a smile. 'I'll see you when I see you.'

22

PAULA

As soon as Paula gets back from school, she hurls her school bag into the corner of her room and reaches for the shoebox under her bed.

Tossing the lid to one side, she removes the contents and spreads them out on the duvet: a glittering swirl of coins, interspersed with a couple of crumpled notes. Painstakingly she starts to count. From saving her pocket money and most of the cash from her Saturday job in the Walthamstow branch of Clintons Cards, she has saved £63.45. She folds the notes into her leather purse, but the coins are too heavy and bulky to fit, and she has to tip them into a plastic sandwich bag and shove them to the bottom of her handbag. Then she changes out of her uniform and into denim cut-offs and a baggy T-shirt, slings her bag across the front of her chest and sets off to the bus stop.

It takes a frustrating fifty minutes for the bus to get to Brent Cross. Paula has very little time to shop and get home before her mother returns, and the ticking clock flusters her, turning her mind to an inefficient blank.

She darts into Boots, which seems an obvious place to start, and stands staring at the confusing array of products in the Baby & Child aisle. 'Breast pads'? She has no idea what they are, or what 'cradle cap shampoo' could be for. She decides to concentrate on the most basic items, picking up a pack of newborn nappies and nappy sacks, some baby wipes, cotton wool and lotion. The till assistant gives her a knowing smile and glances at Paula's midriff as she packs the items into a large carrier bag.

Emboldened by her success, and with £51 still to spend, Paula goes to Mothercare and picks out a multipack of onesies, a few babygros, a changing mat and a couple of cotton blankets. Then she hauls her purchases up to the top deck of the bus and sits there impatiently as it toils its way through rush hour traffic. It's after six o'clock by the time she gets to Hornsey. She'll just have to hope her mother is late.

'Need a hand with those?'

She looks up as she stumbles off the bus, bumping her carrier bags against the other commuters, to see Johnny Shepherd standing on the pavement, cigarette in hand.

'No, it's… I'm fine.' Paula blushes furiously. She can see him glance at the pack of nappies and the Mothercare logo. It's one thing for the cashier in Boots to assume she's pregnant, but she doesn't want Johnny Shepherd thinking that. In fact, that's the last thing she wants.

'Just been doing some shopping for a friend,' she says. It sounds untrue, and the heat in her cheeks intensifies.

'I can help you get those home if you like,' Johnny offers. 'I'm meeting Karen off her bus, but I can always meet her halfway; she lives near yours.'

Paula shakes her head. 'No, don't worry,' she says, quickly. 'This stuff's not too heavy.'

Johnny shrugs. 'All right then, kiddo.' He pats her shoulder. 'You take care now, okay?'

Her eyes downcast, and her face still pink, Paula toils up Green Lanes and back to the flat. She knows before she has even turned her key in the lock that her mother is home. She can hear the radio and smell the faint whiff of frying onions. She thinks about turning tail and hiding her purchases in the building's ground floor laundry room, but her mother has heard her footsteps and flung the front door open. Too late.

'There you are! I was wondering where you'd got to.'

Her eyes flick down to the shopping. 'Mothercare?' she demands. 'What the hell have you been doing at Mothercare?' She rips the bag roughly from Paula's hand and rifles through the newborn-size garments. 'Bloody hell, Paul, please don't tell me you're pregnant!'

Paula shakes her head, but she knows her expression is one of pure guilt.

'What's all this stuff for then?'

Wendy Armitage pulls herself up to her full height, which is not much taller than her daughter. She's of slighter build, wiry rather than stocky, and her hair, which is the same colour and texture as her daughter's, is dyed a vivid auburn to cover the grey. 'You'd better not be lying to me, young lady!'

'They're for someone at school,' Paula mutters. 'A girl in Year 12. She gave me some money and asked me to go shopping for her.'

'What girl?' demands Wendy, 'And why's on earth's she asking you?'

'Umm, Lauren Billings,' Paula says, hastily. She's sure she heard a rumour somewhere that Lauren was pregnant, so this probably doesn't count as a lie.

'Hmmm,' says Wendy, unconvinced. 'Well, go and put it in your room and give me a hand with supper.' She narrows her eyes, and glances down at the waistband of her daughter's shorts. Paula wants to protest that she can't possibly be pregnant if she's never had sex, and disconcertingly finds her mind flashing back to her encounter with Johnny Shepherd. She breathes in hard, to make her stomach look flatter.

*

The next day is Wednesday, which means Wendy is working a half-day.

Knowing her mother will be at home when she gets back from school makes Paula drag her feet, literally and metaphorically, as she trudges up Green Lanes.

Wendy is wearing a velour tracksuit and a very self-satisfied expression. 'Kettle's on, sweetheart.'

They usually have a sweet treat on Wednesday afternoons, and today is no exception. There's a plate of Penguin biscuits on the table, but when Paula reaches for one, she sees that there's a white paper packet set out deliberately in her place.

'What's this?'

'Go on,' says Wendy, pouring boiling water into the teapot. 'You may as well open it.'

Inside the paper bag there's a pregnancy testing kit.

'Mum!' Paula hurls herself down into her chair. 'I told you! I'm not pregnant!'

'In that case you won't mind doing a test then, will you? Let's just settle it, once and for all, and then we don't need to talk about it again.' Her mother holds out a paper cup for her to use.

'Fine!' shouts Paula, snatching up the rectangular box and stomping into the bathroom.

'There are instructions in the packet,' Wendy shouts through the door. But Paula already knows how the kit works. She was there when Debbie Ashcroft had a scare after she'd slept with Jason Shepherd and did a test in the girls' toilets during lunch break.

She's dying to pee, which makes collecting a sample a bit messy, but she manages to catch some in the paper cup and stick the tip of the test stick in it. Squinting at the instructions, she checks the amount of time she needs to wait. Three minutes.

Stomping back to the kitchen, she hands over the test stick and sits down to eat a chocolate biscuit, ignoring her mother. She knows exactly what the stick will say, so there's no point giving this charade any more of her attention.

'Well,' says Wendy eventually, throwing the test into the bin. 'That's that, then.'

Paula grunts and takes a second biscuit.

'I still think it's a bit strange you doing that girl's shopping for her. Who is this girl, anyway? You've never mentioned her before.'

'Lauren Billings. I just felt sorry for her, okay?'

'Seems a strange reason to me,' sniffs Wendy.

'You said taking the test would settle it,' Paula snarls through a mouthful of chocolatey crumbs. 'So just shut up about it, okay?'

She has decided she'll take the baby stuff to Lizzie the following evening. The supermarket where Wendy works is open late on Thursdays, and she's often not home until 9 p.m.

Lizzie opens the door to her, but she's swaying back on her heels, and stumbles down the hall, giving off fumes of White Lightning. Over her shoulder, Paula can see the hunched shape of Macca rolling a joint, lager can in hand, his long greasy hair grazing the collar of his denim jacket.

Paula drops the shopping bags in the hallway, and pushes past her sister, snatching the beer from Macca's hand and tipping it down the sink.

'What the fuck d'you think you're doing, you moron?'

Macca stares up at her blankly with bloodshot eyes, probably unable to remember who she is.

'Lizzie's pregnant!' Paula hisses. 'She's having your baby. She shouldn't be drinking or smoking weed.'

Lizzie appears behind her shoulder. 'Hey, Paul, chill out, we were just taking the edge off a bit. Nothing heavy. It's fine.'

Paula ignores her, scruffing Macca by the back of his jacket and hauling him to his feet. He's a good twelve inches taller than her, but his body is wasted by alcohol abuse, while Paula is sturdy and strong. She hauls him into the hallway and pushes him out of the front door of the flat, slamming it in his face and putting the chain on. Then she whirls back into the living room, scoops up the half-rolled joint and throws it into the bin. Lizzie's scrawny cat winds its way around her ankles, mewling plaintively, so she rummages through the fridge and finds a half-eaten can of tuna, which she puts in the cat's empty bowl.

Lizzie stands in the doorway, immobilised by her drunkenness. 'You can't chuck that stuff out,' she whines. 'That was good grass.' She's as thin as ever, but her pregnant belly has expanded rapidly, even in the few weeks since Paula last saw her. She looks almost ready to give birth. Paula takes her by the shoulders and guides her to the sofa, lowering her onto it. With her hands still on her sister's thin frame, she looks her in the eye.

'Lizzie. You're expecting a baby. You're putting it at risk if you smoke weed.'

Macca starts hammering on the door to be let in, but fortunately Lizzie is becoming sleepy, slumping back onto the cushions. Paula fetches the stained duvet from the bedroom and drapes it over her sister, removing her shoes and positioning a cushion behind her head. She can't leave now, not while Macca's still hanging around outside. Lizzie might end up letting him in, and if he's got more alcohol on him she might drink even more. She might drink too much. Like all relatives of alcoholics, Paula is only too aware of the risk of alcohol poisoning, and that every binge can potentially be lethal.

There's no working phone in the flat – Lizzie was too disorganised and too broke to pay the bills, so BT long since cut off service – but Paula knows that there's a payphone on the ground floor of the building. She waits until Macca's footsteps have retreated, then goes downstairs and phones her home number. Her mother's not back from work yet, so she leaves a message on the answering machine.

'Mum, I'm staying over at Carly's tonight… we're going to watch the DVD of Ocean's Eleven*… I'll go straight to school in the morning, so I'll see you tomorrow. Okay, bye.'*

She added in the detail about the DVD because her friend Carly had been talking about the film at school and she thinks it will make her tale more plausible. She doesn't have her uniform or her school books with her, but she can skip first period and go home to fetch them after her mother's left the flat.

When she gets back upstairs, Lizzie is in an alcoholic stupor and the cat is scratching to go out. Paula lets it out of the fire escape door and sets about cleaning the kitchen and then clearing out a drawer at the bottom of the wardrobe and arranging the baby clothes and bedding neatly inside it. The baby still needs something to sleep in, but she should have time to save enough for a cheap Moses basket before it arrives. She's seen some pretty ones in the market.

Around 10 p.m., Macca starts hammering on the door again. Paula sits hunched in the armchair watching *Big Brother* with the TV sound on low, waiting for him to leave. Eventually there are raised voices as one of the neighbours complains about the noise, then all goes quiet. Paula eventually takes herself off into the bedroom and falls into an uneasy doze.

At school the next day, all she can think about is Lizzie's baby. She's promised not to tell anyone about it, but someone needs to know; she realises that now. Maybe not the authorities, but *someone*. The child is at risk, that much is clear. Would her mother want to help? She doesn't want anything to do with Lizzie, but her own grandchild would be different, surely? Her brother Steve might listen, but he's too far away to be able to do anything. She remembers her father being a little less harsh to Lizzie in the days when her parents were still married, so she phones him after school, before Wendy gets back.

Colin Armitage doesn't like being interrupted at work, and his tone is brisk.

'Something wrong, love?'

'Dad, I wanted to talk to you about Lizzie.'

'Paulie, we've been through this before. As long as she's drinking, I don't want anything to do with her, okay?'

'But, Dad, she's—'

'I'm sorry, love, but you know what was decided after she stole your mum's ring.'

When it happened, it was her father who had been less upset about the ring, more inclined to forgive. But since the divorce and the start of his life with Estelle, he seemed to find it easier to distance himself from his elder daughter. She represented an earlier, messier time he wanted to forget.

'But, Dad, this is really important. Can't I at least come over at the weekend and talk to you?'

'Estelle and I are having a weekend away, on the Norfolk Broads.'

'Something's happened. She's—' Paula stops herself abruptly. She's suddenly hearing Lizzie's fearful voice, begging her not to tell anyone. And Colin's reaction would almost certainly be to arrange for the baby to be taken away from Lizzie.

Her father is still talking. 'Anyway, as far as I'm concerned, Lizzie is nothing to do with me any more, so I really don't want to hear about her latest disaster. Your sister's no longer part of this family.'

23

MARIAN

Since her permanent mission is to lose weight, Marian shouldn't really be eating a third chocolate chip cookie.

The packet is open on her desk and she has been dipping into it mindlessly as she attempts to draft a Section 47 investigation report. When she realises what she's doing, she tosses the remains of the third cookie into the bin in disgust. The departmental office is quieter than usual, with most of the caseworkers on house calls or attending a child protection case conference. Marian stares intently at the screen, but her attention is wandering, her mind elsewhere.

Brushing the biscuit crumbs from her keyboard, she pulls up Internet Explorer and types in the web address for Tom's firm: Cavendish Partners. She clicks on the link to 'Our People' and scrolls down the list until she finds what she's looking for.

Vanessa Rowley.

Vanessa joined us from Lidgate Morris Architects in December 2002. She graduated from Newcastle University in 1988 and worked as a trainee at Razzini Associati in Milan before joining Lidgate Morris in 1994. In her spare time, Vanessa is a keen skier and enjoys tennis and wine tasting.

Enjoys wine tasting, thinks Marian scornfully. *Who says that on their company profile?* Is it code for being a bit of a lush? She looks at the profile photo. Vanessa has dirty-blonde hair, a square brow above a broad nose and large, wide-spaced grey eyes. Her lips are full, with an upward tilt at the corners. None of her features are perfect, but the appeal of her face is greater than the sum of its parts. In other words, she's very attractive. From the dates on her bio, Marian estimates her to be around thirty-five.

Yes, she can see why Tom might be drawn to her. She's not stupid. But ultimately what has Vanessa got to offer him? What Tom wants is a family and she – Tom's wife – is about to make that a reality. A fling with a flighty single girl-about-town can't possibly have the same appeal, not once they have a baby. This Vanessa is no threat. Or at least she won't be once Marian is pregnant.

There's a party at Cavendish Partners that evening to celebrate the construction team breaking ground on one of the firm's high-rise hotels in the Gulf. The unavoidable case conference Marian has to attend will prevent her from getting home to change before the party, so she'll have no choice but to wear the shapeless denim skirt and floral blouse she left the house in that morning.

Once the meeting is finished, she digs out a pair of high-heeled pumps she keeps under her desk for occasions like this, and rummages in the back of a drawer for a chunky gold necklace. Day-to-evening, isn't that what the fashion magazines call this sort of makeover? She regards herself in the mirror of the dingy ladies' loo and realises that the transformation hasn't really worked. The heels only serve to accentuate the frumpiness of the skirt and the gold jewellery is lost against the busy pattern of the blouse. She considers heading to the nearest parade of shops to buy something new, but it's already six o'clock and she has told Tom she'll be there soon after six. Sighing, she freshens her make-up, adding more lipstick and mascara than she would normally wear, and sets off to Regent's Park.

*

'Anyone here I might know?'

Marian scans the event space behind Tom's shoulder. It's already crowded, and there is a loud hum of laughter and conversation. Black-clad waitresses glide through knots of people, expertly filling glasses from champagne bottles wrapped in white linen napkins. As Marian takes a sip of the icy, sparkling liquid, she catches sight of a long, dirty-blonde ponytail swishing against a slender, elegant neck, and the zipper of a teal-coloured bodycon dress.

Tom places a hand in the small of Marian's back and steers her firmly in the opposite direction. 'Gareth and Farzeen should be here somewhere: I invited them and they said they planned on coming.' A tall, portly man in a loud tie stumbles into their path, clearly the wrong side of a large quantity of champagne. 'Ah, Malcolm!' says Tom, loudly. 'Darling, you remember Malcolm, don't you?'

Marian – who is quite sure she's never laid eyes on the man before – nods.

'Malcolm, this is my wife, Marian. Malcolm works in our Glasgow office.'

'Your wife?' slurs Malcolm, taking in her messy hair and poor attempt at evening wear. He was clearly expecting someone altogether more glamorous. Most of the women are in work wear, but it's the streamlined variety: fitted, figure-hugging dresses and smart suits.

Malcolm clearly doesn't want to talk to Marian any more than she wants to talk to him. He's slurring badly anyway, so as conversations go it's a non-event. Marian makes some excuse about needing a glass of water and slips away. Tom has disappeared, absorbed into the crowd. Searching for any familiar face, Marian's eyes alight on a waitress with a tray of canapés. Suddenly aware that she has barely eaten since lunchtime, she lurches at one of the mini burgers, only to have it drip garlic mayonnaise onto the front of her skirt. She escapes to the Ladies, which is a lot more salubrious than those at Haringey Social Services.

After dabbing her skirt, it now sports a dark water mark on the front of her groin as though she's wet herself. She edges out of the bathroom with her bag clutched in front of her.

And then she sees her.

Vanessa Rowley is standing a few feet away, talking to Tom. Marian knows straight away that it's her, and that she had correctly picked her out from her rear view. The teal dress is made from heavy jersey and fits like a glove over a body that's slim but curvy. The provocative high ponytail is flicked over her shoulder, revealing large silver drop earrings as she tilts her head closer to hear what Tom is saying.

It's as if some sixth sense makes Tom look up. He catches sight of Marian standing there, and his expression tells her that he's embarrassed by her baggy, stained skirt and her glaringly incongruous footwear. He breaks away from Vanessa and comes towards her.

'Ready to go home?' he asks, although Marian has barely been there twenty minutes.

She nods her assent, and forces a smile, but she saw it. She saw Tom's subtle, caressing touch to Vanessa's bare arm as he left her.

When Marian gets back from work the next day, there is a thick envelope from the fertility clinic waiting for her.

She sets her bag down on the kitchen table and sits down to read it. There's a computer-generated report with a list of values for blood and hormone levels, and the doctor has sent a copy of his summary letter to their GP, interpreting the results.

I'm pleased to report that Mrs Glynn's AMH level (indicating ovarian reserve) and FSH level (follicle stimulating hormone)

*are above average for a woman of her age. Unfortunately,
however, the tests on Mr Glynn show azoospermia, which
as you know means that there is virtually no sperm in his
ejaculate. This occurs in 2% of the male population, and is
the reason why conception has not occurred after a prolonged
period of unprotected intercourse.*

*I realise this will be very disappointing news, but there is
a very good chance that Mrs Glynn would be able to conceive
following a course of AID (artificial insemination by donor).
From the blood results and ovarian scans, I would estimate
a 45% probability of achieving a pregnancy after three
treatments of this kind.*

*I will be suggesting we move forward with an appointment
to discuss this further.*

After reading the letter through several times, Marian leaves it
open on the table. When Tom returns from work, she points to
it silently, unable to bring herself to tell her husband something
that she knows will devastate him. She pours herself another glass
of wine and takes out a glass from the cupboard for him, filling
it without uttering a word or even making eye contact. He takes
it from her and gulps down half the glass.

'Jesus Christ,' he says, in little more than a whisper, blindly
sitting down at the kitchen table. His face has grown pale. 'Is this
right? It says here that I'm firing bloody blanks!'

Setting down the wine glass, he covers his face with both hands
and rocks slightly to and fro. When he takes his hands away, Marian
is surprised to see that there are tears in his eyes. She knew he
would mind, but expected him to try and hide it. To shrug it off.
Shrugging things off has been Tom's way of late.

'I really, really wish we'd found out sooner,' she says quietly,
pressing a hand on his shoulder.

Tom pulls himself to his feet and wraps his arm round her. 'I'm so sorry,' he says into her shoulder, with so much regret that Marian wonders for a moment exactly what he's apologising for.

'It's not your fault,' she says, patting him awkwardly. 'And anyway… you read what Dr Dempsey said about AI? He says there's a very good chance of it working.'

Tom releases her and sits down again, taking another mouthful of wine and rereading the letter. 'But that would be with donor sperm?' He looks up at her.

'Yes, but—'

He tosses the letter aside as though their predicament is the fault of the doctor. 'That means the baby would be related to you, but not to me.'

Marian sits down opposite him and takes a deep breath. 'Tom…' She struggles for the most tactful way to make her point. 'If you have no viable sperm, then any solution we go with is going to mean a child that's not biologically yours. But at least the baby will be mine. So half ours. Surely that counts for something?'

Tom ignores this last question. 'I'm sure I've read somewhere that they can harvest just a handful of sperm from infertile men and inject them into the egg.'

'We can certainly ask Dr Dempsey about it.' Privately, Marian thinks that the doctor would have mentioned this if it were an option. 'I'll phone them first thing and make an appointment for a consultation.'

As Marian had anticipated, Dr Dempsey is hesitant about recommending intracytoplasmic sperm injection – he tells her this is referred to as ICSI – for the Glynns, stressing that although all it needed for it to be successful was a single spermatozoon, this needed to be of good quality, and lab tests suggested that the few Tom produced weren't.

He sends them away to discuss the situation for twenty-four hours, but after a long circuitous argument, Tom still insists that he wants to try ICSI rather than donor insemination.

'Are you absolutely sure?' Dempsey probes. 'It's a lot for your wife to go through. Painful daily injections, feeling unwell and out of sorts…?'

'Yes, I'm absolutely sure.' Tom's voice is firm, but he avoids eye contact. 'Marian wants it too, and I'll be there to help and support her.'

Dr Dempsey holds up his hands. 'Fine. I feel obliged to spell out that this is no walk in the park. Of course that's par for the course with in vitro procedures, but with normal IVF at least the success rate justifies it. In your case, the chances of a live baby at the end of all this are pretty low.'

Marian glances at Tom, then back at the doctor. 'We know that. But we want at least to try.'

Three days later, she starts the process of injecting hormones into her stomach daily in preparation for egg retrieval. Tom helps her with the first two, but then makes excuses or manages to be out of the house when they need to be done. Marian persists for the remainder of the twelve days, watching her stomach become mottled with bruises. She's uncomfortable, sweaty and moody, and feeling increasingly lonely. The process of having a baby is finally under way, but Tom is distant and disengaged. He's just worried, she tells herself. Protecting himself against the possibility of it not working.

Thirty-six hours after the final injection, they return to the clinic for her eggs to be harvested. They are pronounced to be of adequate maturity, and the ICSI procedure results in two fertilised embryos.

'Could we have twins?' Marian asks, her eyes shining, when she and Tom return on the fourth day for the implantation procedure.

'I've always loved the idea of twins!' She glances over at Tom, but he still seems absent, shell-shocked.

'Well, yes, potentially…' Dr Dempsey prevaricates, picking up a pen from his desk and twisting it through his fingers. 'But I ought to warn you, that although we've seen cell division, the embryos aren't very good quality. They're graded under the microscope, and in your case the number and quality of the cells in the blastocysts are at the lower end of the scale.' When Marian's face falls, he adds, 'That said, we've had high quality embryos that don't result in a pregnancy, and vice versa, so let's remain hopeful.'

Tom holds Marian's hand as the thin plastic catheter is slid inside her, but he's looking down at his shoes rather than at his wife's face.

For the next twelve days Marian dutifully takes it easy, resting as much as possible.

Her abdomen feels swollen and she's sure her breasts are a little more sensitive than normal. *Could this be it?* she wonders, so excited that her heart flutters from just thinking about it. Is she really expecting a baby after nearly four years of trying? Or are these signs just – as the clinic warned – the result of the progesterone pessaries she's using?

She swings between hope and terror, sometimes sure that they will be lucky, at other times despairing that they won't. At night she has incessant dreams of conception and birth, sometimes disturbing, sometimes tantalising.

'Best not to think about it,' Tom instructs her, whenever she recounts a dream or ventures to raise the possibility that the embryos have implanted. Not thinking about it certainly seems to be his approach, changing the subject every time she mentions some intriguing little sign or symptom.

After what feels like months of agony rather than two weeks, the wait is over: day thirteen of Marian's cycle finally arrives. Her breasts are still tender and she's sure her abdomen is more rounded than usual. This has to be a positive sign, surely? She feels optimistic as she takes a pregnancy test into the ladies' toilet at work, and waits for the result, mentally running through how she will surprise Tom with the news that night.

But the little plastic stick callously foils her plans. Her eyes fill with tears as she stares down at the two words, devastated.

NOT PREGNANT

24

MARIAN

Because it's Saturday, Tom gets up before Marian and brings her a cup of tea in bed. Then, just as he does every Saturday morning, he goes out to buy *The Times* and *Guardian* and pick up fresh bread from the local bakery and deli items for lunch.

As he returns, Marian has just come out of the shower and is towelling her damp hair. 'Shall I put some coffee on?' she asks. They usually have coffee when he comes back with the papers. Frequently they have pastries too; one of many reasons her waistbands are all too tight.

'I was going to head out,' he says vaguely, not meeting her eye.

'Head out?' she queries, sounding shriller than she intended. He's been doing this quite a lot recently; disappearing for a few hours at weekends for no apparent reason. Since the negative pregnancy test, it's been worse.

'I need to run a couple of errands. We need a new extension cable for the lawn mower.'

'Can't you do that after coffee?' Marian insists, tipping grounds into the coffee pot and reaching for mugs. 'We need to talk about what we do next.'

'What we do next?' Tom asks, though from the way he avoids eye contact Marian is convinced he knows what she means.

'About treatment. About having another try at ICSI.'

Tom is already shaking his head. 'No,' he says, firmly. 'I don't want to go through that again. Not when you found it so gruelling, and the chances of it working are so small…' He takes the mug of coffee Marian has handed him and gulps it quickly. 'And before you ask, no, I don't think we should try donor insemination. I'm sorry, but I don't want you giving birth to another man's child.'

He colours slightly underneath his weekend stubble, as though he's said something unacceptable, but there's a defiance in his eyes that Marian has never seen there before.

'There's still adoption,' Marian says, plaintively. 'Then the baby wouldn't be related to either of us, so we'd be in the same position. We really need to talk about that as an option, surely? That's all that we have left if we're going to be parents.' She's on the edge of tears, sniffing slightly as she reaches into the pocket of her threadbare dressing gown for a tissue. The dream of her, Tom and a child biologically related to them both – a blissful family unit – has been snatched abruptly away. She's clinging on to whatever straws are left. It's a miserable prospect.

Tom softens slightly. 'Okay,' he says grudgingly, giving her shoulder a quick squeeze, before placing his half-drunk mug of coffee in the sink. 'But later. I really need to get going.'

As she dries her hair and puts on a load of washing, Marian turns over in her mind what she and Tom have just discussed. It didn't take them very far, especially when she raised the subject of adoption. She can feel him pulling away from her, and as he does so, the golden ideal of motherhood – so vital to her for so many years – recedes into the distance. She feels weighed down, heavy and hopeless.

Once the washing is churning in the machine, Marian checks the contents of the fridge. There's the bread Tom bought earlier, plus some ham and antipasti, and she can make a scratch salad.

They can have a proper talk over a civilised weekend lunch. She sends her husband a text.

What time will you be back? Have got lunch here. X

Her phone pings almost immediately, but when she checks it, the text is not from Tom. It's from Farzeen.

Doing bit of shopping in Muswell Hill, wondered if u fancied meeting for a coffee? F x

Marian ignores it for a while, deciding she should make time with Tom a priority. Also, she doesn't need her nose rubbing in the fact that Farzeen is happily pregnant. But Tom doesn't reply to her text, and when she tries phoning him, her call goes straight to voicemail.

She texts Farzeen back as she heads for the door, grabbing her bag and pulling on a cardigan over her baggy jeans and shapeless T-shirt.

Meet me @ Hilltop Café. Walking down now. M.

Farzeen is waiting for her when she arrives. She's had her glossy hair cut short into a sharp jaw-length bob. Her slenderness only seems to accentuate how pregnant she is. It's several weeks since Marian has seen her and her bump has 'popped', pushing out against her chic grey shift dress. She's sipping on a herbal tea, but stands up to embrace Marian. 'You look well,' she says, untruthfully. They both know Marian looks a mess.

'So do you,' says Marian, pulling back so that her flabby belly doesn't make contact with Farzeen's neat, hard little baby bump. She goes to the counter and fetches a latte, and sits down again.

'Well, this is an unexpected pleasure.' She eyes Farzeen a little warily. They normally only socialise as a four, when their partners are present.

'I've been thinking of you and wondering how it was going.' Farzeen sips her tea with a dainty movement. 'You know, with the IVF and everything.'

'Oh, well, you know, early days…' Marian launches into a summary of their treatment so far, making the picture rosier and their chances of conception better than in reality. 'And of course there's always the possibility of adoption, which is something we're considering.'

'I suppose in your job you'd know quite a bit about the ins and outs. I expect it comes in handy.'

'Exactly,' says Marian, forcing a smile and dipping her free biscotti in her latte.

'The thing is…' Farzeen purses her lips, looking troubled. 'The reason I've asked to meet you is… not that it's not great to see you anyway…' She gives a self-conscious smile. 'It's just there's something I need to talk to you about.'

Marian feels colour flooding to her cheeks as though she's done something wrong, which is ridiculous because of course she hasn't.

'Go on,' she says, her voice faint.

'The thing is…' Farzeen repeats, then pauses, lowering her hands to her pregnant abdomen and holding it protectively, before letting her words out in a rush. 'There's a rumour that Tom is having an affair. With someone at Cavendish.' Avoiding Marian's eye, she colours slightly before continuing: 'Actually, it's more than a rumour. Tom confided in Gareth. Told him that that he's seeing someone.'

'Vanessa Rowley,' Marian says. The name hangs there between them.

Farzeen is surprised. 'You know about this?'

'Sort of. I suspected there was… something.'

Farzeen reaches for her hand and squeezes it. 'You poor thing, I'm so sorry. Gareth didn't want me to say anything, but I was adamant that you had a right to know. And quickly, given the fertility thing.'

Marian widens her eyes slightly. 'Fertility thing?' She's pretty sure what Farzeen means but is determined not to show it. Not to capitulate. She closes her eyes for a second, and the image of a rosy, chubby baby recedes even further.

'Obviously, now you know what's going on, you might not feel the same about continuing with the attempt to conceive. Or adopt.'

'Why not?'

Farzeen's smooth golden skin flushes faintly pink. 'Well, because surely it would be wrong, in the circumstances, for you and Tom to become parents. In such an… unstable… setting.' She checks herself. 'I'm sorry, maybe I'm speaking out of turn. I don't mean to judge, but… well, parenthood is a big deal.' Her hand reflexively cradles her bump. 'I just thought you needed all the facts, that's all. Whatever you decide to do.'

Marian forces a smile. 'Thanks, Farzeen, but I'm quite sure this thing with Vanessa is just a fling. Nothing serious. It will burn itself out.'

'Yes. Of course, I expect you're right.' Farzeen doesn't sound convinced. 'Let's hope so.'

Marian stands up. 'Now, if you don't mind, I'd better get going. Tom's expecting me,' she lies.

Outside the café she leans against the wall and closes her eyes. Her mind is churning, trapped in that painful place between anger and hurt. *This is not going to derail me*, she tells herself over and over. *I can afford not to care about Vanessa Rowley, as long as she doesn't stop me becoming a mother.*

Tom eventually returns halfway through the afternoon, brisk and cheerful but avoiding any meaningful interaction. He sets himself a list of domestic chores – cutting the grass, clearing the guttering, fixing a sagging shelf – and devotes the rest of the weekend to accomplishing them. Marian watches him from the sidelines in silent agony, arranging her features in a smile whenever Tom looks in her direction.

At work on Monday, she makes herself do something which, if she is entirely honest with herself, she has been procrastinating over for some weeks. She's going to pay a home visit to Lizzie Armitage.

The early July day is sultry and humid, and Marian's back and armpits are sticky with sweat as she climbs the four flights to Lizzie's flat: the lift, as ever, is broken. She knocks on the door several times, and is about to turn away when the door is pulled open a crack.

'Who is it?' croaks Lizzie.

'It's Marian Glynn. Can I come in?'

Lizzie yanks the door back then stumbles towards the lounge. Marian can tell instantly from the swaying gait that she has been drinking. The curtains are drawn over closed windows, making the room both dark and swelteringly hot. It's only when her eyes become accustomed to the gloom that Marian realises what she's seeing. Lizzie is not only drunk, but pregnant. Heavily pregnant, making her condition unmistakable.

'Goodness, Lizzie… how long have you… when are you due?'

Marian visited a few months earlier, but Lizzie had been on the sofa, her mid-section covered with a duvet and her condition disguised.

Lizzie shrugs. 'Dunno. Whenever, I guess.'

'Any day, from the look of you… Have you seen your GP? Or a midwife?'

Lizzie shakes her head, her eyes unfocussed.

'Lizzie, it's important you register your pregnancy. The baby's health needs to be checked, and there's money you're entitled to – there will be extra benefits, and there's a pregnancy grant for you to buy what you need.' She fishes in her bag and starts to pull out forms. 'Let's make a start on the paperwork now, and I'll arrange for you to be seen on the Whittington maternity unit as soon as possible. You and the baby need to be checked over.'

'No.' Lizzie shakes her head vigorously. 'No. Don't want you telling anyone. They'll take it away from me if they know. The baby.'

'You know I can't keep a secret like that; I'll lose my job. How about your mother? Will she be able to help?'

'She won't want anything to do with it. In fact she'll probably want it taken off me… Please, Marian!' Lizzie pleads. 'You've always been good to me. I trust you like a friend. Don't let them take her.'

'I'll do what I can, I promise. But you have to stay off the drink.' Marian lowers herself onto the edge of the squalid sofa, her sweaty thighs sticking to the fabric. Lizzie drops down beside her and closes her eyes. 'Lizzie, I need you to focus… who knows about your pregnancy?'

'No one. Just Macca, but he's not bothered. And my kid sister.'

'You mean Paula?'

'Yeah. She's helped with getting stuff ready.' She jerks her head in the direction of the bedroom. Marian goes to look, and finds a flimsy Moses basket, lined with broderie anglaise and trimmed with white ribbons. It's placed in a corner and stacked neatly with nappies and baby clothes. It wasn't Lizzie who did this, Marian is sure of that, it was young Paula. A labour of love. Marian picks up a small white babygro and marvels at its size, feeling tears prick her eyes as she imagines the soft, perfect baby skin inside it. She goes back into the living room. Lizzie is stretched out on the sofa, barely conscious.

'Lizzie!' Marian holds out the forms. 'I'll fill these in for you and make a start on getting you the proper care. Okay?'

There's no response.

Marian leaves her, her clammy thighs chafing uncomfortably as she hurries down the stairs. She goes to the back of the building where the communal wheelie bins are housed, their stench attracting flies.

And there, with no one looking, she rips up the request for a pregnancy booking appointment and throws it into the bin.

So now no one will know about Lizzie's imminent arrival. No one but her and Paula – and Macca, that waste of space. As she walks away, Marian tries telling herself that she is merely doing what Lizzie wants. She's keeping the pregnancy secret, ensuring she can give birth without the intervention of the authorities. But even as she tells herself this, another thought is planted at the back of her mind, taking root and growing despite the knowledge that it is wrong. Because she knows full well this baby can't be left with Lizzie. It simply wouldn't be safe. This child needs help, needs someone who can offer that safety. Someone Lizzie trusts.

And if the child's life was at stake, then giving that help wouldn't be wrong, would it? Quite the opposite: it would be the right thing to do.

Back at the office, Marian goes in search of Angela. She finds her sitting at her desk, eating a doughnut and drinking a Diet Coke, a desk fan fluttering the halo of tight curls around her hairline.

'Vile, isn't it,' she says, with a sympathetic glance at the sweat patches under Marian's arms. 'This weather.'

'Awful.' Marian fans herself. 'Ange, will you do me a big favour?'

'Course I will,' says Angela, through her doughnut. 'Shoot.'

'Well, you know…' She becomes self-conscious. 'You know that Tom and I have been trying to have a baby?'

Angela nods.

'We just did a round of IVF, and it didn't work.'

'Oh, you poor love. I'm so sorry.'

Marian bites her lip, remembering the negative pregnancy test. 'Thanks. I'm afraid we've been told the chances of it working in the future are nearly non-existent, so we're looking at adoption. And I wondered if you wouldn't mind coming round and doing a sort of mock interview with Tom and me. Putting us through the type of questions an adoption panel would ask. So we're prepared.' She blinks at her colleague earnestly, rubbing the sweat off the back of her neck.

'Sure,' says Angela, easily. 'If you think it would help. But you do realise that in reality nothing's going to happen for ages. Even when you've passed the official screening, you're likely to have to wait a long time. Especially if it's an infant you want.'

Marian flushes slightly. 'Yes, I do realise. I mean, I know the process inside out, but this is all new to Tom. This would be for his benefit, obviously. To help him get his head around what's involved.'

Angela shrugs. 'Well, all right then, if you think it would help. The next couple of weeks are a bit chocka though – can it wait?'

'No, not really,' says Marian, firmly. 'It can't. It needs to be right away.'

25

MARIAN

'Let's go and wait in the garden. How about a cold drink?'

Marian leads Angela outside, and fetches a tray with a jug of icy cold home-made lemonade and three glasses. It's a hot midsummer's evening, the sun still hovering in the sky, and several hours to go before it reaches the horizon and the air temperature starts to drop to more bearable levels.

'I'm sure Tom will be back any minute,' she tells Angela, smoothly, although she's not sure at all. 'He must have been held up at work.'

As she speaks, she hears the sound of the front door being slammed.

'Ah, there he is now.'

Tom appears in the open French windows and does a double take of surprise.

'Darling, you remember Angela Dixon, don't you? From work. She's here to do our pre-adoption interview.'

Angela gives an awkward half-wave.

Tom stares back blankly. 'Our what?'

'Remember, I told you!' She shakes her head indulgently as though she's told him about this appointment and he's forgotten about it. 'Angela's going over some of our screening paperwork for us now, to try and speed things up. She's very busy at the moment – aren't you, Angela? – so she's doing us a huge favour fitting us in so quickly. Most couples have to wait several months at least,' she says, as though this explains the ambush.

'But—' Tom loosens his tie and tugs it off, tossing it over the back of a kitchen chair. 'Marian, could I have a quick word, please?' He looks in Angela's direction. 'Excuse us a minute, Angela.'

Marian comes in from the garden. 'What is all this?' he hisses, keeping his voice low so that they can't be overheard. 'We haven't decided on adoption, not yet. I told you I wanted time to think. We still need to talk about it properly.'

'I know, but Angela could see how upset I was about the failed ICSI attempt, and she just wanted to help. This doesn't commit us to anything, it just speeds up the paperwork in case it's what we *do* want.'

Marian doesn't know if she sounds desperate, but that is exactly how she feels. For her incipient plan to work – and in her mind it would really only be adoption via a different route – she and Tom have to look like approved candidates.

Tom scrunches up his face in that way he does when he's annoyed, turning away from her.

'Please,' she begs. 'At least we'll be doing something positive towards becoming parents. And I need that so badly at the moment, I really do.'

Tears prick her eyes, unprompted but genuine. Tom turns back towards her, and sees them.

'Okay, Marrie,' he says with a shrug. 'If it means that much to you, then let's do it. If I'm firing blanks, I guess it's my only option at the end of the day, whatever happens.'

Marian decides against exploring the meaning of these last two words, instead beckoning Angela in from the garden and ushering her through to the sitting room.

Sensing Tom's reluctance, Angela says cheerily, 'Sorry to spring this on you, but really it won't take long at all. It's really just a few questions, then I'll have all I need and be out of your hair.' She brandishes a clipboard with an official-looking form on it.

'Might as well get the red tape out of the way, I suppose.' Tom forces a smile and arranges himself stiffly upright on the sofa opposite Angela.

A series of questions follows, aimed at both of them, and all fairly predictable. Marian has heard them all many times before in the course of her career. They're asked about significant medical history, religious beliefs, support from wider family and employers, any specific concerns they have about their role as parents. This last question seems to faze Tom, who shrugs and turns to Marian. She produces her pre-prepared answer about not having sufficient energy as an older mother.

'And what age of child would you like, ideally?' asks Angela.

'A baby!' Marian exhales immediately, her eyes wide with longing. 'Wouldn't we, Tom?'

He nods woodenly.

'Although, of course we are aware there are fewer of them to adopt,' Marian chimes in, reaching across to squeeze his hand. Her fingers are clammy with sweat and he recoils slightly.

'Well, I think that's everything,' says Angela, gathering her things and heading for the front door with a quick, meaningful glance at Marian.

After she has gone, Tom turns to Marian, frowning. 'Is that normal – for someone you work with to do an adoption interview?"

'As an employee of Haringey Social Services, I get fast-tracked,' Marian says simply as she clears the glasses. 'It's a sort of professional courtesy.'

Tom follows her into the kitchen and takes the tray from her, placing it on the table and turning her round so that she's facing him.

'Look. Marrie…' He uses her pet name for the second time that evening, even though it's a rarity these days. She stares back at him in alarm, her lip quivering.

'I'm still not sure that adopting is the right thing for us at this point in time. Or at all, really.'

'Why not? If you won't use donor sperm, then it's our only chance for a family.'

'Because…'

Because you've been seeing someone behind my back for months and you want to be with her.

Marian feels the tears return. She clutches at the sleeves of his shirt. 'Please don't say that, Tom,' she says, in a low voice that comes out as a croak. 'At least give the idea a chance. Otherwise you're taking away my chance of becoming a mother.'

'Marian, this isn't your only chance. You can have a child with someone else, a biological child. Just not with me.'

Her crying intensifies, and she staggers, as though her legs are giving way beneath her.

Tom grabs her under her elbow and helps her to a kitchen chair, handing her a glass of lemonade from the tray. 'Why don't I run you a nice hot bath?' he asks, patting her ineffectually to try and stop her hysterical sobbing. 'Then I'll make us something to eat.'

He goes upstairs to the bathroom and Marian hears taps start to run.

'Bath'll be two minutes!' Tom shouts down the stairs.

The loud gushing of the water almost disguises the sound, but not quite. Standing at the foot of the stairs, Marian can hear her husband talking in low, urgent tones. He's on the phone. He's talking to *her*.

26

PAULA

The summer term at Turnbull Comprehensive has finally ended, and for quite a few of Paula's contemporaries, school is over forever.

But not for Paula. In an attempt to please her parents rather than through any academic aspirations of her own, she is returning in September to start her A levels. Or she will be if her GCSEs are good enough.

'A bunch of us are going down to Regent's Canal,' Paula's friend Carly tells her. Carly is one of those who will definitely not be returning to school. She already has spray paint from the art department all over her school shirt and skirt, from creating wild technicolour graffiti.

'Who's going?' asks Paula, though she has guessed the answer.

'Jason Shepherd… Adil.'

'Oh.'

'Go on, Paul!' Carly says, plucking at Paula's sleeve. 'It'll be fun. Everyone always goes.'

The school tradition is for the fifth years to sneak out as much as possible in the way of textbooks and classroom equipment on their last day, then dump it all in the Regent's Canal while getting drunk on a cocktail called 'Headfuck', made of White Lightning and blue WKD.

'No, you're all right,' Paula says, extricating herself. 'There's somewhere I need to be.'

The truth is, she's had a weird, nagging feeling of dread all day. Her mind automatically connects that feeling with her sister. She saw Lizzie a few days ago and she seemed fine; managing to stay sober at least some of the time. But some instinct tells her she needs to go back and check on her.

She doesn't even go back home to change first, but gets straight onto a bus to Tottenham.

There's no answer when she first knocks on the door, so she lets herself in. Lizzie gave her a spare key long ago, which she keeps on the chain around her neck with her own house keys.

'Hello?' she calls into the gloomy flat. It's airless and suffocatingly warm. The cat shoots between her legs, desperate to get outside.

From nowhere, the tall figure of Macca appears, blocking her path.

'Where's Lizzie?' Paula demands.

'In the bedroom. She just needs a bit of a nap.'

Paula cranes her neck past Macca. Through the half-open bedroom door, she can just see Lizzie. Dressed only in a T-shirt, she's gripping the bed frame and rocking rhythmically to and fro. Her belly looks alarmingly large from this angle, as though it contains a Spacehopper.

'You okay, Lizzie?' Paula asks.

'Fine,' she says, through gritted teeth. 'Just a few cramps. They happen all the time.'

'D'you want me to fetch someone?'

'No!' Lizzie says, then forces a smile. 'It's nothing, honest.'

'See? You heard her: she doesn't need anyone. She just needs a rest. Come on now, best we leave her to it.'

Macca has his battered, grimy rucksack in his hand, and is shoving his roll-ups and lighter in his jeans pocket, indicating that he's heading out. He holds the front door of the flat open, waiting for Paula to leave.

'I'll pop back later, Lizzie,' she shouts down the corridor, before reluctantly following Macca to the stairs. He bounds ahead of her and out to the street, climbing into the back of a waiting car, its engine running. The three other men in it look as though they're on a mission, and Paula knows instinctively that it's not a trip to the supermarket or the park, but something altogether darker.

She glances up at Lizzie's window, then turns and heads for the bus stop. *You may as well join Carly and the others at Regent's Canal*, she tells herself. If last year's party was anything to go by, it should be good fun.

27

MARIAN

Marian is shocked when she receives the call. Shocked but inwardly thrilled. It's Lizzie Armitage calling from the communal phone box in her building, to tell her that her waters have just broken.

'Are you alone?' is the first thing Marian asks. 'Is your boyfriend there?'

'He went out.'

'Good. Don't let anyone else in, okay? I'm getting a cab over now. I'll be about fifteen minutes.'

By the time she arrives, Lizzie is clearly well into her labour. She's crouched on her hands and knees in the bedroom, bellowing like a cow. Marian takes some plastic sheeting from her bag and spreads it on the mattress, with a layer of cotton wadding on top. Then she heaves Lizzie onto the bed and props her against the headboard. Her face is bright red, and she's sweating.

'Have you been drinking?' she asks.

'No, but I need some vodka,' Lizzie wails at the top of her voice. She leans over to the messy nightstand beside the bed and rummages amongst the overflowing ashtray and empty lager cans. 'I can't handle this!'

'Not now,' Marian says, calmly. 'It's bad for the baby.'

She glances up at Lizzie's anguished face, then checks between her legs again. A dark shape is already bulging there, becoming gradually more visible. Taking a deep breath, Marian positions a clean towel on the bed and reaches forward to touch the slimy crown of the baby's head.

When she and Tom were trying to conceive she read every pregnancy book going, and watched endless childbirth videos. As a result, she's more than confident about the stages of labour and delivery.

'I need you to give a strong push,' she tells Lizzie, echoing words she's heard the midwives say on screen. 'Push down as though you need the toilet.'

Lizzie gasps, and with no warning the baby slithers out of her. Marian wraps it and rubs its body briskly, until the crumpled face turns pink and emits a cry. Only then does she gingerly open the towel and take a look. The baby is small – smaller than Lizzie's massive stomach would have suggested – but seems healthy.

'You were right, it's a little girl,' she says, quietly, even though Lizzie does not appear to be listening. She wraps the baby tightly again and lays her on the bed. Marian knows that there'll be the afterbirth to deal with now, and Lizzie is already bearing down again, whimpering with pain, pleading for her bottle of vodka.

A few seconds later, another dark shape emerges, along with a little gush of blood. Marian feels a quiver of panic, concerned that the placenta has somehow ruptured, but realises with a jolt of shock that it's not the afterbirth.

It's a second baby's head.

'Oh my good God,' Marian whispers, grabbing one of the stained towels that she has spread out. 'It's twins.'

Her mind races. Two babies, just as she and Tom had imagined when her embryos were implanted. It's a sign: this was meant to be.

The second baby is smaller, and takes longer to cry. 'You've got a brother,' Marian observes to the first baby, who is pursing her lips and looking up at her with an unfocussed gaze. She examines the baby boy, checks that he is breathing adequately. His size makes her nervous and she feels a rush of anger towards Lizzie, stunting her babies' growth by drinking through pregnancy. Not even being aware that she was carrying two babies.

She fetches soapy water and cleans Lizzie as best she can, helps her into a clean nightshirt and underwear with a sanitary pad, then makes her tea with plenty of sugar. Changing the water in the bowl, she takes swabs of cotton wool and carefully cleans the two tiny bodies, then dresses them in the newborn nappies and clothes that Paula Armitage bought. The 0–3 month sleepsuits are a little too big, and the feet hang empty. But at least the babies being small means that they both fit into the Moses basket together.

She tops and tails them, then tucks a blanket around them. The boy baby is crying. A faint plaintive squawk. They need feeding, but Marian is not willing to risk Lizzie's breast milk, which could be laced with the alcohol still in her system. She'll have to go to the shops, but she can't exactly take the babies with her. On the other hand, leaving them with their mother while they're so vulnerable is far from ideal. Anyone might come to the flat while she's gone; Paula, or even the useless Macca.

'I'm going out to get some formula,' she tells Lizzie, who is half asleep herself, the mug of tea cooling beside her. 'I'll be as quick as I can.'

'Phone Paula,' Lizzie mumbles. 'She came by earlier. Tell her to come back.'

'I will,' says Marian, who has absolutely no intention of doing so. She runs all the way to the local shops, the first time she's done so for years. It's unfamiliar and uncomfortable and makes her sweat, but she's terrified of leaving the babies for longer than she has to. She buys formula milk, bottles and teats, hurrying back again with a growing sense of unease. Sure enough, as she pushes the flat door open, she hears both babies crying.

'Lizzie?' Marian calls, although as soon as she reaches the bedroom door, she knows there will be no answer. Lizzie is passed out on the pillows, the empty quart of vodka beside her on the bed.

Marian sits down slowly next to her, trying to order her thoughts. First she must make up some formula, and feed the babies. Once they're settled, she needs to clear away the mess and paraphernalia of delivery completely, so no one will be alerted to the fact that Lizzie has just given birth.

She bought plastic refuse sacks in the corner shop and, after feeding the babies and putting them down to sleep, she sets about clearing away the bloodstained pads and sheets and double-bagging the placentas. All the waste is taken downstairs and dumped in the communal dumpsters.

The babies are still asleep and Lizzie is sleeping heavily, so Marian has some time to think. The issue of transport needs to be resolved. She has far too much to carry to use the bus. She took a taxi straight here when Paula phoned her, but taking two newborn babies in a taxi would draw far too much attention. She'll need the car, which she will have to fetch from home, and once again she'll have to be as quick as she can to avoid the possibility of someone arriving at the flat while she's gone.

Grabbing her handbag and the makeshift delivery kit she brought with her, she runs out onto the street and hails another cab.

As it turns into her street, she notices with relief that Tom's car is not outside. She doesn't want him to know: not yet. It's going to be the most wonderful surprise.

'Everything okay, love?' asks the cabbie.

'Fine,' says Marian, forcing a smile as she hands him a ten-pound note. 'Everything's perfect.'

When Marian arrives back at the Tottenham flat with her car, Lizzie is still deeply asleep, but the babies are stirring, starting to whimper. Marian changes their nappies, mixes more formula and feeds them. The girl sucks greedily, but the boy fusses and squirms, spitting out the teat repeatedly. She sits for a while watching them sleep as the sky outside turns dark, waiting for Lizzie to wake up. As soon as she does, Marian will tell her that unfortunately she has no choice, and that the babies are being taking into care. But Lizzie doesn't wake. In fact, her breathing is so faint that Marian has to check her pulse a couple of times.

She can't leave the babies here: that would not be an option whatever the circumstances. Lizzie is in no fit state to look after them and, whatever happened, would never be able to keep them. It's better, surely, that they're with someone Lizzie already knows and trusts? And no one could dispute that she, Marian, is better placed to care for them.

She knows, of course, that what she should really do is remove them now and take them straight to the local hospital, report the birth. But isn't this the perfect solution? A ready-made family for the Glynns, no questions asked. A secure and comfortable home for the babies that will be better than any foster care social services could provide. One that will keep the twins together.

The ugly thought that Tom won't want them because he no longer wants her, bobs up in her brain like a piece of cork she's tried to force underwater. She ignores it, moving around the flat in a brisk, organised fashion. She drops the dirty nappies down to the communal bin, then loads the Moses basket containing both babies, all of Paula's baby purchases and the milk and bottles into the back of her car. She goes back upstairs one more time to make sure that there is no remaining evidence of the babies' existence, then drives slowly and carefully back to Muswell Hill.

It's late enough for there to be no sign of activity on her street. Marian gets out of the car and checks that none of her neighbours are around before lifting the Moses basket out of the car. Four tiny sets of fingers wave up at her and the discontented whimpers start up.

'Shhhhh,' she whispers to them. 'No need to cry now. We're home. Home to see your daddy.'

28

PAULA

Someone has brought a ghetto-blaster to the banks of the Regent's Canal, and it's playing Lil' Kim loudly and with too much bass. A handful of soggy exercise books floats on the scummy water, their pages catching against an upturned supermarket trolley. Paula sits and watches as a two-litre bottle of cider is spiked with 95% proof vodka from the Polish shop.

This lethal cocktail is passed around and gulped down amid giggling from the girls and raucous chants of encouragement from the boys. Carly is drunk, singing in a slurring voice and flashing her knickers, before stumbling and falling over on the sun-scorched grass verge. Debbie Ashcroft is already vomiting.

'Here, Paul.'

Adil passes the bottle to Paula but she shakes her head, standing up and smoothing down her school skirt. 'No, I need to get going.'

'Pau-ulll!' Carly slurs, reaching to grab her hand, but missing.

Paula ignores her and stomps down the tow path. She can't quite get the sight of Lizzie out of her head, or the sound of her. The catch in her throat as she gasped with pain.

She has to wait ages for a bus, and by the time she reaches the flat in Tottenham it's almost dark. She rings the bell a couple of times, but the lights are off and there is no reply.

'Hello? Lizzie?'

The silence is ominous. She looks around the door of the lounge, but there is no one there. The cat is curled up on the grimy sofa and raises its head to look at her, its eyes glowing like tiny headlamps.

In the bedroom, she can just make out the shape of her sister, curled up under the duvet. Paula expects switching on the light to wake her, but it doesn't. She remains deeply asleep.

'Lizzie!'

Paula shakes her shoulder, but although she rolls onto her back with a snorting noise, she does not open her eyes. Paula's foot makes contact with an empty vodka bottle, which rolls noisily across the floor. Some instinct makes her pull back the duvet. Lizzie is dressed in a clean nightie and the huge dome of her stomach is gone. There's still a discernible bump under the fabric but it's much smaller, like a balloon that's had half the air let out of it. The bed sheets are clean and the room seems unnaturally tidy.

Paula strides quickly to the wardrobe, where she stored the Moses basket, nappies and baby clothes she bought. They're gone. All of them.

Hurrying back to the lounge, Paula switches on the light and starts to search the room. She pulls the sofa away from the wall, startling the cat, but there's nothing behind it. Nothing in the kitchen either, although that too looks cleaner than normal.

'Lizzie, for God's sake!'

She shakes her sister more vigorously this time, but she's passed out cold, only giving another nasal snore. Paula leaves a glass of water next to her bed and heads out into the night. There's a bar on the estate – the Rumsden – more of a working men's club than a pub, and she knows that Macca often drinks in there with his dodgy associates. It's thick with smoke and a faint smell of dirty clothes.

'You old enough to be in here, love?' asks the barman.

'I'm looking for Macca,' she tells him. 'You know: tall guy, mixed race. Lives on the estate.'

'I know Macca,' the barman says, with a grimace. 'He's not been in. Not tonight.'

Paula thinks for a moment. Her mother will be wondering where she is by now, probably furious that she's out this late without saying where she was going. But she can't just leave this.

'Do you know a pub called the Half Moon?'

'I've heard of it. Over Muswell Hill way, I think. On Alexandra Park Road.'

'Do you have an A–Z?'

He pulls a yellowed, much-thumbed copy from under the bar. 'You'd be amazed how many times I get asked for this.'

Paula flicks through the pages and finds what she's looking for, memorises the route for a few seconds then hands the book back.

'Should I tell Macca who was looking for him if he comes in?'

'No.' She shakes her head. 'Just tell him he needs to go home to his girlfriend.'

29

MARIAN

During the drive back to Ranmoor Road, Marian decided she would tell Tom that the twins have already been named. That way they will avoid them being lumbered with Victoria and William. Noah for the boy: she's always liked the solid, biblical feel of it. And the girl will be Saffron. The Indians called it 'red gold', and per ounce it's more valuable than the metal itself. More precious than gold. That seems fitting.

Carrying the blanketed bundle up the steps to the front door also feels entirely right.

'Saffron, Noah, this is your new home,' she whispers. But as she turns the key in the lock and pushes open the door, it's clear the house is empty. It's dark and silent. No Tom.

Her heart pounding, she leaves the Moses basket in the hall and hurries into the kitchen. There's a piece of white paper propped against the salt and pepper mills, next to Tom's set of house keys. She recognises his handwriting instantly.

M, I know this isn't the nicest way to tell you, but I've moved out. I need some space to think, and to make decisions before the adoption process has the chance to get underway. I'll be in touch. T x

She stares at it blankly, then races upstairs to the bedroom. The clothes from Tom's armoire and his half of the wardrobe are gone. His shaving stuff is gone, his precious Dell laptop, and his camera.

Shaking with shock, Marian walks back onto the landing. Hanging on to the banister like an octogenarian, she staggers down the stairs and fumbles for her bag. Both babies are sleeping, making the silence palpable. She jabs at Tom's number on her phone, but the call goes straight to voicemail. She keeps trying him over and over again for nearly an hour, but still he won't pick up.

When the doorbell eventually sounds with a shrill squawk, she jumps, dropping her mobile. One of the babies stirs.

Whoever is there will go away, she tells herself. It can't be the Jehovah's Witnesses that roam the neighbourhood; it's too late even for them. The bell rings again. And again. And it suddenly occurs to her that it must be Tom. He left his keys, after all, but he probably still wants to talk to her. He might even be having second thoughts. She carries the Moses basket and the nursery supplies through to the kitchen and closes the door, before yanking the front door open.

It's Paula Armitage.

How on earth did the girl find her? She must have asked the office, though they're not supposed to give out staff addresses. Then Marian vaguely remembers once telling Lizzie which street she lived on when they were discussing North London pubs. Lizzie could have mentioned it to Paula. And once on this street, she would have recognised the car parked outside from Marian's frequent home visits.

'Something's happened to Lizzie,' Paula blurts out. She's out of breath. 'I've been round to her flat and she not pregnant any more!'

'Lizzie isn't expecting.' Marian keeps her voice calm, though her heart is thumping in her chest. 'She isn't on my list of clients receiving antenatal care.'

'She was! I know she was. And I went round there just now and her stomach's gone down but there's no baby in the flat.' Her tone is accusing.

'I think you must have been imagining things, Paula. I saw her a couple of days ago and she wasn't pregnant then.'

'She was; she just hid it. She didn't want anyone to know so it couldn't be taken away from her.'

Marian shakes her head. 'That can't be right. Lizzie was probably telling one of her tall tales. You know how she gets when she's been drinking. She often doesn't make a lot of sense.'

'But I definitely saw her baby bump. And what about all the baby stuff, then? The basket and the nappies and stuff I bought. It's not there now.'

'I really wouldn't know about that,' Marian says, stiffly. 'More than likely that boyfriend of hers has taken it and sold it for his next fix.' This, at least, is a credible scenario. 'And if you're right, and she really has given birth, well... the absence of the baby should tell you all you need to know.'

The girl is confused, and stares hard at Marian. 'What do you mean?'

'I mean that the child might not have survived, and maybe your sister... arranged to, you know...'

Paula is still staring blankly.

'...dispose of it. With or without her boyfriend's help. That does happen, unfortunately, especially with addicts.'

'But why—'

'I'm afraid I have to go now. I have things... things I need to do.'

'I'm going to tell someone,' Paula says desperately. 'I'll ask the police.'

'I'm doubt they'll be able to help any more than I can.'

'You're her social worker! Surely you should try and find out what's happened?'

'I will, I assure you. As soon as I'm back at work on Monday, I'll go and check on her. Now, if you don't mind…'

Marian closes the front door quickly, just as there is a thin, insistent wail from the direction of the kitchen. She hurries in there to see little pink fists being pressed into hungry mouths. Both babies are squirming and making hungry sucking and grunting noises. The primal sound wraps around her heart and tugs at it, opening the floodgates of the maternal feelings she's suppressed for so many years. The babies. The babies are still here, and they need her. They need someone responsible to care for them. It was she, Marian, who saw them safely into the world, and that seems like fate: like a sign that they are meant to be hers.

She has no way of knowing that she will eventually wish that they weren't.

30

PAULA

That Friday night, Paula lies awake until nearly 3 a.m., turning over and over in her narrow single bed.

She and her mother had the inevitable row when she returned to the flat just before 11 p.m.

'You didn't tell me where you were!' Wendy stormed. 'If you're going to be out after eight p.m. you're supposed to tell me first! Honestly, I just can't bloody trust you.'

'Because I didn't know,' Paula said, truthfully. 'I went down to the canal with a load of people after school, and... I don't know... it just got late.'

'And you were drinking, is that it? Is that what's going on behind my back?' In the wake of Lizzie's problems, Wendy has been paranoid about Paula being around alcohol.

'Other people were, I didn't. That stuff was revolting.'

Wendy had leaned in and smelled her daughter's breath. Slightly mollified by scenting only Impulse body spray and chewing gum, she went on: 'Anyway, you know why I wanted you back early tonight. We're going to Auntie Cissie's tomorrow morning. You need to pack, and we need to head for Liverpool Street in time to catch the ten o'clock train. Please don't tell me you've forgotten!'

Paula had forgotten, in fact. Forgotten that they were going to spend a week in Frinton-on-Sea with her mother's elderly aunt,

Cissie. Which made no sense given they went every single July, as soon as school had broken up for the summer. But Paula has had other things on her mind.

She replays the sight of Lizzie lying in her bed over and over, as though it's a loop of video tape. Had her stomach really been that much smaller or was it a trick of the light? Or had the baby somehow shifted into a position that made it stick out less? Her conversation with Lizzie's social worker confused her even more. At first she seemed to be suggesting that Lizzie couldn't have been pregnant. And then it was as if she was accusing Lizzie and Macca of concealing the birth; of giving away the baby, or even worse. Which was it?

At least she had promised to go and check on Lizzie. Paula is grateful for that, because with the taxi arriving at 8.45 next morning, there will be no chance for her to visit Lizzie herself until she's back from holiday. If she could avoid going to Frinton, she would, but Wendy won't hear of it.

The week in Frinton-on-Sea drags, but in that respect it's no different from every other year. Cissie, a sprightly seventy-two, lives in a bungalow just off the promenade. She's kind, but very set in her ways and has never had children. Paula finds it hard to imagine Cissie having been a child herself, because she seems oblivious to how boring Frinton is for a sixteen year old: she thinks mini golf or the antiques centre or a visit to Felixstowe museum are appealing activities.

In Paula's opinion, the beach is the only good thing about Frinton. She spends the start of the week stretched out on a towel on the sand, reading *Smash Hits* and trying to get a tan. On Tuesday evening the weather breaks suddenly, with torrential downpours and forecasts of flash floods. They are condemned to spending all of Wednesday in Cissie's bungalow playing dominoes, and when the forecast confirms rain for the rest of the week, Wendy decides to change their train tickets and travel back to London on Thursday morning instead of Saturday.

Paula is relieved, not just to get away from the dominoes and the antimacassars and the kippers for breakfast, but also to have a chance to call on Lizzie. Now, finally, she will be able to get answers to the questions still dominating her thoughts.

'I'm just going to go and meet Carly,' she lies to Wendy, as soon as their suitcases are through the front door of the flat.

Wendy frowns. 'I thought you said Carly was going to Tenerife?'

Paula colours slightly. 'She's been. She got back this morning.'

'Well, at least stay long enough to have a cuppa with me.' Wendy bustles into the kitchen and switches on the kettle. 'I think there are still some Penguins in the biscuit tin.'

Paula hesitates. 'Thing is, I really want to get going before—'

The doorbell rings, loudly and insistently. And then again.

'At least see who that is before you go.'

Paula lifts the intercom. A man's voice speaks, and her heart leaps in response, thumping against her ribs.

'Mum. He says it's the police.'

Wendy stares, the milk jug in her hand. They both know nothing good ever comes from a house call from the police. 'Go on then – let them up.'

There are two of them, a man and a woman, both in uniform. Paula instinctively knows that this is bad.

'Mrs Armitage? Wendy Armitage? Would you like to sit down?'

Wendy obeys. Paula's heart hammers harder, so hard she can hear it in her head.

'It's about your daughter, Elizabeth. I'm afraid we have some bad news.'

'Lizzie. She's always known as Lizzie,' Wendy says, stubbornly.

Paula's hands fly instinctively to her ears, to block out what she already knows they're going to say.

'Mrs Armitage, I'm afraid that Elizabeth… Lizzie… has passed away.'

The use of the euphemism throws Paula temporarily. 'You mean she's died?' Her voice sounds strange to her own ears, unnaturally high.

The policewoman puts a hand on her shoulder, leads her to a chair. 'I'm afraid so, yes.'

The policeman is talking now, telling her that a neighbour noticed the curtains had remained closed for a few days and called the on-site caretaker, who had a key. Lizzie was alone in the flat, and she was dead.

'When did you last see your daughter?' he asks Wendy.

She shakes her head mutely, staring straight ahead at the wall as though it can somehow give her answers.

'Mrs Armitage?'

'Not for a long time. Years.'

'And you?'

This is directed at Paula. She knows you shouldn't lie to the police, but she also knows that this is not the time for her mother to find out that she's defied her instructions and been visiting Lizzie. 'Same.' She shrugs. 'Long time ago.'

But she's betraying her sister, and the shame of this betrayal brings a sudden torrent of tears.

'I'm so sorry.' The policewoman is squeezing her hand. 'It must be a terrible shock even if you weren't close.'

'Is there anyone we can call? To come and be with you?' the other officer asks.

'No.' Wendy shakes her head, her eyes still fixed on the wall. 'It's too late for all that. Far too late.'

31

MARIAN

It takes Marian a while to realise that the shrill sound is not part of her dream, but the front doorbell ringing.

She opens her eyes and glances at the bedside clock: 8.15 a.m. She finally got the babies to sleep just before five. This followed a nightmarish seven-hour game akin to musical chairs during which she climbed constantly in and out of bed, picking up first one baby then the other, feeding them, changing them, attempting to settle them, moving one then both of them into bed with her before returning them either together or separately to the Moses basket. And so on, endlessly throughout the night. If one of them squirmed and wailed in the basket, it would always set the other one off. Eventually, somehow, they had both sunk into a deep sleep and so, drained beyond belief, had she. It was like that the night before, and the one before that, and the one before that. For a whole week.

The doorbell rings again insistently, and Marian climbs groggily off the bed and throws on her tatty dressing gown. Even though she's attempting to be quiet, the babies start to whimper. When she visited clients with new babies, they always seemed to sleep like statues through any amount of domestic chaos. *Her* twins – as she is starting to think of them – are disturbed by the slightest noise.

By the time she's reached the front door, they're both screaming angrily. She comes out onto the step and pulls the front door to behind her so that whoever it is won't hear. It's only the postman, holding out a large cardboard box.

'Thank goodness,' she says to him. 'I only ordered this yesterday, but I really need it.'

Inside the box is a second baby basket, a sturdier one, ordered from an upmarket online store. And packed inside it, wrapped in finest white tissue, are two cashmere blankets: one shell pink, the other palest blue. The pink one is appliquéd with an 'S', the blue one with a 'N'.

Marian ignores the crying long enough to make herself a strong cup of coffee, which she downs in one go before warming two bottles of formula and carrying them upstairs. She changes two dirty nappies amid a cacophony of yells, then sets about trying to feed the babies, a process she never dreamed could take so long. Saffron first, because she always seems the hungriest and drinks the quickest. Noah doesn't suck very well, and it takes forever to feed and burp him. She watches him anxiously, taking in every suck.

Come on, she urges him silently. *Drink it up. You need to start putting on some weight.* Still he fusses, refusing the teat and turning his face away.

She is aware that she should probably bath the babies, but she lacks the energy. Instead she carries them downstairs in the white ribbon-trimmed basket that Paula Armitage bought, and transfers Noah to the new, plainer basket. She tucks the blue blanket around him and the pink one around his sister and waits a few seconds to see what happens. Each baby squirms and reaches out their limbs for their missing twin, but eventually, after a few half-hearted cries, they both fall asleep. Marian darts upstairs to run a bath for herself, but before the tub is half full, Noah has started wailing. She recognises his cry: thinner and weaker than his sister's.

She storms downstairs again. 'Stop it!' she hisses at him. 'You'll wake your sister. Please, please, just stop it!'

Then she bursts into angry, exhausted tears.

*

The following day, Saturday, she phones the local branch of Mothercare, gives them her credit card details and arranges for a wheeled carrycot to be delivered to the house that afternoon.

One obvious problem is that she can't just walk out of her front door and push the twins down Ranmoor Road. People will see her; questions will be asked. She is forced instead to drive a distance in the car, and then take them for a walk. This involves removing the body of the carrycot from its wheels, struggling to collapse the frame and loading both into the rear of the car. She doesn't have car seats yet, and hasn't quite resolved how she can fit them in the car without people noticing them. So for now the babies have to travel in the carrycot, with the rear seat belts lassoed around it in a makeshift restraint. And of course she has to time leaving the house with the carrycot for a rare moment when there are no neighbours within sight. All of which is so exhausting that by the time she parks up on the edge of Hampstead Heath early on Sunday morning, she barely has the energy or will to walk.

But walk she does, her feet falling heavily in time to the grizzling of the babies, arranged top to toe. Eventually they fall quiet, and all she can hear is her own footsteps.

A woman walking her dog comes over and peeps into the carrycot.

'Oh, my goodness, twins! How old are they?'

'Nine days,' Marian replies, flatly.

'And you're out and about already? I wasn't even out of hospital after five days when I had my two…'

Marian forces a smile.

'And a boy and a girl?'

Marian nods.

'Gosh, aren't you lucky!'

Lucky, Marian repeats to herself. *I'm lucky*. I've finally got the children I longed for all these years. She stares down at them, desperate to feel something – anything – other than overwhelming anxiety. If only she had Tom, she thinks. Tom would share the feeding, and bring her cups of tea, rock the babies while she took a shower, cook them both supper. That was the family life she had always pictured. Not doing it like this, alone. She has been too exhausted to mourn the collapse of her marriage, but now as she pictures her husband holding the twins, the tears course down her cheeks.

Should she tell him about the babies anyway, feeding him the line about a specially fast-tracked adoption? Would that persuade him to return? Would it lure him away from the glamorous career girl Vanessa? Because she is convinced that *she* is why he has left, even though his note didn't mention her.

Then her thoughts turn to Lizzie Armitage. These are really Lizzie's children. Maybe if she were to dry out, she could be a half-decent mother to them. Perhaps she should have had the chance to at least try, and fail. Because some women seem to have a knack with babies and small children. They just do. And she, Marian, does not appear to be one of them. For all she knows, Lizzie could be. Her younger sister is a bright, sensible girl. Her brother has a good job, by all accounts, and from what she's heard, the Armitage parents are decent, hard-working people. They are the twins' family. And a proper family is something she, Marian, will struggle to provide. Her parents are dead and her sister lives in New Zealand.

As if reading her mind, first Saffron and then Noah begin to cry. *Maybe they're trying to tell me something*, Marian thinks miserably. Her rational mind tells her this is nonsense, but she's so wretchedly tired that her rational mind has become detached from the rest of her, and seems to be floating somewhere above her head like a balloon.

The babies cry most of the way back to Muswell Hill, and she has to drive round and round the block until they are quiet enough for her to sneak them back into the house. Even then, she's sure she sees the curtains twitching at number twenty-five. Marian feeds and changes them both, and Saffron settles for a while, but Noah screams and screams all afternoon, pulling his tiny knees up to his chest. He appears to have diarrhoea, constantly filling one nappy after another. She bathes him and finally gets him to sleep only to have Saffron start screaming for another feed. It's two days since Marian has had the chance to wash herself, and she hasn't eaten anything other than biscuits, crisps and apples since she brought the babies home.

After another terrible night, during which she manages a total of one hour and forty minutes' sleep, she makes a decision. She will make up some story about the babies needing to be checked over in hospital, or temporarily fostered, but the babies will have to go back. She's going to take them back to Lizzie.

Three days after the babies were born, Marian phoned in sick to work, claiming a bout of gastric flu. It's now Monday morning and she's been off since the previous Monday. Her colleagues will be expecting her back, so she will have to phone again and claim she's still ill. She doesn't want to speak to Angela, because Angela knows her well enough to sniff out the lie. Angela might ask awkward questions. So she asks for the extension of the head of department's assistant, Sally.

'Sally's phone.'

Christ. Marian recognises the voice straight away.

'Who am I speaking to?' she asks, though she knows.

'It's Angela Dixon… Marian, is that you? I was just passing Sally's desk when her phone rang. She's just popped to the Ladies.'

Angela sounds so energetic, so upbeat. She sounds, in fact, like someone who has spent most of the night asleep in bed.

'I was ringing to say that I'm no better,' Marian said. At least she didn't have to play-act sounding rough. 'I'll have to get a sick note from my GP,' she fibbed.

'Actually, Maz, I'm quite glad you phoned…' Angela lowers her voice slightly. 'Something absolutely terrible happened on Thursday. With one of your clients.'

'Which one?' *Please don't say it, please don't say it.*

'Lizzie Armitage. The manager of the flats found her.'

'Found her…?' Marian's voice is little more than a whisper.

'Dead. In her bed. There's going to be a post-mortem, but apparently it looked like she'd had some sort of haemorrhage. Apparently it happens quite often with alcoholics when they have a drinking binge.'

'Oh. God.'

'I know. Such a shame. She wasn't all that old, was she? If she'd managed to get sober, she could have had her whole life ahead of her. She might even have had a family and stuff.'

Marian's voice box makes a strange sound, a sort of muffled groan.

'You okay, Maz? I'll try and find out when the funeral's going to be, if you like?'

'I've got to go.' Marian covers her mouth with her hand. 'I'm going to be sick.'

When her phone buzzes with a text later, Marian thinks it might be from Angela with more details about Lizzie Armitage.

It's from Tom.

On my way round. Need to pick up a few things, and also we should talk. T x

32

PAULA

'Get the door, will you?' Wendy Armitage says wearily. 'I can't face it.'

Paula opens the door of the flat to find yet another neighbour bearing yet another piece of ovenware covered in foil.

'It's Mrs Braithwaite,' she calls to her mother. 'She's brought lasagne.'

This is what happens, Paula is discovering, when somebody dies. People cook stuff and bring it round.

'Tell her to come in,' her mother calls back. Wendy likes Joyce Braithwaite, who's a calm, sensible sort of woman. 'And put the kettle on.'

Paula makes yet another pot of tea. That's something else that happens when a family member dies. You have to drink a lot of tea. In her case, it's something to do with her hands, something to stave off the terrible sadness and sense of discomfiture she feels at her sister's squalid end.

Three of Wendy's colleagues from the supermarket arrive next, then her cousin Gloria, and soon the small living room is packed with people.

'What about the funeral, Wend?' Gloria asks, passing around the plate of shortbread biscuits that she brought. 'When is it?'

'Colin's taking care of all the arrangements,' Wendy says, her jaw clenched with tension. She's finding it hard, Paula knows, to play the role of the grieving mother when most people know that she and Lizzie had been estranged for years. Most of the time she just sits, silently, and stares.

'Can I go out?' she asks.

Wendy frowns. 'Where to? I'm going to need help clearing up all this lot.'

'It's all right, let her go,' says nice Mrs Braithwaite. 'We'll help you.'

'I'm just going to Carly's,' says Paula. 'I won't be very long, I promise.'

But she doesn't go to Carly's. She takes the bus to Wood Green police station. She has lied to the police, and that was wrong, but now she's going to try and make amends.

The desk sergeant has white hair and a drooping moustache that makes him look like a walrus. 'And how can I help you, young lady?' He's brisk, a little impatient when it's eventually her turn to be called to the desk. There are still several other people waiting.

'It's about my sister. Lizzie Armitage. Elizabeth Armitage.'

'And you are…?'

'Paula Armitage.'

'Address?'

She gives it, and he writes it down, slowly, laboriously. 'Is your sister missing?'

Paula dips her head, feeling her lip tremble. 'No. She's dead. She died four days ago.'

The man softens slightly. 'I'm sorry to hear that… so, do you have a crime to report that relates to her death?'

'It's about her baby. She had a baby, but when they found her in the flat, they never said anything about what had happened to the baby.'

'When you say "they" found her…?'

'The police. The caretaker called the police and then they came and told us. Me and Mum.'

'Hold on a minute… let me just go and speak to someone.'

He returns a few minutes later. 'I've spoken to the officer in charge of that case over in Tottenham CID, and apparently there was no report of a baby at the premises when your sister's body was found. Was this child a boy or a girl?'

'I don't know.'

'You don't know? How old was the child?'

Paula calculates. 'They would have been only a couple of days old.'

'And who's the father?'

'He's called Macca. I don't know his full name.'

Recognition dawns on the sergeant's face. He turns the computer screen so that a mugshot is visible. 'This him?'

Paula nods.

'Yes, we know young Macca. He's had a few overnighters in our cells in recent years. If he's the father, might he have taken the baby?'

'I suppose so. But I don't know where he is. I mean, he lived with Lizzie some of the time, but I don't know where he was when he wasn't with her.'

The desk sergeant types something into his monitor. 'Says on his record "No Fixed Abode"… Oh, no – wait a minute. His new lodgings are courtesy of Her Majesty at Wormwood Scrubs. Arrested for conspiracy to commit armed robbery on the eighteenth of July.'

'That was the day the baby was born.'

'So I think we can conclude it wasn't him that took it. What about his family then? Do you know them? Might the baby be with a grandmother? An aunt?'

'I don't know. I don't know how to find out.'

The desk sergeant looks past her at the growing queue of people waiting to be helped. 'I'll tell you what, I'll ask the boys to keep an ear to the ground, and if they find out anything, we'll be in touch. Okay?'

Paul nods miserably and walks out onto the High Road, and heads towards the bus stop. A car horn honks, and she glances round to see Johnny Shepherd at the wheel of a sleek silver sports car.

'Hop in, kid!' he says with his usual brio. 'I'll give you a lift.'

She climbs in, turning her head to look out of the window because she feels the tears coming again. She doesn't have a handkerchief, and is forced to sniff to stop her nose running.

'You okay, Paul?' Johnny asks gently. He reaches into the glovebox for a tissue and hands it to her. 'What's up?'

She thinks about telling him that her sister has just died, but she can't really do so without having to answer a barrage of questions, and right now she's not in the mood for talking about it. That's all that anyone's talked about for days – all the well-meaning neighbours, relatives and friends – how awful it is to drink yourself to death at the age of twenty-four.

'Nothing,' she says thickly. 'I'm all right.'

He studies her face in profile for a few seconds. 'Well, if you're sure.' He pulls up outside her block of flats and waits for her to open the door and climb out. 'But if you ever need anything, you just tell me, okay?'

33

MARIAN

Marian returns her husband's text immediately.

What do you need to collect?

Her phone starts flashing with an incoming call a few minutes later.

'Look, I'm in the car now so I can't text… I want to get my ski stuff and my old vinyls. They're in the loft. And my cufflink box.'

She closes the door of the sitting room behind her so that Saffron and Noah won't be audible. 'How long will you be?'

He hasn't told her where he's staying, and she doesn't dare ask in case the answer is something she can't face.

'About ten minutes or so.'

Not very long at all. She considers letting him see the twins, telling him that she's going ahead with adoption, with or without him. Maybe the reality of them will persuade him to return after all. But if he refuses to come back, then he might still have questions about how the 'adoption' has gone ahead so suddenly and with so little bureaucratic input. Also, she looks absolutely terrible. Her hair is greasy, her clothes are grubby and she smells stale. If he were to think she's not coping as a single parent – and what other conclusion could he possibly reach – he might report her to someone. One of her colleagues, perhaps.

No, the babies are going to have to be well out of sight. She considers putting them in the back of the car. But a neighbour or passer-by might see them and raise the alarm. Then it comes to her, prompted by the call from Tom. They need to get the loft open anyway, so she'll put them up there and bring down Tom's vinyls at the same time. It'll only be for a few minutes; they won't come to any harm.

Marian shoves nappies, muslins and all the other baby paraphernalia behind the sofa, and hides the bottles, formula and sterilising equipment in the cupboard under the sink in the kitchen. Then she lifts Saffron carefully into Noah's basket, and lugs it awkwardly up the loft ladder. Fortunately, they're both asleep and stay asleep, despite all the movement.

Up in the loft, the air is thick with dust, and it's stuffy. Marian places the basket carefully at the far end of the space, then drags Tom's box of vinyls to the loft hatch. It's very heavy and she struggles to get it down the ladder. Her face and hands are covered with dust and her hair is damp with sweat, but she manages to drag the box down onto the landing and retract the ladder.

Because she will have to leave the hatch open to allow air to circulate, she realises she can't have Tom going upstairs. She fetches the bag containing his ski equipment from the spare room, puts his leather cuff link box in it, and carries the bag downstairs with the box of records, arriving in the hall just as the doorbell rings.

As soon as she sees Tom, her heart lurches, despite her exhaustion. His handsome face is well-rested, and he has the beginnings of a tan, as though he has been sitting outside in a garden somewhere. She wants him back. She needs him back.

'Sorry,' Marian says, indicating her dishevelled appearance. 'It's filthy up in the loft.'

'You should have let me go up there.' Tom recoils from her slightly. 'There was no need for you to do it.'

'It's fine,' she says, quickly. 'I wanted to see what was up there, anyway. Would you like some tea? Coffee?'

He shakes his head. 'No, thanks.'

'Only you said we needed to talk.'

Tom sighs. 'I suppose we should,' he agrees, without enthusiasm.

They go into the kitchen and Tom sits down while Marian sets the kettle to boil, visually sweeping the room for any remaining baby equipment. There's an empty feeding bottle on the draining board, and she quickly puts it into the dishwasher. Then as she turns to take the mugs from the dresser she spots a flash of pink out of the corner of her eye: Saffron's blanket, which must have fallen somehow when she was lifting her into her brother's basket. She scoops it up and with one seamless movement pushes it out of sight behind the back of the dresser.

'You look tired,' Tom observes, when she eventually sits down with a pot of tea and two mugs.

'I've not exactly been sleeping well.' She drops her chin, self-conscious about her filthy hair and grey skin. 'A lot on my mind, you know?'

Tom opens his mouth to speak, but she cuts him off, blurting out in a rush: 'They've found us twins to adopt. Newborn babies. A boy and a girl.'

Despite her decision not to mention Saffron and Noah, she feels now that she has to. That offering a ready-made family is her only hope of hanging on to him. He's never going to come back for her alone. Just look at her, for God's sake.

He smiles sadly, and places his hand briefly over hers. 'Marrie, you must know that's not a possibility.'

'But you said you needed to think things over. I thought—'

'I'm with someone else.'

She stares at him. 'Vanessa,' she says, flatly.

'Yes.'

'Are you living with her?'

He nods. 'In her flat, yes.'

'So you and I… we're never going to be a family?'

Tom shakes his head. He seems genuinely upset. 'I'm sorry. I'm so sorry.'

She's crying now, her sheer exhaustion making her crumble. 'But the babies, what about the twin babies?'

'Someone else will give them a wonderful home, I'm sure of it. There are always queues of people wanting to adopt newborns. You said so yourself.'

Marian thinks of the two tiny humans hidden away in the corner of the loft, and her weeping intensifies. This isn't the wonderful home Tom's referring to. She isn't what the babies need.

He fetches a tissue from the box on the dresser and hands it to her. 'Remember what the IVF consultant said, Marrie? It's me that's infertile, not you. You could still have a baby if you met someone else. There's still time.'

She simply scowls at him and shakes her head.

'Look, we'll talk about what to do with the house at some point, but now obviously isn't the time. Let's leave it till things have settled down a bit, okay?'

Tom goes into the hall and is hefting the box of vinyls when a distinct screeching sound floats down from the top floor. He straightens up and looks back up the stairs.

'What the hell was that?' he asks, startled.

'Oh, it's that wretched Burmese cat from number twenty-seven,' Marian says, quickly. 'It's taken to sitting in our garden and howling.'

'We should go out there and chuck cold water over it,' Tom says. An awkwardness descends with his use of the word 'we'. 'I'll do it if you like. You don't want the thing coming in and spraying everywhere.'

'It's fine,' says Marian, firmly. She places her body so that she's blocking his route to the garden.

'Okay then.' Her husband gives her a long, thoughtful look, before carrying his things out of the house and driving away.

Marian watches the car through the sitting room window. *Don't go,* every cell in her body is screaming. *Don't leave me alone with them.*

Once the car has rounded the corner onto Alexandra Park Road, she dabs her eyes with the tissue Tom gave her, and walks slowly up the stairs. There's a cry; a cross, indignant cry.

Saffron, she thinks. *That's the sound Saffron makes when she's hungry.*

She yanks down the loft ladder and climbs up into the loft, pausing at the top to give her eyes time to adjust to the gloom. The dust in the air makes her cough. Saffron is still crying, tiny hands and feet waving.

Marian reaches instinctively to pick her up and calm her before carrying the basket back to the ladder.

And then she sees that something is very wrong.

34

MARIAN

'Who's the patient, is it yourself?'

The nurse on the end of the line at NHS Direct speaks the words in a sing-song voice, sticking to her script. Marian's first instinct had been to phone her GP, but of course her GP knows that she's been going through fertility treatment, and has not recently given birth to twins.

'No. No, it's my son.'

'And how old is your son, please?'

'Ten days old.'

'And can I take your name please?'

'Um, Cathy. Cathy Smith.'

'And the baby's name?'

'Noah.'

'Right, Cathy, can you tell me what the problem seems to be.'

'Um, he's... he's not breathing properly, and—'

'Let me just stop you there, Cathy... he is breathing?'

'Yes, it's just... he's a bit blue around the lips. And his breathing is a bit shallow, a bit rapid. A bit like an asthma attack.'

'Did he have breathing difficulties at birth?'

Marian hesitates. 'No.'

'Is he premature?'

Was he? She didn't know. Nobody knew Lizzie's dates, not even Lizzie.

'No, but he's on the small side. He's one of twins.'

'In that case I think you should take him straight to hospital and get him seen by a neonatal specialist. There are several reasons for a baby turning blue, including heart problems, but they all need immediate attention.'

Marian says nothing. She can hear nothing, except for the thumping of her own heart.

'Cathy? Cathy… are you still on the line?'

'Yes, yes, I'm here. Okay, thank you, I will. I'll take him straight to A and E.'

She hangs up the landline. She'd withheld the number just in case. The trouble with going to her local A and E is that they'll want to look up Noah's birth record. They'll want details of her midwife, who should have been doing daily home visits. It won't take much to raise their suspicions that this is not really her child. And then the police might be called. And the local social services, where she herself is an employee. Oh, the irony. The tabloids would lap it up.

She reaches down and picks up Noah. His colour has improved, and his breathing is a little less shallow. Perhaps he just got a bit of dust in his lungs when he was in the loft, and it was stuck in his airway. He grimaces and squirms in her arms.

'Hungry, little man?' she asks. He's still a lot less interested in feeding than his sister, and she's sure he's lost weight rather than gained. Marian fetches a bottle and coaxes him into drinking a few ounces before he falls asleep, the teat slipping from his lips. She lays him down in his basket and feeds and changes his sister. Saffron screams on and off for what feels like hours before settling, though the clock says it's only forty minutes. Once she's finally asleep, Marian places her basket on the bedroom floor next to her brother's. Noah's chest is rising and falling rapidly, but he looks peaceful. She makes herself some toast, has a quick shower and then collapses into bed, delirious with exhaustion.

Her first thought on waking is that this is the longest period of sleep she's had all week.

The clock tells her it's well over four hours since she turned out the light. Until now, she's rarely been more than an hour and a half without one of the twins waking. The startling thing is what a difference this makes. A stretch of deep, dreamless sleep has reset her brain.

One of the babies is crying now, however. From the volume and the indignant tone, it has to be Saffron. Marian tugs on her dressing gown and walks over to the baskets. As she bends down to lift the little girl, she freezes. Noah is completely still, and there's something about the stillness that feels quite wrong. She's seen enough newborn sleep in the last few days to know how it looks. And instinctively she knows this is not it.

This is not sleep.

With Saffron draped over her shoulder, she reaches down and touches Noah's cheek. It's cold, despite the warmth of the July night. Icy cold.

The shock is visceral, like a physical blow to her body.

It takes her a long time to accept it. To accept that he has gone. At first she just stands there staring down into the bassinet, at the tiny waxen figure. Willing him to move. But of course, he doesn't. He won't.

Saffron twists in her arms, rooting against her chest for milk, stuffing her curled fist into her gummy mouth. Marian puts her back into her own basket and, when she begins to wail, takes the basket into the spare room and shuts the door. She can't deal with another baby right now. She has to think. She has to act.

Lowering herself onto the edge of her bed in the silent room, Marian buries her face in her hands and tries to order her swirling thoughts. She could take Noah's body to the hospital, anonymously of course, and leave him where he would be found. But if they somehow manage to trace her afterwards, they will think that she killed him. Even if she could persuade them it was a natural death, they'll take Saffron away, and possibly send her to prison. And it would make no difference to Noah, not now. He's gone. She consoles herself that if he had been left alone with Lizzie, this would still have happened. It might even have happened sooner. Marian wasn't the one who drank her way through her pregnancy.

It's not her fault.

From her work at social services Marian knows only too well that the bodies of newborns are found in all sorts of places: toilet blocks, dumpsters, storm drains. But she could never do that. *Would* never do that. She has to give him some dignity. She pulls on tracksuit bottoms and a T-shirt and, ignoring Saffron's discontented murmuring, goes out to the garden. There's a light fitting in the shed, but she doesn't dare switch it on. She mustn't do anything that will attract the attention of the neighbours. Instead she gropes around in the dark until she finds the spade that Tom used to dig the flowerbeds.

She knows the perfect spot. At the far end of the garden is a large, overgrown ceanothus bush. Its flowering has just come to an end, but in bloom its stems are heavy with blue flowers. She digs a hole behind it, with difficulty, because she has to angle the spade past the branches and can't get enough downward purchase. Eventually she abandons the spade and resorts to a large trowel, getting down on her knees and hacking away at the topsoil. The earth beneath is heavy London clay, and she struggles to keep going. But keep going she must, because the hole can't be too shallow.

It takes her about an hour, by which time Saffron has given up crying and gone back to sleep. Marian rinses the mud off her hands, and with tears half blinding her, gently wraps Noah in the blue cashmere blanket, covering his face. She remembers a wooden wine box that contained a magnum of champagne, given to Tom by a client, and retrieves it from the back of a cupboard in the utility room. The blanketed bundle fits inside it perfectly.

She carries the makeshift coffin across the moonlit lawn and lowers it with infinite care into the grave. Filling it in does not take quite as long as digging it, but she takes pains to flatten the surface of the earth as much as possible. The overhanging branches of the ceanothus will mask the disturbance until it settles. And it's not as though Tom is going to be doing any more gardening in Ranmoor Road.

It's done, yet walking away feels impossible. Marian sinks back onto her knees at the edge of the lawn and uses the hem of her T-shirt to wipe away the tears that have been coursing down her face. She feels the need to say or do something to mark the occasion. A prayer, perhaps. She's not religious, but her Church of England grammar school was very big on praying. She reaches back into her memory to try and dredge up something suitable. The only thing that she can recall with any clarity is Psalm 23, so she whispers it now.

"'The Lord is my shepherd; I shall not want. He maketh me to lie down in green pastures: he leadeth me beside the still waters. He restoreth my soul: he leadeth me in the paths of righteousness for his name's sake. Yea, though I walk through the valley of the shadow of death, I will fear no evil: for thou art with me; thy rod and thy staff they comfort me.'"

It doesn't feel enough, yet it's all she has. She drops her head and weeps some more, then walks wearily back to the house to care for Noah's sister.

35

MARIAN

The text message makes her heart leap in her chest.

Am in area, thought I might pop in for a chat. Angela x

Marian has been signed off work with stress for the past month and a half, citing the stress of her marriage ending as the reason. The truth is she doesn't ever think about work, or her colleagues. She thinks of them now as her former colleagues. The only thing occupying her mind is the challenge of new motherhood.

The logistics of caring for one newborn are straightforward, after dealing with two on her own. One set of feeds to prepare, one set of nappies to change. No background screaming from Twin 1 while she attends to Twin 2. But something in Saffron has changed since Noah's death. While she was always the louder and hungrier of the siblings, her needs were simple. She cried when she was hungry, but once fed she stopped. She was easier to settle, and slept for longer periods.

But now it's as though Saffron has taken on Noah's role as the difficult one. As though she senses his absence and is traumatised by the loss. She wails inconsolably for long periods of the day, for no apparent reason. If Marian picks her up, she squirms and arches her back, refusing to be comforted. As if she's angry. At night she rarely sleeps for more than an hour and a half at a time. Marian is so exhausted, her own sleep pattern so disturbed, that she's like a zombie most of the time. She rarely leaves the house, having all her groceries delivered instead. When she can do so without detection, she takes Saffron out in the car, because the sound and vibration of the engine usually soothe her.

And now this. Angela calling round. She thinks about texting her back and saying she's not at the house, but if Angela doesn't check her phone and comes round anyway, that could be a problem. Instead, she'll use the excuse that she's not well and get rid of her as quickly as possible. It's not as if she doesn't look terrible, so her excuse won't seem fabricated.

She puts Saffron in the carrycot and pushes it down to the end of the garden, positioning it out of sight behind the shed. As though sensing the proximity of her brother's resting place, Saffron begins to wail.

'It'll only be five minutes,' Marian tell her. 'Then I'm coming back.'

It's all right to leave her there, she tells herself. *She's only in the garden. People left prams in the garden all the time when I was a baby. Fresh air was considered a good thing. And it's still only September.*

But the memory of leaving the twins in the loft eats away at her. She'd thought they would be okay, but Noah wasn't. Noah had become ill and died. *It's necessary*, she tells herself briskly. Of all the people to discover her with a baby, Angela would be the worst.

In the kitchen she strains to hear, but the carrycot is mercifully out of earshot. She scoops up the feeding stuff and any stray bits of clothing into a wicker basket – a routine that has become familiar – and bundles it into the under-stairs cupboard. Thirty seconds later, the doorbell rings.

'Oh, sorry! Have I woken you up?' Angela takes in Marian's stained dressing gown and wild hair.

'I was just about to have a shower,' Marian replies truthfully. 'I've been a bit under the weather… this bug that's going around… so I won't ask you in if you don't mind.'

'Sorry to hear that.' Angela glances past her shoulder into the untidy kitchen. 'I just wanted to check up on you, see if there was anything I could do. You're obviously going through a tough time, with Tom and everything.'

'Yes,' Marian mumbles. 'It's been really difficult.' Tears well up in her eyes, and to her horror she starts to sob. If she needed to convince Angela that she was suffering with stress, there can be no doubt about it now.

'Oh, you poor love!' Angela reaches in and gives her a hug, stiffening slightly at the smell of Marian's unwashed hair. 'And this situation can't help.'

Marian pulls back, wondering what she means, then realises Angela is pointing to the FOR SALE board nailed to the gatepost.

'Yes, well… it's probably for the best in the long run. Fresh start and all that.'

Marian means it. She wants the house to be sold so she can put an end to this soul-destroying subterfuge. Hiding a young baby in a neighbourhood like this is almost impossible. The business of selling is draining, however. Because of Saffron, she can't be in when potential purchasers come round, and has had to refuse several requests to conduct last-minute viewings herself.

Tom has become angry and exasperated about this. 'I'll come over myself and talk to buyers if you don't want to,' he argued. 'Honestly, Marian, I know this is difficult, but the way you're behaving at the moment, it's like you've lost the plot. I don't know how to get through to you any more.'

She only just succeeded in persuading him that there was sufficient interest in the property for them to be confident of a quick sale. 'Then we can both move on. Which is what we want.'

She knows that Tom and Vanessa are looking at properties in North London together, but she has a different plan. The more distance she puts between herself and London, the easier it will be to blend in as a mother. To have some sort of normal life. She has decided she'll move to Brighton. She used to enjoy visiting when she was a child, and loves the idea of raising a child at the seaside. Fresh air, playing on the beach, freedom from scrutiny. And with her share of the capital from Ranmoor Road she'll be able to afford somewhere decent without the need for a big mortgage.

'Probably for the best,' Angela is agreeing. 'But going through the upheaval must be hard.' She attempts another stiff-armed hug. 'Poor you. Let me know if there's anything I can do. Promise?'

'Promise,' says Marian. She waits until Angela has got into her car, before shutting the front door firmly behind her.

There's a reluctance in Marian as she walks down to the end of the garden to retrieve the carrycot. She feels uneasy at being so near to where Noah's remains are buried.

Saffron was only out in the garden for a few minutes in the end. And her crying has stopped, so no harm done. If she stays asleep a bit longer, Marian might even get to take a shower and put on some clothes. After checking that the neighbours on either side aren't in their gardens, she wheels the carrycot gingerly back to the house.

Just as she is lifting it over the sill of the French windows, Kate from number twenty-three heads out onto her terrace. She turns her head in Marian's direction, sending her scuttling into the kitchen and closing the doors, despite the Indian summer warmth. *This is ridiculous*, she thinks. *I can't live like this. Like a fugitive. And somebody is going to notice something soon. It's only a matter of time.*

She has just stripped off her dressing gown and stepped into the shower when Saffron begins to scream again. According to most of the online childcare tips she's read it won't harm a baby to let it cry for a bit, but it still risks the neighbours hearing through the walls. She wraps a towel round herself, goes downstairs, lifts the small body against her shoulder, and carries her back up to the bathroom, placing her on the bathmat with her jungle gym positioned above her. Saffron ignores the bright shapes and continues to grizzle, but at least in here with the door closed the neighbours are unlikely to hear.

The crying continues intermittently all afternoon, worsening as the day goes on. Saffron's face is bright red, and contorted with rage. Marian phones NHS Direct again.

'It's almost certainly three-month colic,' the nurse tells her. 'Most parents find their baby is worst in the early evening.'

'Does that mean it lasts three months?' Marian bought books on pregnancy but none on parenting, and is having to rely on the occasional foray into online forums.

'It means it's usually over by the time the baby is three months old. Six to twelve weeks is usually the worst time. How old is your daughter?'

'Eight weeks. Nearly nine.'

'Well, there you are then; it'll likely not last much longer.'

This fact – even assuming it is true – is of little comfort to Marian at two in the morning when she has not yet had the chance to fall asleep. Saffron seems incapable of settling for more than twenty or thirty minutes before shuddering into wakefulness and launching into a high-pitched shriek. Every time Marian is just drifting over the threshold into oblivion, she is jolted awake. Over and over again. She remembers that they use a similar technique to torture prisoners of war. Makes perfect sense.

'What do you want?' she hisses at the squirming figure in the Moses basket. 'Why are you doing this?'

Saffron gulps, hiccups, then roars again. Marian lifts the little velour-clad bundle against her shoulder and jiggles her up and down, pacing. It makes no difference. She holds her sideways and rocks her horizontally. The roars persist.

'Oh, for crying out loud!' Normally she would have laughed at this poor choice of words, but Marian's sense of humour has long since abandoned her. She drops rather than places Saffron back in the basket, gripping the sides of it and shaking it violently to and fro so that the little body jolts from side to side.

'Will. You. Stop. *Please.*'

As if Marian's desperate screech has shocked her, Saffron's eyes widen and her sobs subside to a hiccup. Marian jostles the basket roughly again, and strangely Saffron seems calmed by it. Eventually, her eyelids droop, her fists uncurl. Marian gives the basket another tentative jiggle. Nothing. She's sleeping.

Crawling into her own bed, Marian rolls onto her side, dizzy with exhaustion and reaches for the light switch.

And then she hears it. A newborn baby's cry.

She glances down beside the bed, but Saffron is still asleep. And this cry is different: higher, thinner. It's Noah's cry.

She jerks herself upright. There it is again, that distinctive sound. But it can't be; it's not possible. It must be the Burmese cat. Or she must be so sleep deprived, she's starting to hallucinate. That can happen, can't it? People hearing or seeing things that aren't there when they've been under severe stress.

Marian tries closing her eyes, but she is unable to rid her brain of the sound. Pulling on her dressing gown, she creeps out of the bedroom and heads down the stairs. She slides open the French windows and tiptoes out onto the moonlit lawn. A fox trots past her, barely paying attention. The crying is still there in her head, fainter now but still unmistakable. Still Noah.

The ceanothus bush is nothing but a looming black shape, throwing sinister shadows across the lawn. But the grave is still there, still undisturbed; just the faintest mound of fresh-looking earth betraying its existence.

The crying in her head stops. Marian sinks to the ground and gives way to tears. 'I'm sorry,' she whispers. 'I'm so sorry, Noah. I wasn't good enough. I didn't do things right.'

The thoughts tumble through her head, accusing, unforgiving. She should have sought help sooner. She should have taken him to be seen by a doctor. She should never have taken the babies at all.

This is what the crying means, she realises. This is Noah's way of getting her to make a decision about her future. And make a decision she must.

36

MARIAN

'Mrs Glynn?'

It's 8.45 a.m. and Marian has just woken. She fed and changed Saffron at five thirty and managed to coax her to sleep again before dropping off herself.

'Yes,' she croaks.

'It's Tamara. Tamara Granger, from Hendricks.'

The estate agent. She doesn't wait for Marian to reply, but goes on. 'Only I left a message yesterday afternoon, but no one got back to me… I've booked in viewings for ten, twelve fifteen and two. Hope that's okay?'

'Well, no, not really.'

'The thing is, two of these are second viewings and I think there's a very good chance of them offering on the property today. But obviously they're keen to come back and take another look. I know one of them wants to measure for curtains.'

Marian sighs, and pushes herself up on her elbows. The appointment times mean she will have to be out most of the day. On the other hand, if the house is under offer at the end of it, she will be able to halt the viewings entirely.

'All right then.'

She drags her weary body out of bed, and stumbles downstairs to make coffee, just as Saffron wakes and begins to demand feeding again. The mild September weather seems to have come to an abrupt end, with the house feeling chilly and heavy drizzle running down the window panes.

On autopilot, Marian feeds and changes the baby, makes extra bottles and dresses herself in jeans and a shapeless sweater. She tidies away all evidence of motherhood and loads Saffron into her new car seat, with the carrycot and changing bag stowed in the boot. Instead of being calmed by the movement of the car, Saffron seems enraged by it and protests loudly, squirming and kicking in her seat. Driving in heavy London traffic with screams in her ears sends Marian's blood pressure soaring, and she drums her fingernails on the steering wheel. She tries putting the radio on, but that only serves to make the screams louder.

'Will you shut up!' She turns her head and shouts at Saffron while the car is idling at a red light. The driver of the car in the adjacent lane stares at her in alarm, but Marian ignores him. It's still raining, so going for a long walk in Highgate Wood or on Hampstead Heath is out of the question. An indoor option will have to be found. She turns the car onto the A41 and heads for Brent Cross.

Five hours in the shopping centre are all that she can bear.

They're more than she can bear, really, but she has no choice. She pushes the grumbling Saffron around and around shops she has no interest in until her feet are aching. At intervals she sits on a hard bench to feed her. The bottles of formula have gone cold, and Saffron protests by turning her head away from the teat and whimpering. After changing her nappy in a dirty toilet cubicle for the third time, Marian decides to cut her losses and head home.

When they arrive in Ranmoor Road, it's clear the three o'clock viewing is still going on, even though it's now three forty-five. The car with the Hendricks logo is parked outside, and through the sitting room window Marian glimpses a woman with a clipboard in her arms and two other people, deep in conversation. Swearing under her breath, she drives around the block and parks, twisting in her seat to try and pacify the squirming baby.

Please buy the house. Please just buy the sodding house.

Twenty minutes later, when Saffron is building up to a full-blown meltdown, Marian drives back to Ranmoor Road. The agent and her clients are gone. She is so relieved that she doesn't even bother trying to be discreet, carrying baby and changing bag into the house without checking for onlookers.

The NHS Direct nurse said that typically infant colic started in the evening, but as ever Saffron has her own timetable, and starts her chorus of angry screams as soon as they are inside the house. Marian makes up a fresh bottle of milk – warm this time – but after sucking on it hungrily for a few seconds, the milk is regurgitated in a projectile stream, and the screams resume. Subsequent attempts to feed her result in more vomiting, yet after every time Saffron protests that she is hungry. Marian's clothes and the carpet are covered in sour-smelling white curds.

In desperation she tries a bath, but it makes the baby even more distressed. She cries if she's held, she cries if she's put down. Marian's head is filled with nothing but crying. It feels like the middle of the night, but is only seven thirty. Leaving Saffron squirming in her basket, she goes downstairs and pours herself a large glass of wine. She's about to go back upstairs to the scene of the battle when the front door bell rings.

Marian freezes. It rings again. Then again, more insistently. She's intent on ignoring it, but then there is a firm hammering on the front door. It could be Tom. And Tom has a key.

Tossing a milk-stained muslin onto the foot of the stairs, she opens the door a crack, wine glass clutched to her chest. It's Kate, from next door.

'Is everything all right, Marian?'

Marian blinks, takes a sip. 'Yes, why wouldn't it be?' She tries to position the edge of the door so that it hides the huge milk vomit stain on the front of her sweater.

'Only, I…' Kate Fletcher is a neatly dressed, deeply conformist woman who used to work as an accountant and is now, in her own words, 'a full-time homemaker'. She seems embarrassed. 'The thing is, I couldn't help hearing it. The crying.'

'Crying?' Marian feels her cheeks glowing red.

'Yes. Like… like a small baby's crying.'

Marian frowns, feigning confusion. 'A baby?'

'Have you got someone staying with you perhaps, who has a baby?'

Marian shakes her head, starts pulling the door closed.

'But I saw you, Marian.' Kate is flushed now, deeply uncomfortable. 'This afternoon. I saw you come back in the car, and carry a baby inside.'

Marian feels a cold, tightening sensation in her chest. 'I don't know what you think you saw, Kate, but it definitely wasn't that. And I think you must have misheard. There's no baby here.' She slams the door shut with more force than she intended.

Shit. She knows. She'll tell someone.

Saffron is making the little hiccupping noises that precede a full-blown roar, but before Marian can deal with her, the doorbell rings again. She pulls open the door a crack. This time it's a man, one she doesn't recognise.

'Are you from Hendricks?'

He shows a warrant card. 'DC Gary Marsden. Have you got a minute?'

'It's not all that convenient, actually.'

Shit. Whatever he wants, she can't let him come in.

He smiles. 'Sorry, I should have given you a bit of warning. How about we fix a time for you to come down to the station? Or I could call back? I just need to take a statement from you.'

A statement?

'What is this regarding?'

'Your client through social services, Elizabeth Armitage. Now deceased. At the inquest the coroner requested an investigation into some matters… surrounding her passing.'

'Fine. How about you give me your number and I'll arrange a time.' She accepts one of his business cards and closes the door.

This is it. This is a sign. I have to do it now.

Upstairs, Saffron screams angrily.

After she's finished her wine and managed to get Saffron to keep some milk down, Marian looks out of her bedroom window, onto the street.

It's dusk now, with a gauzy autumn mist hanging in the air. Kate's little red hatchback is parked directly outside, with her husband Michael's car behind it. They're unlikely to be going out for the evening now; it's too late. She'll just have to wait until they, and everyone else, have gone to bed.

Saffron dozes on and off for the next few hours, between periods of grizzling. Her crying is half-hearted as if now that Marian has given up, she's giving up too. Marian picks her up and holds her across her lap, admiring the curve of her cheek, the delicate perfection of her eyelashes, the golden glow of her skin. She feels a lot heavier now than she did on the day she was carried out of Lizzie Armitage's grotty flat in Tottenham. Despite the colic, she's thriving.

Lifting her gently onto her changing mat, Marian puts on a clean nappy and onesie and dresses the baby in her favourite babygro: white, dotted with little coral-coloured starfish. She fetches a piece of paper from the desk in the spare room and writes on it in clear capital letters.

MY NAME IS SAFFRON, BORN 18th JULY

She wraps Saffron in a white cotton blanket then lays her in the Moses basket that she originally took the twins in. The second bassinet she bought for Noah is bigger and sturdier, but since his death she hasn't liked using it. She tucks a thicker cot quilt over the white blanket. Finally, the piece of paper is slipped down the side of the mattress, and Saffron's favourite yellow stuffed duckling placed by her feet. She stretches and then settles into sleep, as though enjoying the extra warmth.

It's midnight now. This feels like the right time. Marian tucks her hair into a beanie hat, picks up her coat and keys, then takes the basket out to the car.

'It's for the best,' she says out loud into the rear-view mirror. There's no answering flutter of a hand or even a cry. 'Why couldn't you have behaved like this all along?' Marian asks, her voice thick with tears. 'Then that busybody Kate would never have come round.'

She parks a short distance from Whittington Hospital, not wanting anyone to see her car and trace its number plate. With the hood of her coat pulled down low so her face is obscured, she carries the basket to the entrance of the maternity unit. Through the glass doors, the lobby is in half-darkness, but there's a bell for mothers arriving in labour after hours. Marian places the basket in front of the door, rings the bell then darts around the side of the building, and down the path that skirts the car park. Instinctively she listens for Saffron's cry. There is no cry.

Don't look back, she tells herself, stumbling out onto Highgate Hill. *Whatever you do, don't look back.*

37

MARIAN

For the past two months, Marian has not slept for more than four hours in a night. All she has wanted, for the whole of that time, is to sleep.

Now, finally, she is alone in a silent house. No babies. Just her. And yet, still she can't sleep. She switches off her phone, then showers, puts on clean pyjamas and crawls under the duvet. Lies there for hours, staring at the ceiling. Listening. She can't make her brain stop listening for the babies, even though they're not there. Even when her eyelids become heavy and she starts to drift off, she hears it again. The sound of Noah's cry.

Eventually, at 5 a.m., she falls into a deep sleep and sleeps until after midday. When she wakes, she still feels tired. But not that hallucinatory brain fog of a person whose sleep is constantly interrupted. Not the prison camp torture tiredness. She makes scrambled eggs, toast and coffee and eats it slowly and with enjoyment.

For the first time in what feels like weeks, Marian washes her hair and dries it properly. She even puts on a bit of make-up. Once she's dressed, she strips off the greasy sheets that have been on her bed for at least a month and puts them in the machine. Despite feeling rested, she moves slowly, her limbs leaden, as though weighed down with sorrow. Every cell in her body longs for Saffron; the smell of her, the softness of her skin. The magical, miraculous smiles she bestowed on Marian when the attacks of colic abated. The way she had learned to clutch her fluffy duckling toy between her fingers and stare at it in amazement.

Eventually, once the house is clean, she gathers the larger items of baby equipment, toys and clothes, and takes them up into the loft. Bottles, nappies and formula are thrown into a bin bag and taken out to the dustbin. With rubber gloves on, she washes down the kitchen surfaces and mops the floor. Keeping the rubber gloves on, she positions herself on the sitting room window seat and waits. Having sacrificed Saffron to prevent discovery, she needs to make sure it pays off somehow. To vindicate herself.

Kate Fletcher pulls up outside just before three o'clock, dressed in gym gear, fresh from her weekly Pilates class. She'll be heading off on the school run shortly. Nothing if not predictable.

Marian grabs a duster and a bottle of Brasso and, opening the front door wide, gets to work on the brass door knocker and numbers '2' and '1'. She glances up as though she has only just noticed her neighbour.

'Hi, Kate!' She waves the duster brightly, despite feeling hollow inside. 'Got time for a cuppa?'

Kate hesitates, glancing through the open front door.

Look, you nosy bitch. And listen. No babies here. See?

'Thanks, Marian, that's very kind, but I'd better get on.' She continues looking past Marian's shoulder and into the hallway. 'How's everything with you?'

'Fine,' says Marian briskly.

'Only, we heard… we couldn't help noticing that Tom's not here.' She gives an awkward grimace. 'That he's moved out. And obviously…' She gives a meaningful nod in the direction of the sale board.

'Yes, well,' said Marian, with more sangfroid than she has ever felt about her husband's defection. 'Things change. People change. But I'm moving on. And at least we don't have children.'

'No,' concedes Kate. 'At least there's that.'

*

That night, Marian takes a sleeping pill and passes out for nearly eleven hours.

Although she feels slow and groggy when she first wakes up, the feeling eases once she's had coffee. Physically she feels like a human being again, even though her heart is a void.

After hoovering all the carpets in the house, she's just about to tackle the bathroom with bleach and scouring pads when her phone rings.

'Mrs Glynn? Tamara Granger from Hendricks.'

'Oh. Hi.'

'Is this a good moment?'

'Yes.' *For once*, thinks Marian. 'What can I do for you?'

'I've got some great news. One of the couples who came on Thursday, the Evershotts, have offered full asking. And they've already sold, so they'll be able to complete quickly.'

'Goodness,' says Marian, sitting down on the edge of the bath. 'That *is* great news. Thank you.'

After she's finished cleaning, she goes and sits at the desk in the spare room. The silence in the house is unnerving her, as is her relative leisure. No bottles to make up, or nappies to change. She opens her laptop to draft her letter of resignation to Haringey Social Services, then gets distracted looking at property in Brighton. She's calculated exactly what she will be able to afford with half of the huge sum they have just been offered but nothing much appeals, until she scrolls down to a pretty early Victorian villa, rendered in palest blue with a bright red front door. It's near the seafront, and has a small, enclosed garden.

Marian clicks through the photos. There, in the garden, is the most adorable little purpose-built Wendy house. And sure enough, one of the bedrooms has been decorated for a girl, with walls painted sugar pink. There's a rocking horse in the window and a doll's house next to the canopied bed. It's the perfect room for a little girl to grow up in. A little girl like Saffron.

She slumps back in her chair, the ache in her chest so overwhelming, it's as though she has been violently struck. What has she just done? She acted when she was out of her mind with tiredness, not thinking straight: only thinking of the now, not the future. Yes, babies cry; they're hard work. Everyone says so. But the point is that they don't stay babies forever. They grow into little girls; little girls who play with dolls' houses and rocking horses. And yes, Kate Fletcher's curiosity was a problem, but she could surely have come up with a solution. She and Saffron could have gone to stay somewhere else while the house was sold. A hotel perhaps, or a holiday let. They still can.

Hurrying out to the car, she drives straight to the Whittington and dumps the car haphazardly in the car park. Marian has avoided reading or listening to the local news, in case there's an appeal for an abandoned baby girl's mother to come forward. Too painful, too shaming. But if Saffron's still here – and where else would she be? – she'll be in a nursery on the postnatal ward, being cared for by midwives. The possibility that she has already been fostered looms in her mind, but no, it's too soon for the local social services to have organised that. She should know.

The maternity unit has a security lock, but Marian tags along behind a group of visiting relatives with armfuls of flowers and helium balloons, and follows them in to the ward. She knows from having visited her clients in hospital in the past that the nursery is somewhere near the central nursing station. She marches down a corridor as though she knows where she's going, but only finds four-bedded bays full of new mothers lying on their beds like beached seals, their babies beside them in their clear plastic cribs. It must be in the other direction.

As she turns back, she hears it. A strident cry, different from the muffled mewing of the newly born. Marian has enough first-hand experience to recognise the cry of a nine-week old. It's her. It's Saffron, it has to be. She heads in the direction of the cry, reaches the door marked 'Nursery' and grabs the door handle.

Saffron. I'm here. Mummy's here.

Suddenly, a midwife is at her elbow, her face stony.

'Excuse me? Can I ask where you're going? Are you visiting someone?'

'Yes. A friend.'

'And her name?'

'Um, she's...' Marian's mind goes completely blank. 'Farzeen. Farzeen Coker.'

Farzeen's baby isn't due for another few weeks, but she's the only pregnant woman Marian can think of. She tries to scuttle back down the corridor, but the midwife blocks her path. 'Just a moment, please.'

Eye contact is made between her and the midwife at the nursing station, and she mouths 'Code Blue' to her colleague. Suddenly, seemingly out of nowhere, a security guard appears.

'I'm afraid I'm going to have to ask you to leave the premises, madam.' He grabs her elbow and steers her in the direction of the lifts, ushering her into one and riding with her down to the ground floor.

'This way.' He shepherds her towards the exit door, adding in a slightly kinder tone, 'I wouldn't go up to the maternity floor without authorisation if I were you. They've got cameras everywhere.'

Afraid to walk straight back to her car in case the guard takes a note of her registration, Marian loiters at the side of the building until he's moved on. The last thing she can afford is for the hospital authorities to identify her, for someone to pay her a visit. They'll be waiting for the abandoned child's birth mother to come back for her, as they so often do.

Only when she's sure he must have gone does she cross the car park and slide into the driver's seat. She hangs her head, beating the steering wheel with frustration, and weeping.

When Marian gets home, the browser on her laptop is still opened on the online details of the lovely Victorian villa in Brighton.

Marian shuts it down hastily, before the picture of the little girl's bedroom can torment her further. There's no point requesting a viewing now. She could never be happy in a place like that: not on her own. No, a property suitable for a middle-aged single woman awaits her. A nice, low-maintenance flat.

The doorbell rings. She splashes cold water on her face and goes down to open it. Probably Kate from next door, checking that she's not harbouring illicit children.

It's Tom.

'Hi!' He's looking conspicuously tanned and healthy, and wearing a shirt Marian has never seen before. Her husband hates shopping for clothes, so *she* probably bought it. 'Can I come in for a minute?'

She steps back and lets him in without speaking.

'The agent said we've had an asking price offer… so we need to go ahead and formally accept, sign the memorandum of sale or whatever. I take it that's okay.'

'Yes. Fine.'

'And we need to have a discussion about the house contents. Apart from my desk there isn't really any furniture I want. So take what you want with you and get rid of the rest… maybe to charity? Apparently the buyers want us to include the kitchen dresser in the sale.'

Marian shrugs. 'Okay. I don't particularly want to keep it. It's too bulky to take to a smaller place.'

'Great. We can get it added to the list of fixtures and fittings.' Tom forces a smile, but there is anxiety below the surface. She senses it. 'The other reason I've called round is... look, this is awkward, but I had a phone call.'

She raises an eyebrow, but says nothing, folding her arms across her chest.

'Your colleague, Angela, called me. She said she'd been round here to see you, and the visit had left her very concerned. You've not been to work in over two months, apparently? She was... well, quite frankly, she was worried about your mental state.'

'My mental state is fine,' Marian says tightly. 'I've just had my marriage fall apart on me, that's all. Not like that's a big deal or anything. I mean, why on earth would I be upset?' She marches to the front door and yanks it open, stands there waiting for him to leave.

'Marrie, if you need professional help or anything—'

'I don't. I'm fine.'

Tom gives a helpless shrug and heads towards the door. 'All right, I just wanted to check. I do still care about you, you know.'

He heads down the path towards the car. Marian squints after him, trying to work out why what she's seeing is disturbing her. And then she realises. There's now a child seat in the back. A chill runs up her spine.

'Hold on a minute!' She follows him outside. 'Why the hell have you got *that* in the back seat?'

'It's for Lucy.'

'Lucy?'

'Vanessa's daughter from her first marriage. She's just turned four.' He has the grace to look sheepish.

Marian stumbles backwards, as though someone has punched her in the solar plexus. The glamorous Vanessa, in her mind, had always been the single-minded career woman; the girl about town that Tom will eventually tire of. But no. Vanessa is a mother. He now has his family. Just as she's lost the chance to have hers.

He unlocks the car. 'I'll give you a call about the paperwork, and collecting the desk.'

'No!' Marian spits. 'From now on, anything to do with the house sale needs to come from the solicitor. I don't want to hear from you directly again. Not ever.'

And she picks up a plant pot from the front step and hurls it in her husband's direction with as much force as she can muster.

PART THREE

2019

38

PAULA

Paula opens the door to leave for work, and finds DI Stratton on her doorstep.

'Morning, Mrs Donnelly,' he says cheerfully. He looks dapper in a dark grey overcoat. 'Thought I'd come and update you in person.'

'Come in.' She beckons him through to the hall. 'But please, call me Paula.'

He follows her into the kitchen and she puts the kettle on. He notices the tangle of school bags and sports kit in the corner, the artwork pinned to the fridge door with a random assortment of magnets. 'You've got kids of your own?'

'Two,' Paula tells him. 'Fourteen and twelve. And if they don't get going, they're going to be late for school.'

'And your husband… what does he do?'

'I'm divorced.' She holds up a packet of teabags, and he nods.

'So the man who came to the station with you… Mr Shepherd… he's your partner?'

Paula turns away to fill the teapot, feeling her cheeks go pink. This is ridiculous, she thinks, they're both consenting adults. They're not kids. 'Um. Sort of. Well, not really.' They haven't slept together, after all. 'More of an old family friend.'

He raises his eyebrows fractionally as she hands him the tea, but does not pursue it, instead waiting for her to sit down opposite him at the kitchen table.

'Okay… the first thing. The forensic lab has done testing on the infant's remains. Comparison with your DNA confirms twenty-five per cent of it is shared with you, which is consistent with a match to the child of your sibling. In other words, we are confident this was your nephew.'

Paula hangs her head, feeling tears closing off her throat. So it was true. Johnny's hunch had been right.

'The size and level of decomposition of the bones are consistent with a child no more than a few weeks old being buried somewhere between ten and twenty years ago. Obviously, with decomposition over a long period, it's difficult to be more accurate about how long they… he… had been there.'

Stratton pauses like the experienced professional that he is, to give her time to absorb this news.

Paula sniffs and drags a tissue over her eyes, before lifting her head to face him again. 'So, what about her? The social worker, Marian Glynn. He was buried while she lived at that house and she was Lizzie's caseworker when he was born; that can't be a coincidence. It has to be her doing, surely?'

'Ah, well, that was the next thing I was coming to. Officers from Sussex Police went round to Mrs Glynn's flat in Hove, but she wasn't at the property. Eventually they forced entry, but the place was empty. Her car isn't there, and items like phone and laptop were missing, implying she had left the place voluntarily. We spoke to her neighbours, and no one recalled having seen her lately. That said, she seems to have kept herself to herself anyway. She had no visitors apparently, and was described by the people my officer spoke to as a "loner" and an "oddball".'

'So she's just vanished? What happens now?'

'I've managed to get a detective based at the cop shop down there, one DC Jasmine Khatri, interviewing her colleagues and examining as much local CCTV as she can get her hands on. She's checking for the car, and also any footage from local railway stations. We'll obviously stay in close contact with them in the meantime. But with just one officer allocated to the case… nothing's going to happen very quickly, unless we get a lucky break. Or…'

Paula was one step ahead of him. '*Crimewatch*, that kind of thing.'

'Exactly. We break the story in the news, name her as a person of interest and ask people to come forward. It usually brings results. But…' He turns down the corners of his mouth in an expression of regret. 'It will mean mentioning the baby being found. And any story like that, as I'm sure you're aware, generates a huge amount of press interest.'

Paula pictures her children being pursued as they leave school, seedy reporters hammering at her mother's door. Her mother will be furious, with her and with Lizzie. 'Do you have to involve us? My mum's health isn't the greatest. She's suffered badly with depression. Since my sister died.'

'For the time being, I think we can avoid naming your sister as the birth mother. But probably not forever. Let's see where we get with finding Mrs Glynn first, and what an appeal for her whereabouts throws up. An investigation like this involves pulling on more than one loose thread.'

'Speaking of which…' Paula stands up. 'D'you mind just waiting here a minute.' She runs upstairs to the airing cupboard and comes downstairs again with the pink baby blanket. 'Look,' she says, pointing to the embroidered letter. 'It's exactly like the one the baby boy was wrapped in, except it's an "S" rather than an "N".'

Stratton reaches into his pocket for a pair of latex gloves before taking it from her and examining it. He goes outside to his car to fetch an evidence bag. 'And you got this… where exactly?' he asks, when he comes back into the house.

'Twenty-one Ranmoor Road. Alice Evershott gave it to me. She found it there when she moved in.'

'I'll get forensics back to Ranmoor Road for a full search, but if we don't turn up any evidence there, I'm not sure we'll be able to get far tracing a second baby. At least, not without talking to Marian Glynn.'

'What about her ex-husband?'

Stratton gives a brief smile. 'We're already making arrangements to speak with Mr Glynn.'

As soon as he's left, Paula phones Johnny and repeats as much as she can remember from her conversation with DI Stratton.

'That's where the plod's wrong,' Johnny says, confidently.

'What is?'

'Saying there's no chance of finding the other baby. I reckon we can do it. We've done it once; why shouldn't we do it again?'

'Okay if I leave a bit early?' Paula asks Calum.

'Sure, Jody will buzz people in,' he replies. Jody often covers reception for Paula when she's not there.

It's four thirty, and Johnny has asked her to meet him at Wood Green library before it closes at six o'clock.

'You look nice,' he says with a grin, when he meets her. He looks her up and down, taking in the grey fitted dress and high heels she wore to work.

'So, why are we here?'

'Today, young Paula, we are taking it old school, doing proper research the way it was done before the world wide web.' He takes her hand and almost pulls her into the area for journals and newspapers, an urgency in his step.

He knows something, she thinks.

Johnny sits down in front of a large computer terminal on an ancient wooden desk, polished to a sheen by the elbows of decades of users. 'I went online at home, searching for "Lost baby girl North London July 2003". There were loads of results, all of them unhelpful. So to try and narrow it down, I looked on the website of what would have been Lizzie's local paper: *The Tottenham and Wood Green Independent*.'

'And?' Paula takes off her jacket and scarf and sits down next to him as he switches on the terminal and starts scrolling through blurry black and white images.

'As luck would have it, they only have articles going back to 2005 on their website. But I phoned the paper and they told me that older stuff, including 2003, is still available on microfiche in the library.'

'I'm impressed,' Paula smiles. 'You have been a busy boy.'

'One of the advantages of being your own boss. Okay, confession time.' He turns to face her. 'I came in here earlier today and found this. I've already read the relevant stuff.' From the light in his eyes, the energy his body language is generating, she can tell he's excited. 'Only I wanted to show you this in person rather than just tell you about it later.'

'Oh my God…' Paula stares at him.

He points her back to the screen and finishes scrolling, stopping the cursor on an article dated 19 September 2003.

New appeal for abandoned Saffron's mother

Police have issued a new appeal for the mother of a two-month-old girl who was abandoned at a North London hospital to contact them. Saffron, who was born in July, is in the care of Haringey Social Services after she was found on Tuesday night outside the Whittington maternity unit. A spokesman for the police said, 'The baby is being well cared for, but we want to know that her mother is also safe and well.'

There's a photograph of a baby lying in a wicker Moses basket.

'So I'm thinking,' Johnny says, 'born in North London in July, abandoned several weeks later… this could be her.'

Paula has gone pale. 'It *is* her,' she says in a voice barely above a whisper. 'It has to be.'

'How do you know?'

She points at the picture. 'That basket. With the white eyelet lace and the little satin ribbons round the rim. That's the exact same one I bought for Lizzie! I got it at a Cypriot stall on Archway Market. It was quite distinctive.'

'Good God, Paul.' Johnny puts his arm around her shoulders. 'So this is her. Lizzie's other baby. She's alive.'

They drive back to Palmers Green in Johnny's car. 'You coming in for something to eat?' Paula asks him.

'Kids around?'

She shakes her head. 'Ben's gone out with one of his friends and is going to sleep over. My mother-in-law collected Jess today, and she's having her overnight.'

Johnny grins. 'I was kind of hoping you'd say that.'

Paula takes off her coat and goes straight to the fridge, pulling out a bottle of vodka. 'Don't know about you, but I need a stiff drink.' She puts it on a tray with glasses and tonic water, but instead of carrying it through to the living room, she heads for the stairs.

'Where are you going with that?' Johnny asks, surprised.

She throws a smile over her shoulder, giving a little wiggle of her hips as she walks up the staircase. The high heels she's still wearing add to the seductive effect. 'I thought we might have it in the bedroom.'

He grins, and follows her, tapping her playfully on her backside. 'Thank God for that. I was worried you were never going to ask.'

*

As they're lying in bed afterwards, Paula is silent, her eyes turned to the ceiling.

Johnny touches her arm. 'You okay, Paul?'

'I'm sorry, I can't stop thinking about Lizzie's baby. Wondering where she is now.'

'Well, there's nothing in that article about her being reunited with her mother, obviously. We already know her birth mother was dead, and it's not like Marian Glynn could have claimed her. My guess is she must have been adopted.'

Paula leans back on the pillows, covers her face with her hand. 'So how do we find out what happened to her?'

'I've no idea,' Johnny says, sombrely. 'But we'll give it a go.'

39

MARIAN

Now that it's on the plate, the meal looks uninviting: a single lamb chop, and a couple of boiled potatoes. With some tinned vegetables, because that's all Marian has in the flat. She makes as few trips to the supermarket as she can get away with, as grocery shopping for one is such a hollow experience. No one pays attention to a drab, slightly overweight fifty-seven-year-old woman; till assistants barely even make eye contact. She is invisible.

Marian wonders whether to make gravy, and decides she can't be bothered. She digs out an old, dried-up jar of mustard instead, places it on the tray and carries her lunch to the table in the living room's large picture window. When she bought the flat, she sacrificed space for location, choosing a flat in an elegant mansion block close to Hove's seafront. The magnificent sea views were what clinched it. But today, on a blustery November Saturday, sea and sky are one indistinguishable grey strip.

As she eats the chop, she flicks through the *Brighton Argus* in an attempt to find something to do, something that will fill at least part of her weekend. She doesn't enjoy her job, resents it even. From Monday to Friday it feels as though she does little but clock watch, waiting for the end of the working week to roll around. But on a Saturday, once she has enjoyed a modest lie-in and done some housework, the rest of the weekend stretches ahead like a prison sentence.

Her experience as a social worker qualified her for the job as librarian in the social studies department of the local university. At least, her experience was sufficiently relevant for her to be picked out of what was an unimpressive shortlist of candidates. As librarian, she's treated by her colleagues as separate; not quite a regular member of the department. Most of them are at least ten years younger than her anyway. Sometimes she overhears them talking about social events they're planning: bar crawls and pub quizzes. If she's within earshot they'll make a token attempt at including her ('Not sure it's your thing, Marian, but of course you're welcome to come along'). But she never goes. She knows they don't want to be seen out and about with a dowdy, grey-haired matron. The label 'spinster' probably applies in their minds, though strictly speaking she's a divorcee. There are a few people in the department who are around her age, but they all have families, grown-up children and even grandchildren. Which she does not. Without that shared ground, she has no value in their eyes.

When she first arrived in Hove, with the vestiges of optimism still intact, Marian signed up for an online dating site. Meeting online didn't have the common currency it enjoys now, sixteen years later, but it was starting to take off. Even though she was a lot younger then, the pickings were still slim. There was nobody Marian could remotely have fallen for, but a romantic connection was not her agenda. Her agenda was to try and become pregnant while she still could. Because, as Tom had been at pains to point out, it was his infertility that had left them childless, not hers. She still had two or three years in which she could conceive.

After six months of unspeakably awkward dates, Marian met Clive. He worked in administration at a local insurance company, a dull, timid man in his late thirties who still lived with his mother. At Marian's instigation they engaged in coitus a few times, back at her flat after what Clive liked to call 'a meal out'. He was so inept in bed that she suspected he might even have been a virgin. After the last of these unsatisfactory couplings, her period was late. Convinced she was pregnant, Marian made the mistake of telling an appalled Clive. They never used contraception, but it seemed it had never occurred to him that at nearly forty-three, she could still conceive.

Her period eventually arrived a week later, and her GP informed her in a dismissive fashion that this irregularity was probably the onset of perimenopause. Clive melted away into the ether, refusing to take her calls or answer her texts. Marian kept her profile on the matchmaking site for a further year and a half, but subsequent encounters never led to her kissing any of her dates, let alone sleeping with them. Eventually, as her forty-fifth birthday loomed, she accepted that pregnancy was no longer a possibility and deleted her online profile. Her waistline thickened further, her hair grew greyer and she remained alone.

The Events page in the *Argus* has a feature on a folk art exhibition at the Wagner Hall. Marian is not much interested in folk art, but decides she may as well go. It will give her a reason to leave the flat, if nothing else. After she has cleared up her lunch things, she puts on her shapeless blue anorak and sets off into the town centre.

'Oh my goodness, it is you! It is!'

The woman that she sensed was following her around the exhibition plants herself in Marian's path. The broad smiling face and braided grey hair do register in her memory, but it takes a split second for her mind to catch up.

'Angela! Angela Dixon!'

'Yes.' Marian smiles back, trying to hide her discomfort. 'Of course. It's been a while; I wasn't sure…'

'Gosh, yes, *ages*. I remember hearing you'd moved down here. I would have got in touch when I decided to come to this exhibition, but obviously I didn't have your address. How *are* you?'

'Well, you know… fine.'

'And are you enjoying this?' Angela waves expansively at an arrangement of carved wooden figurines. 'Wonderful, isn't it? I've always had a passion for folk art.'

'It's certainly… interesting.'

'Shall we head to the café and have a catch-up?'

'Yes, all right then,' agrees Marian, who has had enough of childlike pictures of farm animals and disembodied carousel horses. 'A cup of tea would be great.'

'So,' Angela says comfortably, once they're seated at a window table with a pot of tea between them. 'Tell me all about life in Brighton.'

'I live in Hove.' Marian's response is automatic.

'How are you finding being away from London? Do you miss it? I must say I can't imagine leaving the place, much as I moan about it. We all do.'

'Are you still at Haringey Social Services?' Marian asks, trying to remember how old Angela is.

'Retired last year. Just as well, really; the place was even more chaotic than when you were there. You probably got out at the right time. Still working?'

Marian tells her about her job at the university.

'Great.' Angela slurps her tea noisily. 'New job, new start. Best thing after a divorce. I gather Tom has a new family now?'

'I wouldn't know.' She stiffens. 'Once I'd moved out of the old house, I only ever heard from him through his solicitors. No more direct contact. Which was my decision.'

Angela lowers her cup slowly. 'Oh, so you wouldn't know about the adoption?'

Marian's heart rate speeds up, and she balls her paper napkin in her fist. 'Like I said, we've had no contact.'

'Oh my goodness… it was rather incredible, really. Do you remember that newborn baby that was left at the Whittington? It was in all the news, around the time you moved. A little girl. Well, we found a foster placement for her, and Tom and his new partner adopted her when she was about six months old…' She pauses. 'Marian, are you okay?'

'Yes,' she says faintly, as the blood drains from her face and her extremities begin to tingle. 'I just had no idea… they'd adopted.'

'They were lucky to get a baby as soon as they were approved. She already had a little girl, which probably helped: they were a ready-made family unit. Well, you don't need me to tell you all this; you worked in the department long enough. Lovely little thing the baby was, really gorgeous. And a few years later they adopted again: a little boy.'

Marian pushes her chair back and stumbles to her feet. 'Sorry, Angela, I've got a headache coming on. I've got to go.'

When she emerges from the building into Regency Road it's growing dark. She turns right and heads for the seafront, barely noticing the chilly, horizontal drizzle blowing off the sea. With her hood obscuring her vision, she staggers like a drunk along Kingsway. Other walkers have to swerve to avoid her, but she is barely aware of her surroundings. One thought alone is repeating and repeating in her brain.

He has Saffron. Tom has taken Saffron.

40

PAULA

'We've got to tell them. Surely we don't have a choice now?'

Paula and Johnny are sitting in her kitchen, surrounded by greasy cardboard boxes, finishing the dregs of a bottle of red wine. It's Monday, and since she's been at work all day, Johnny offered to treat her and the children to a pizza delivery. The children, replete with stuffed crust and fizzy drinks, are comatose on the sofa watching Netflix. They seem to like Johnny, for his easy-going manner as much as his generosity with takeaways.

They haven't told anyone about the newspaper article that Paula is convinced identifies her sister's baby girl. She believes that now she's raised the possibility of the dead baby being one of twins, she's duty bound to share their discovery with the police.

'If she was adopted, which we're pretty sure has to be the case, then the police can easily access adoption records to find out. They'll soon know if it checks out.'

'That's true.' Johnny picks at a stray piece of pepperoni. 'The thing is, though, Paul, they're not going to share that information with us, are they? Even if they wanted to, they can't. Adoption records from back then are almost always sealed. So it doesn't help you, does it? You still won't know where Lizzie's kid is. You could only hope that when she's eighteen and can access the information herself, she comes looking for her mother's family.'

Paula shrugs. 'Looks like that will have to be good enough, then. At least it's not that long to wait now.'

'Assuming she does go looking. There's no guarantee of that.'

'So what, then?' Paula looks at Johnny, raising an eyebrow. She knows him well enough by now to know when he's plotting something. There's a certain tilt of the head, a gleam in his eye.

'I've got this mate, okay, from when I worked in the Specials. Used to be a cop, now works private security.'

'Oh, yeah?' Both Paula's eyebrows go up now. 'Why's that?'

'He got in a spot of bother. Bit of a misconduct issue.' Johnny grins, his expression sheepish. 'I know what you're thinking, but Tony's a good guy, honestly. And he just happens to know people. People who can access various official databases. Such as adoption records.'

Paula sips her wine, shaking her head. 'I think we should go straight to the police. I'd feel wrong if we didn't tell them.'

'How about we tell them after we've found out where your niece is? That way they can do their thing with their investigation, but it won't matter that they can't disclose adoption information because we'll already know.'

'I'm not sure, Johnny. I'm really not.'

The following evening, Paula finds herself on the pavement outside a pub in Islington.

'At least come in and meet him,' Johnny urges. 'It doesn't commit us to anything.'

'I still think it would be better to involve the law first, Johnny.'

'Why, though?'

'Because…' She shrugs. 'I'm scared, I suppose.'

'What of?'

'I don't know, I just am.' Because she's wanted to find out where Lizzie's daughter is for so long that she's terrified of disappointment.

Of reaching a dead end. Of this shadowy person becoming real at last. But she can't explain this to Johnny. 'I suppose it won't do any harm just to talk.'

'That's my girl.'

Johnny leads Paula inside and introduces her to his friend, Big Tony Barlow.

Big Tony is – unsurprisingly – huge, with a missing front tooth and a neck as thick as his bald head. He drinks his way rhythmically through a pint of stout, his face expressionless, while the problem is explained to him.

'So could you do it, Tone?' Johnny asks. 'If we wanted you to?'

'Not personally, no. That kind of job needs a specialist. Adoption files and that. Especially if you don't have exact names and dates.'

'But you know someone, yeah?'

Big Tony wipes a huge paw across his mouth, then belches. 'Sure. I know someone.'

Johnny looks over at Paula. 'So… are we doing this?'

She hesitates a few seconds. 'Go on, then. I suppose we have to at least try and find out.'

He reaches into the pocket of his velvet-collared covert coat and brings out a wad of notes, which he slides across the table. 'There's a ton there, and there'll be more if your contact can come up with the goods.'

'You have to pay him?' Paula demands, looping her arm through his as they walk back up Upper Street to where Johnny has parked his car.

'Sure,' says Johnny, easily. 'Think of it as a professional service, like a lawyer or an accountant. You pay them for their expertise, don't you? This is the same thing.'

'Hmm.' Paula remains dubious. 'It still feels dodgy to me. Still think we should have gone straight to DI Stratton.'

When Johnny appears at Paula's house forty-eight hours later, brandishing a manila envelope, despite her misgivings she can't avoid a frisson of excitement.

'You ready for this?' Then he lowers his voice. 'Kids around?'

'They're with Dave… have you already looked?'

Johnny shakes his head, following her into the living room. 'I wanted you to be the first to know; it's only fair.'

Paula sits on the edge of the sofa and turns the envelope over and over between shaking fingers. She's strangely nervous about opening it.

'You do it,' she says eventually, handing it to Johnny and walking over to the drinks cupboard to pour herself a brandy.

He takes out two pieces of paper, running his eye briefly over the first one before handing it to Paula. It's a confidential memo from an independent reviewing officer appointed by Haringey Council. The officer in question endorses an adoption order in the case of a female infant known only as 'Saffron', abandoned at Whittington Hospital on 16 September 2003 and believed to have been born on 18 July 2003.

The second document is salmon pink, a certified copy of an entry in the Adoptions Register, dated 22 February 2004. Paula's eyes widen as she reads the entry out loud.

'"Name and surname of child: Charlotte Saffron Glynn. Sex of child: Female. Name and surname: Thomas Michael Glynn, Vanessa Jane Glynn. Address: 35 Laurel Road, London N19. Occupation of parent(s): Architectural consultant, chartered architect."'

Johnny reaches for the certificate and stares at it. 'Hold on a minute… Glynn. That's the surname of the social worker who took the babies. The one from Ranmoor Road. Marian.'

Paula nods. 'And I'm sure Alice Evershott said her husband was called Tom.'

Alison James

Johnny presses his fingers against his temples. 'Can't be a coincidence, surely? One baby ends up dead in his garden, and he and his new missus adopt the other one? He had to have been in on the abduction.'

Paula sips her brandy, her expression dazed. 'No, I doubt that. If it was a bitter divorce, then why would she want him and the new wife to have one of the twins? And anyway, these records are legit. Adoptive parents don't have any control over which baby they're given. It's all decided by a panel made up of third parties.'

'Perhaps he coerced her somehow into handing over the female twin. Blackmailed her. Remember she worked for social services herself, an insider. Maybe she rigged the system somehow.'

Paula shrugs.

'However it happened, the evidence is here in black and white. The child that was stolen from your sister by Mrs Glynn has ended up a Glynn herself. I can hardly get my head around it.'

'I know one thing,' Paula says, grimly. 'We have to tell the police now.'

41

MARIAN

It isn't too difficult to track down her ex-husband.

Tom moved on from Cavendish Partners seven years ago. Marian knows this, because she googled his name and found a whole page on him at a firm called AQA Architecture.

Tom Glynn came to AQA from Cavendish Partners in 2012. A native of North London, Tom leads the Commercial Environments team…

North London. As she suspected, he hadn't moved far. She reads the rest of the profile. *Tom is married with three children.*

Three? That seems almost greedy. No matter. She will find him. And she will find Saffron.

The bag of clothes at the back of the wardrobe hasn't been touched in years. Marian deposited it there when she moved into the flat; things she knew she would no longer wear but couldn't quite bring herself to throw away or give to charity. It contains the satin brocade coat dress she bought for a wedding about twenty years ago. She still thinks the duck-egg blue embroidered with gold and silver is beautiful. There's also a black wool crêpe party dress she bought from Jil Sander: a splurge buy that she quickly grew too heavy to fit into, and a pretty Jaeger chiffon blouse, also far too small now. And the wig.

When Tom first started work at Cavendish they used to throw extravagant parties, and to celebrate the new millennium, the theme was Hollywood Royalty. Marian decided she would go as Marilyn Monroe, and ordered a shoulder-length blonde wig from an online party shop, only to find when it arrived that the colour was different to that depicted on the website. Instead of platinum blonde, it was a darker, strawberry-blonde colour.

'Actually, Marilyn's real hair colour was something like this,' Marian told Tom. 'And if I wear it with the iconic white halterneck dress…'

But he had been dismissive, shaking his head. 'Nope. No one will know who you're supposed to be. No offence, but you don't look anything like Marilyn. Except for the hips.' He slapped her playfully on the backside.

In the end Marian admitted defeat and went to the party as Charlie Chaplin, in a baggy man's suit, bowler and fake moustache. But she kept the wig. It was made of real hair and had been expensive, and she was reluctant to throw it away. You never knew, she had reasoned then, it might prove useful one day.

The wig smells a little musty, but is otherwise in perfect condition. Marian brushes it carefully and lays it out on the bed, while she packs a bag with toiletries, underwear and a few changes of clothes. Then she sits at her dressing table and for the first time in ages, puts on a full face of make-up, including bright red lipstick. When her frizzy grey hair is pinned to her head and the wig settled into position, the effect is dramatic. True, her plus-size body remains unchanged, but otherwise she is transformed. The strawberry blonde hair falls to her shoulders in attractive waves and flatters her skin tone. It detracts from the frown lines and drooping eyelids. She looks at least a decade younger.

She squeezes herself into what is euphemistically called 'shape-wear' (her mother would have referred to it as a girdle) and dresses in a plain white blouse and her favourite navy trouser suit. It's the only decent outfit she possesses that still fits her. For her work at the university library she usually wears a skirt with an elasticated waist under an equally shapeless top. For a brief moment she considers adding a jaunty beret to the outfit, but decides it will attract too much attention. She wants to blend in, not stand out.

Taking the car is out of the question. It doesn't matter how you alter your appearance, if you are in your own vehicle it's easy for your movements to be traced. Nevertheless, she wants the obvious assumption to be that she has taken a trip in it, so after putting on her best winter coat she drives her car from her allotted parking space and leaves it, unlocked, at the end of a cul-de-sac a few hundred yards away. Then she walks the mile to the station, wheeling her case. The only stop she makes is to use the cash machine in the local convenience store, withdrawing a large amount of cash and making just one purchase.

Abshir, who mans the till from dawn to dusk seven days a week, does a double-take. 'It's you, innit?' He points to the wig. 'Hair's different, though.'

Marian often calls in there for bread, milk or teabags, usually picking up a bar of milk chocolate at the same time. The fact that he's recognised her leaves her slightly flustered.

'You sure that's all you want, love?' he asks. 'No chocolate this time, not like usual?' He adds with a grin.

'This is it, thank you,' Marian replies, forcing a smile.

It's Tuesday morning, and she blends easily into the crowds of commuters catching the train from Hove to London. She buys a coffee from the concession on the platform and, once on the train, sips it while she opens up her laptop on the small table. Nobody speaks to her, or appears to notice her, leaving her to use the journey time to find temporary accommodation. After a few false starts, she finds a small bed and breakfast hotel in Russell Square whose website claims it will take cash.

She takes the tube there from Victoria, after first phoning to check that the place has rooms available. Reserving a room via their website had to be avoided because it would have meant inputting too much personal data.

'Name?' asks a bored receptionist, without looking up at her.

'Webber,' says Marian giving her maiden name. 'Anne Webber.'

She is handed a form to fill in, and writes down a fictitious address.

'ID?'

'I'm afraid I don't have my driving licence or passport with me,' she says, adding quickly, 'but I'm happy to pay with cash up front.' To prove the point, she pulls out her purse and extracts a fold of pristine £20 notes.

'We're supposed to get the manager's approval if there's no ID.' The receptionist looks up at her for the first time. What she sees is a respectable-looking middle-aged woman in smart clothes, and she clearly can't be bothered to hunt down the manager. 'Do you have enough for the four nights' room rate?'

'I do,' says Marian with a smile. 'And I'm happy to add a damage deposit for peace of mind.'

A key is handed over and she's left to drag her case up to the room on the first floor. It's stuffy and claustrophobic, with crimson walls and fussy furnishings, but Marian doesn't care. She hangs her clothes in the tiny wardrobe, arranges her wash things in the bathroom and then sits down on the bed with her laptop. All she needs now is to input the wi-fi password.

And then she can set about finding her daughter.

42

CHARLIE

Bonnie whimpers in her sleep, her arms twitching and her little fingers fanning out like starfish.

Charlie watches her for a while, then gets back to the business of trying to pack up and clean the flat. She bundles anything belonging to Jake into black plastic bin bags, and starts emptying the bathroom cupboards of toiletries and make-up. She's just starting to make headway when the doorbell rings.

The woman who's standing there is middle-aged and heavyset. She's wearing a coat in a strikingly ugly yellow colour.

'Are you Charlotte?'

Charlie frowns. 'Yes.'

'My name's Angela Dixon. I'm from Haringey Council.'

'Oh. I think there might be a misunderstanding. This isn't council property any more. It's rented privately.'

'Actually, it's not about the flat. Well, not directly.'

Charlie tilts her head in the direction of the stack of cardboard boxes. 'Can't this wait? I'm a bit busy.'

'The thing is, we routinely follow up on all children under eighteen living apart from their parents. To assess—'

'No offence, but I'm about to move back in with my parents anyway, so…' Charlie shrugs.

'May I ask when?'

'This weekend. Sunday probably.'

Charlie just wants the woman to leave but, not wanting to appear rude, she opens the door wider and waves her hand in the direction of empty cardboard boxes.

'I'm supposed to be packing, only my sister called round to see the baby and distracted me.'

'The baby?'

Behind her, Bonnie gives a restless little squawk, an early indication that she's about to need feeding. The woman jumps slightly and stares in the direction of the bassinet, taking a step forwards as if to get a better look. Charlie experiences a flash of annoyance. Clearly, she feels Charlie is too young to have a baby. Probably thinks she can't look after her properly.

'If you don't mind, I really need to get on before she wakes for a feed.'

'Of course… I'll call back another time.'

Charlie stops herself from rolling her eyes. Don't social services have anything better to do than interfere in the lives of two people who don't need their help?

'No offence, but there's really no need. I won't be here from the day after tomorrow.'

Her mouth opens as though she is about to say something, but then she closes it again, gives a curt nod, and leaves.

Charlie lifts Bonnie from the crib and sits down on the sofa to feed her. 'It's okay,' she soothes, 'the funny lady's gone now.'

Bonnie fails to settle, launching into an uncharacteristic crying jag and refusing to be comforted unless she's being held.

Charlie phones her mother. 'Mum, I can't get Bonnie to go off… if I bring her over would you or Lu mind having her for a bit? Just so I can get this packing done. I'm never going to get finished by Sunday, otherwise.'

As she pushes the buggy over to Laurel Road, she mulls over the visit from the woman in the yellow coat. Why, she wonders, would social services be making such a check on her now, months after she left home? She has been seen by midwives and a health visitor, all of whom have been employed to check on her welfare, and that of her baby. There has never been any official concern expressed about her living arrangements, and why would there be? She has a perfectly nice flat, and the support of her family.

As she approaches the front door, there is someone leaving the house: a man with ginger hair that she doesn't recognise.

'Who's that?' she asks her mother, who is standing in the hall watching the man go.

'Just someone who wanted to talk to Dad, but obviously he's in the office at the moment.' Vanessa puts an arm around her briefly before reaching down to lift her granddaughter out of the buggy. 'How's my chubby little munchkin?'

Charlie is about to tell her that she has also had a stranger call round that morning, but since she will no longer be living in the flat on her own, the whole issue seems redundant. And she doesn't want to worry her parents any more than she already has. Best not to mention it.

43

MARIAN

Yellow, Marian decides, as she sits on her hotel bed sipping her tea.

She doesn't care for the colour, not on herself, anyway. She never wears it because it washes her out and makes her look sallow. But Tom knows she hates yellow and would never expect her to be wearing it, however deep that idea is buried in his subconscious. Therefore, she will wear yellow.

Breakfast is included in the room rate, so Marian sits alone in the dark, depressing dining room on the ground floor, ordering coffee and boiled eggs with toast. When it eventually arrives, the coffee is acrid and the eggs have been boiled so long that the yolks are rimmed with grey. She eats them anyway, disguising their texture by slathering the toast thickly in butter, and sips slowly on her coffee. She can afford to take her time today. She takes the copy of the *Metro* offered by the waitress and flicks through it. And then the blood in her veins turns to ice, and she drops the coffee cup into the saucer so abruptly that it slops everywhere.

North London police find body in garden

The remains of a newborn baby boy have been found in a garden in Ranmoor Road, Muswell Hill. The child is believed to have been buried there between fifteen and twenty years

*ago. Detective Inspector Kevin Stratton, leading the enquiry,
said: 'We are urging people who lived in the area at the time
to come forward if they have any information.'*

Noah. Her mouth forms the word silently. She never said it out
loud to anyone, she realises, apart from Noah himself. Nobody
knows his name but her. This thought calms her and her breathing
returns to normal. Her name isn't mentioned in the piece, so it
could even be a different house in the road. She's done nothing
wrong anyway, she reasons. Noah was given a lovely burial when
he died, and he died because he was ill. The fact that he was sickly
was the fault of Lizzie Armitage. She was the one downing alcohol
while pregnant.

The timing of the news item is unsettling, but she's not going
to let it put her off. After all, nobody knows where she is. She folds
the paper over again, collects her coat and bag from her room and
heads on foot to the Brunswick shopping centre. Blending in with
the other shoppers is easy. Christmas decorations have just been
put up, people are busy and purposeful, despite the bitter cold.
Nobody gives her a second glance.

Marian goes into Next and buys an overcoat in mustard yellow
wool, and a dark grey bobble hat. She puts on the hat as she leaves
the store, pulling it on awkwardly over the blonde wig. The wig
is starting to itch now, but she is resigned to wearing it, especially
after seeing that article in the paper. As long as she's in the wig,
there's little chance of being recognised. She heads back to the
hotel to prepare for the next stage of her plan.

At four o'clock, Marian puts on the hat, a scarf and her new mustard-
coloured coat and takes the Northern Line to Camden Town.

The offices of AQA are in a modern, glass-fronted block on
Parkway. It's dark by the time she gets there; car headlights are

bouncing off the damp street, and the sky is streaked grey and gold. Marian positions herself in the entranceway of the building, close enough to see who's emerging from the brightly lit foyer. Employees come out in twos or threes, often chatting to one another, hugging their arms around themselves for warmth. Quite a few light up immediately and take a few meditative puffs of their cigarette before strolling on, laptop bags slung over their shoulders.

At 6.15, Tom emerges. She knows it's him immediately. At fifty-five, he has lost some of his hair, and what's left is greying, but he still has a buoyant, vital energy. Still walks with the same purposeful stride. So much so, that Marian struggles to keep up with him at her safe distance of a few metres. She has the hat pulled down low, a scarf pulled up over her mouth, and with the yellow coat and waves of strawberry blonde hair escaping onto her shoulders, she's confident that even if he turns round, he'll have no idea who she is.

At Prince Albert Road, he boards the 88 bus. Marian waits for him to start up the stairs before boarding herself and staying on the lower deck, hanging on to one of the metal poles near the exit door. Just as the bus is reaching its destination at Parliament Hill Fields – by now almost empty – Tom thunders down the stairs and grabs the same pole she is gripping. Shaking at the unexpected physical proximity of her ex-husband, Marian swivels around abruptly so that her back is turned to him.

He leaps off the bus and she gets off after him, keeping him in her sightline while staying as far back as she can. These streets are nearly empty, and if he looks behind him, it will be obvious she is following him. He heads into Dartmouth Park, turning into Laurel Road. Of course. Marian remembers him telling her that he loved this particular tree-lined street, especially the pretty Victorian villas towards its eastern end. It's outside one of these that he slows down and pulls out a bunch of keys, before walking up to the pale blue front door and letting himself in. The blinds in the house are lowered, and lights behind them glow invitingly. There are raised voices, and the garlicky smell of something cooking hangs in the air. It's a family home, Marian thinks bitterly. Just what she – what *they* – always wanted.

Marian makes a mental note of the door number: thirty-five. But there is little point her waiting around on this occasion. They'll be making supper and settling in for the evening, discussing Tom's work, or maybe *her* work. She was an architect too, wasn't she, Vanessa? Instead, Marian walks back to Highgate Road and flags a cab back to the hotel.

At six the next morning an alarm wakes her. Dressing exactly as she did the day before, she catches the tube to Tufnell Park and walks back to Laurel Road. The sun is just rising as she arrives, commuters emerging from their homes into the chilly air. Number twenty-nine has a huge privet bush growing over its wall, providing something of a screen, and Marian places herself behind it and waits, sipping from the takeaway coffee cup she bought on the way from the tube. A cup of coffee makes her seem more normal, she calculates. Wrongdoers don't go round drinking coffee.

At seven forty, Tom emerges and walks briskly in the other direction, towards Highgate Road. Fifteen minutes later a woman appears, with a boy of about twelve dressed in school uniform. Marian recognises Vanessa, who has gained a little mid-life weight but kept her mane of blonde hair. She and the boy climb into a car, with her saying something about rugby training, and drive off.

Saffron is school age too, Marian thinks. So she will be emerging some time in the next hour or so and heading off to the local comprehensive or academy. On her own. But nine o'clock comes and goes, and there is no sign of her. A few people glance in Marian's direction, but she sips on the empty coffee cup and pretends to be looking at the screen of her phone, as though she's waiting for someone. Which, in a way, she is.

By nine thirty she's starting to need the loo quite badly. Just as she's weighing up whether to return later in the day, the door of number thirty-five opens and a young woman emerges, tall and slim with long blonde hair. Marian's heart pounds. Is this her? Is this her own Saffron?

In her agitation, Marian starts following too close. So close that she can hear when the girl pulls out her phone and starts having a conversation.

'Hi… it's Lucy.'

She feels a jolt of disappointment. Lucy, she now remembers, is Vanessa's daughter from her first marriage. She must be about twenty.

'Yes,' the girl is saying, 'I'm just on my way to see Charlie.'

Charlie is probably a boyfriend, Marian reasons. She's decided she has no choice but to head back to the tube station. Lucy also appears to be catching the tube, so they continue walking the same way.

But at the intersection by the station, Lucy keeps going along Tufnell Park Road. Instinctively Marian continues to follow as she turns left and comes to a stop at a large council block; the sort that is now largely privately owned and has been smartened up a little. Lucy goes into the lobby and calls the lift. Pressing one of the top buttons, Marian notes.

Her need to empty her bladder is now extremely urgent. Reasoning that there is probably a toilet for the cleaning staff or caretaker, she goes into the building and through the door at the back of the lobby. To the right is the access to the emergency stairs, and next to that a locked door with a sign saying: 'Private – staff only'. At the very end of the corridor is the fire door to the outside, and just before that, to the left, is an unmarked door. To Marian's relief it contains a sluice with buckets, broom and mop, and a toilet.

On her way out of the building, something catches her eye as she passes the row of mailboxes. The postman has inserted mail haphazardly, and where the tenant hasn't bothered to empty their box, letters and flyers are spilling out. Protruding from the box for flat 504 is a white, typed envelope. The name startles Marian so much that her heart jumps in her chest.

Miss C. S. Glynn

Marian rips open the envelope. It's a promotional offer from a mobile phone provider.

Dear Charlotte…

Charlotte. Charlie. That must be the Charlie Lucy was referring to. Her younger sister. And if Tom is a father to three, and the youngest is a boy, then Charlotte can only be the baby he and Vanessa adopted when Lucy was a few years old.

The baby once known as Saffron.

But why on earth is she living here, away from her family, if she only turned seventeen a few months ago? It makes no sense. Marian flicks through the rest of the bunch of mail and finds what looks like a bill, addressed to a Mr Jake Palmer. Is that why she's left home, to live with a boyfriend? She makes an involuntary scoffing noise in her throat. How typical of Tom and his laissez-faire attitude. She, Marian, would never have allowed Saffron to do that. Never.

The lift shaft clanks, and Marian darts back into the rear passage just before it arrives on the ground floor. When she emerges, she sees Lucy Glynn – or is she still Lucy Rowley? – leaving the building. She takes a few steps out of the passage, and presses the button marked 5.

'Hello?'

The voice, heard before the door is fully opened, sounds annoyed.

The girl who eventually stands in front of her is of medium height, with light brown wavy hair worn very long, as teenagers do these days. The hair is similar to Lizzie Armitage's, but Marian can see no further resemblance. The dark eyes and the olive skin must come from her birth father, who Marian remembers was of mixed heritage. She's wearing far too much make-up, but she's very pretty.

She's Saffron.

Marian rehearsed what she was going to say while in the lift, but the reality of seeing her child in the flesh leaves her mouth dry. 'Um…'

'Can I help you?' The enquiry is polite but impatient.

'My name's Angela Dixon. I'm from Haringey Council.'

Saffron doesn't ask for her ID, which an adult would probably do. But she frowns. 'I'm a bit busy.'

'The thing is, we routinely follow up on all children under eighteen living apart from their parents. To assess—'

'No offence, but I'm about to move back in with my parents anyway, so…' She gives a pretty shrug.

'May I ask when?'

'This weekend. Sunday probably.'

Saffron steps back and opens the door wider, waving her hand in the direction of empty cardboard boxes. 'I'm supposed to be packing, only my sister called round to see the baby and distracted me.'

The blood rushes from Marian's face, and her fingers turn numb. 'The baby?'

Only then does she notice the array of pink-themed cards on the windowsill: 'Welcome to your baby girl', 'Congratulations, it's a girl!' At the centre of the open-plan living area is a little crib on a stand. A white-wrapped bundle. And Saffron's own fluffy yellow duckling. The bundle emits a little sound. She flinches visibly.

Saffron. The memories flood her brain, making her almost giddy.

Baby Saffron. There she is, and she's well, thriving.

She tries to step closer, but the girl blocks her path. 'If you don't mind, I really need to get on before she wakes for a feed.'

'Of course... I'll call back another time.'

'No offence, but there's really no need. I won't be here from the day after tomorrow.'

Marian gives what she hopes is a reassuringly official nod, and turns to go, but only after she has craned her neck and caught the most tantalising glimpse of the infant's sleeping face.

44

CHARLIE

At nine on Sunday morning, her father arrives in the family estate, which he manages to park directly in front of the building.

Charlie has been up several times in the night to feed and settle Bonnie, and is feeling lacklustre and heavy-footed.

'Can't we just have a coffee before we start?' she wheedles. 'I've been awake since five.' The baby is in her arms, twisting her head restlessly in the quest for milk.

'Sure,' Tom says, ruffling her hair. 'You get madam here fed and off to sleep and I'll shoot to the coffee shop on Tufnell Park Road and get us caffeine. Caramel latte? That still your favourite?'

By the time he returns with two takeaway cups, Bonnie is sleeping peacefully in her crib, and Charlie is in rubber gloves, wiping down the kitchen countertops.

'We'll put Bonnie in the car last, save disturbing her,' Tom says, as they both drink their coffee. 'It shouldn't take us too long to load up the rest of your stuff.' He surveys the massed bags and boxes. 'I'm not sure we're going to get all of this in the boot in one go, but we can always come back for the rest another time. Just make sure we have everything you need for the next day or so.'

They start the laborious process of taking the boxes down to the ground floor. The lift is tiny, so they have to travel separately and with one box at a time. Once most of Charlie's belongings are in the lobby of the building, her father starts packing them into the boot of the car while she returns to the top floor to bring more bags and boxes.

'Baby still asleep?' he asks over his shoulder when Charlie comes through the entrance door with her laptop bag and make-up case.

'Out like a light, thank God.'

'She'd sleep through a marching band, that one – like your brother. You're lucky.'

Charlie is about to head back to the lift when she sees a familiar figure. The hat throws her at first: a baseball cap pulled low. But the hovering figures behind him are the giveaway. His henchmen, Mikey Tomas and Scott King.

She's too numb with shock to speak, but her father has no such inhibition.

'What the hell are you doing here?' he asks Jake.

Jake shrugs. 'My name's on the lease, I've got every right to be here.'

'Not after you stole my daughter's money, you don't.' Her father steps forward aggressively.

'Dad, don't,' Charlie pleads. She can't bring herself to look directly at her former boyfriend. The father of her child. A complex array of emotions fights for space in her brain. She's longed for him to return, but now he has, is she pleased to see him or not? She doesn't know. The surge of adrenalin makes her stomach do somersaults.

'I didn't steal nothing,' Jake says. 'That money was legit mine, yeah?' He glances around, looks into the back seat of the Subaru. 'Where's the kid?' he asks accusingly.

Neither Charlie nor her father answer.

'Where is she?' Jake snarls. 'Where's my little girl?'

'Oh, so she's *your* little girl all of a sudden,' Tom sneers.

'He's got the right to see his own kid,' Scott grunts.

'Piss off!' Her father advances threateningly. 'This is a family matter, nothing to do with you.'

Jake makes a gesture with his head and Mikey and Scott obediently slope off. 'Come back to the flat in a bit, yeah?' Jake says, looking at Charlie as he speaks. *I'm still in control*, the look says.

Seeing his daughter's look of confusion and doubt, Tom snaps. He lunges at Jake, grabbing the collar of his T-shirt and twisting it, lifting Jake off his feet. Jake fights back, bringing his fists up and jabbing at the older man's face. He's fended off and within seconds they are in a full-on brawl, with Jake being knocked off his feet and Tom on top of him, pummelling him.

'Dad! Stop!' Charlie shrieks at the top of her voice. She grabs at the back of her father's jacket and attempts to pull him off. Passers-by in the street are slowing down to stare, one of them pulling out a mobile phone as though to call the police.

Thinking better of assaulting a teenager, Tom stands up, smoothing down his shirt and wiping sweat from his forehead with the back of his hand. Jake rolls around on the ground melodramatically, clutching his jaw.

'That's assault, mate,' he groans. He spits on the pavement and it's streaked pink with blood. 'I ought to get the filth on you.'

Tom hauls him to his feet. 'What you need to do – *mate* – is clear off sharpish and stay well away from my daughter.'

'I live here,' Jake whines.

Tom indicates the boxes he's cramming into the boot. 'Well, as you can see, from today, Charlotte doesn't. What you do after she's left is up to you, given the flat's paid for until next spring. But for now, until she's gone, please do us a favour and stay away.'

Jakes spits again, but he picks up the baseball cap from the pavement and slopes off. Charlie and her father watch until he's disappeared from sight.

'Right.' He sighs heavily. 'You'd better go back up and fetch Bonnie, then we'll get going. Make sure you don't leave anything that you don't want *him*' – he jerks his head in the direction Jake went – 'getting his hands on.'

Charlie takes the lift up to the fifth floor, her legs still shaking as she walks back into her flat. She'd left the heavy front door of the flat propped open with a box of books, because the spring closure is impossible to negotiate while carrying an armful of belongings. She reaches for the changing bag that she left hung over the back of a dining chair. It's not there. Her father has probably taken it down without her noticing, and stowed it in the car. She goes into the bedroom.

The crib is there, exactly as she left it, but the baby and her stuffed yellow duckling are gone.

She looks around wildly, as though she might mistakenly have put her daughter somewhere else: the bed, the floor, the changing table. She runs back into the living room, murmuring 'No, no, no, no, no…'

Bonnie's not there.

Her heart is hammering with panic, but she places her hands on her knees and takes slow breaths to try and calm her racing mind. *Think. Think clearly.*

Her father must have moved her, is the thought that comes. That's the only logical explanation. He probably put her into her buggy and wheeled it out of the way of all the toing and froing. That must be it. She darts out to the lift, jabbing at the buttons, hyperventilating at the slowness with which it ascends to the fifth floor.

Outside, her father is yet again leaning into the open hatchback, moving boxes and bags to pack them more efficiently.

'Dad, where've you put Bonnie?'

He twists round, alarmed. 'What d'you mean? She was upstairs with you.'

'You haven't moved her?'

He shakes his head, taking a step towards her as her face crumples. 'Lottie—'

A scream pierces the cold air. It takes a couple of seconds for Charlie to grasp that it's coming from her.

Her father looks genuinely frightened now. 'What the hell's happened?'

He's already running back into the building, Charlie stumbling behind him. Her voice comes out as a gasp.

'She's gone! Somebody must have taken her while I was down here!'

Tom ignores the lift and races up the back stairs, taking them two at the time.

'The door was open?' he demands, when they reach the flat.

'I propped it, just while I went down. I thought I'd only be gone thirty seconds, then I'd be straight back up, but then Jake came…'

'He's got something to do with this,' Tom snarls. He's checked the bedroom and the bathroom, fruitlessly. There's no baby. 'He picked a fight with me as a diversion tactic, while those gormless friends of his went round to the back of the block, went in and took Bonnie. That has to be it.'

'You picked the fight, Dad, not him.' Charlie's face is ghostly white, streaked with tears and dust.

But he already has his phone out and is dialling 999. 'Police, please, quickly… my baby granddaughter's been abducted.' He gives the address and hangs up. 'They're on their way.'

Charlie shakes her head mutely, tears coursing down her face. Her father gathers her into a tight hug. 'Try not to worry, she can't have gone very far. They'll find her, I promise.'

45

MARIAN

Marian pushes the buggy down Kentish Town Road, pausing occasionally to tuck the pink blanket more tightly.

She's brought a pacifier with her just in case the baby is hungry or fretful, but she sleeps on, her perfect rosebud mouth pursed.

'You're such a good baby, Saffron,' Marian murmurs. 'Such a perfect little angel.'

In the end, buying the buggy had proved a very good idea. Someone carrying a small infant in their arms would instantly draw attention, where a woman pushing a buggy does not. She toyed with the idea of carrying Saffron in one of those very large, PVC-coated zipped laundry bags, but if she started crying, that would have been a problem. She also considered walking with her just as far as Highgate Road and flagging a cab. The risk then would be the taxi driver remembering her in the event of an appeal for a missing baby.

So instead, on Saturday afternoon, she walked down from the hotel to Oxford Street and bought a trendy all-terrain buggy in one of the department stores; the type that doubles as a car seat. She paid with cash and insisted on taking one of the display models rather than waiting for a delivery. While they removed the buggy from the display stand and got it ready, she browsed the department and picked up a few essentials: nappies, clothes, bottles, a baby blanket in pale pink. Saffron's blanket.

On Sunday morning, very early, she took the bus to Tufnell Park and left the buggy a few yards from the rear of the building. At that point there was no plan, other than a vague one to persuade Saffron's mother that the child needed to be taken for a health check, or to try to get her out of the flat on some pretence for a minute or two. When she called at the flat on Friday, the girl had told her she was about to move, and sure enough, from the lobby, she glimpsed her ex-husband's estate car parked outside the front door. He was loading, while the girl was making repeated trips from the fifth floor to the ground.

Marian went up the emergency stairs from the rear lobby and waited on the fifth-floor staircase, peering through the fire door's small glazed pane onto the corridor. After a few minutes, the girl went into the flat and emerged with a couple of small cases, leaving the front door propped open. As soon as the lift door had slid shut behind her, Marian hurried into the flat, her eyes scanning the living room. There was a baby's changing bag, conveniently packed and hung on a chair. She slung it over her shoulder and continued into the hall. The smaller bedroom to the left of the front door was empty apart from a single bed and a few boxes. The larger bedroom had just a stripped double bed, and on top of it a bassinet. Saffron lay sleeping peacefully inside it.

'Hello, my darling,' Marian whispered. 'Have you been left all alone?'

Very carefully, and with the utmost tenderness, she scooped up the white bundle and cradled her. That new baby smell transported her instantly to another time and place.

But there was no time to waste. She grabbed Saffron's yellow duckling and shoved it into her coat pocket, then walked quickly out of the flat and down the emergency stairs, through the fire door and out of the back of the building. She had to climb over a low railing and a two-foot-high privet hedge, before emerging onto the street at the back of the apartment complex.

It was still early on Sunday morning, and none of the residents were about. It took a mere twenty seconds to reach the bush where she had hidden the brand-new buggy from view and place Saffron in it, tucking the pink blanket over her to keep out the wintry drizzle that had just started to fall. Then she started walking briskly in the direction of Bloomsbury, via Kentish Town and Camden. She was not in the yellow coat this time, but her drab, formless blue anorak, with the hood pulled up to obscure her face. Nobody spoke to her. Nobody noticed her.

46

CHARLIE

The uniformed officers who arrive at the flat in Tufnell Park mean well, but they're young and hopelessly out of their depth.

Charlie is too traumatised, too paralysed with fear to make much sense, but her father manages to give them Jake's details and his mother's address. Along with the number plate for the Audi TT, which disappeared when Jake did.

'We'll put out an APB, and liaise with the major incident team,' the fresh-faced constable tells them. 'Don't worry, we see this happen all the time with separated dads. They decide they want some time with their kid, but quickly change their mind when they realise there's work involved.'

If this is intended to reassure, it falls wide of the mark. Charlie bursts into tears again, and she can tell her father is struggling to stay calm himself, still promising her that Bonnie will be returned soon. There's nothing for them to do but drive back to Laurel Road with the car full of baby stuff, which feels horribly wrong.

A few hours later, a female officer called Teresa Sanchez arrives at the house.

'This is our family liaison officer,' her mother says, bringing the woman into the kitchen.

'No more police.' Charlie buries her head in her arms. 'I can't.'

'She needs to speak to all of us, darling. It's important.'

DC Sanchez tells them that they are still searching for Jake Palmer, but a visit to his mother's flat has confirmed that Bonnie is not there. Jake's friends vehemently deny any involvement, or any knowledge of where Jake is. According to DC Sanchez there is no evidence so far that leads them to believe Jake would want to arrange the abduction of the baby.

'Except that the boy's a thief and a fraud,' Tom says hotly. 'He took a large sum of money from my daughter and just disappeared.'

'Exactly,' says DC Sanchez. 'From what we know so far, he's not in the slightest bit interested in parenting Bonnie. Apparently he's been in Ibiza for the past three months, partying. Only came back here when the funds dried up.'

'So where does that leave us, if we can't find Palmer?'

Charlie's level of fear is increasing rapidly. If the police don't think it's Jake, then the alternative is far worse. A random stranger walking in off the street, someone who will never be traced?

'Well, we're interviewing all the other residents of the block of flats, in case anyone saw anything, and examining as much CCTV footage of the area as we can. But obviously that takes time. In the meantime, Charlotte, we need you to think back, try and remember anyone else that might have given grounds for suspicion. Anyone acting strangely, taking an interest in the baby.'

A different policeman arrives only an hour after Sanchez has left.

Charlie has rushed down the stairs at the sound of the doorbell, and sees the man with the ginger hair who called on Friday morning. He's holding up a warrant card. 'DI Kevin Stratton. Could I come in for a minute?'

'Is it about Bonnie?' Charlie says, her hand flying to her chest. 'Have you found her?'

'Actually, I'm sorry but this is about a different matter. I've been needing to speak to your dad about something and I'm afraid it can't wait.'

'Come through.' Her father beckons DI Stratton into the kitchen dining room at the back of the house and Charlie follows. Her mother has told her to go up to her room to rest but she can't. She just can't.

'I've just made tea if you're interested…?' her father asks Stratton.

'Thank you. White, one sugar.'

He sits down at the large table, takes out a notebook and pen and waits for the tea to be poured.

'How can I help you, DI…?'

'Stratton. I'll come straight to the point.' His pale grey eyes are magnified by the horn-rimmed glasses, making him look like one of Charlie's teachers rather than a detective. 'You used to live in Ranmoor Road, N10, I believe?'

'Yes, but ages ago. With my first wife.'

The man glances at Charlie. 'I'm not sure if it's a good idea for your daughter to stay for this, in the circumstances. Given what she's going through.'

'It's fine,' says Charlie, heavily. 'It's not like I could get any more upset than I already am.'

'Okay then… I want to speak to you about the discovery of a baby's remains in the garden there. Historic remains, not recent,' he adds quickly.

'Dear God.' Tom leans back, recoiling automatically. 'I read something about that on the news but to be perfectly honest, it never occurred to me that it was my old house… Are you sure? That it's a baby, I mean?' He glances over at Charlie, who is pale but calm.

Stratton avoids eye contact, keeping his voice neutral. 'Yes, we're quite sure. The body of a male infant. The forensic tests suggest that it was buried getting on for twenty years ago. Which means during the time when you and your former wife lived there.'

Tom stares, rubbing his hand through his hair. 'But that's impossible.'

'You and your ex-wife... you didn't have any children?'

'No. We tried, but it didn't happen.' He flushes slightly, glancing at Charlie again. 'It was me. Me that couldn't have them. We considered adopting, but then I met my second wife and moved out.'

'And when was that, exactly?'

He thinks for a moment. 'It would have been in the July of 2003.'

'But your wife was still living there?'

'Yes. Yes, she stayed on until the house was sold, around October I think.'

Stratton sips his coffee and picks up his pen again. 'And... this might sound like an odd question... When you moved out, is there any chance your wife could have been pregnant?'

'Well, if she was, it wasn't by me...' He shakes his head ruefully. 'But no, surely not. Although...' He pauses, looks up at the ceiling.

'Go on,' Stratton prompts.

'Well, I do remember she was behaving very oddly at the time. Of course the separation was upsetting for her, but it seemed like more than that.'

'In what way?'

'She seemed unfocused, distracted. And she looked awful, as though she never slept.'

'And if she wasn't pregnant, was there someone else she was close to who might have had a new baby that she was looking after? We spoke to a Mrs Maud Pinker, who recalls seeing her carrying a baby into the house. And a former next-door neighbour, Kate Fletcher, has given a statement about hearing a young baby crying. Inside your house. This was around August or September of that year.'

Charlie is staring at her father intently. He shakes his head slowly, shocked. 'I know nothing about anyone having a baby there. Hold on…' He pauses, remembering.

'Go on.'

'There was this weird thing with the cat.'

'A cat?'

'Yes, I went round to speak to my ex-wife after I'd moved out and I heard a strange screeching sound. She told me it was a neighbour's cat, but it sounded like a baby.'

'I see.' Stratton makes a note.

'Surely you've asked her about all this?'

Stratton gives a rueful shake of the head. 'I was just coming to that… I'm afraid your ex-wife has gone missing. She's not at her home in Sussex, and so far we've not been able to find anyone who knows where she is. I don't suppose you would know where she might have gone?'

Tom sighs, standing up to clear away the tea mugs. 'I'm sorry, I don't. We've not had any contact since the divorce; I don't even have a mobile number for her any more; she changed it years back and didn't give me the new one. My friends Gareth and Farzeen Coker might know it; you could ask them.'

'Do you have any recent photos of her?'

'Not recent ones, no. I'm happy to show you what I have got.'

Tom disappears into the study and comes back with a sheaf of photos, which he spreads out on the kitchen table.

'To be honest, I'm surprised I still even have these. This is our wedding photo… this was one Christmas towards the end of our marriage… and these were taken on the last holiday we ever had together, in Kefalonia.'

Charlie is looking at the photos too, and her heart rate speeds up, so fast that she can hear it. She points, her finger shaking.

'That's her! The woman in the yellow coat!'

'Which woman?' Tom asks.

'I've been so completely out of my mind I forgot all about it… it was a couple of days ago, just after Lucy left, when I was making a start on packing. This woman knocked on the door of the flat and wanted to come in, said something about being from the council. Checking up on teens who didn't live with their parents. I told her I was moving out, and got rid of her. But that' – she stabs the photos with her forefinger – 'that's her. She had on lipstick and her hair was different… blonde… but it's definitely the same woman.'

47

MARIAN

At the hotel, Marian wheels the buggy quickly into the lift.

The bored girl on reception glances in her direction.

'My godchild,' Marian says. 'I'm babysitting for a couple of hours.'

The girl just grunts and goes back to looking at her phone.

In her room, Marian examines the contents of the changing bag. There's one bottle of what appears to be expressed breast milk, some muslins and wipes, a few spare nappies. There's a towelling bib with 'Bonnie' embroidered on it. Marian looks at it with distaste and throws it into the bathroom bin, setting the bottle in a sink full of hot water to warm it.

Saffron is stirring now, so Marian picks her up.

'Hello, beautiful girl. Remember me?'

Saffron screws up her face at the unfamiliar voice, the unfamiliar scent. Her mouth opens in a howl of protest. Marian reaches for the bottle and inserts it into the baby's mouth. Instantly she latches on and sucks hungrily, draining all the milk in a few minutes. She allows Marian to wind and change her and put her down again, with no further complaint. Almost immediately, she is asleep.

'Such a good girl,' Marian murmurs, before pulling out her phone. She knows she has to act quickly, before anyone has the chance to take Saffron away from her. She needs a car, but she can't use her own in case it's recognised, and she can't go to a car rental because that will involve producing her driving licence and giving personal details that match them. It won't be how it was when she arrived at the bed and breakfast, where they didn't bother to check.

She phones the number for her motor insurers.

'Hi… I need to report my car stolen.'

She gives the details of her own car, still parked in the street behind her flat in Hove. It will be found soon enough, no doubt, but by then she'll be long gone.

'Yes,' she says. 'I've filled in a police incident form online… yes, I have a crime number.'

She reads out the number the local police had given her a couple of years ago when one of her car windows was smashed, saved on her phone. 'The thing is, I've got the extra cover that allows me a courtesy car straight away, delivered to my home… only I'm in London on business… would it be okay for it to be brought to my hotel?'

The woman on the other end of the phone assures her that it will, but that since it's Sunday, a vehicle won't be available until first thing Monday morning. Will that be all right? Marian, who has little choice in the matter, assures her that it will.

She has no option now but to stay here with Saffron for another sixteen hours or so. Leaving the baby sleeping peacefully, she hurries to the nearest supermarket and buys some formula, boiling the flimsy plastic kettle in the hotel room to make up some more bottles. She could perform this task in her sleep, having already made so many bottles of milk for the twins.

Saffron wakes at intervals to be fed and changed, but otherwise displays an extraordinarily placid temperament. *This is the baby I was supposed to have*, Marian tells herself. *This one. That is why this all makes the most perfect sense.*

*

She's well rested in the morning, but restless, pacing the small, womblike room while Saffron lies on the duvet waving her little hands at the ceiling. The breakfast news programme says nothing about a missing baby. *Quite right too*, thinks Marian, *since she's really only back where she belongs.* Eventually, at nine thirty, there's a call from reception.

'Car for you,' the bored girl says.

Marian puts on the blonde wig and hurries down to reception where a courtesy driver is waiting for her. She signs the paperwork and takes the keys, and within ten minutes she has loaded the buggy and their luggage into the car. The top part of the buggy is strapped in, after a few minutes of fiddling and swearing, to form a rear-facing child seat.

'Nice and safe for you,' she tells Saffron. She pulls off the wig and throws it onto the passenger seat before turning round in the driver's seat to look at her. 'We've not got far to go. Not long till you reach your new home.'

48

CHARLIE

DI Stratton returns to the house the next day with a colleague in tow – a petite woman with ginger hair tied up in a high ponytail. Charlie wonders if he chose her for this reason: that her hair is the same colour as his. The two detectives looked like a matched pair.

'This is DS Emma Ross,' he says, 'one of the team that's been working on the Ranmoor Road case. After Charlotte identified Mrs Glynn – Marian Glynn – as the woman who came to her flat, we're combining that enquiry with the search for Bonnie.'

'Are you going to be okay to talk?' her mother asks her. 'You look wrung out.'

Charlie, who has not slept a wink and feels torn up with fear and anxiety, nods mechanically. 'Of course. If it's about Bonnie. I need to know. I need to know everything.'

They sit down at the kitchen table as before, and Vanessa makes coffee.

'First of all,' says Stratton, 'although we'd more or less ruled him out at this point anyway, I ought to tell you that we've tracked down Jake Palmer. We had an alert on all the airports, and his name came up on a flight manifest to Ibiza. Interpol arranged for the local police to check on him, and he doesn't have Bonnie. He's just there to party.'

Tom rolls his eyes in disgust.

'Secondly, I think your FLO was planning to come and talk to you about doing an appeal on TV. Do you think you'd be up to that, Charlotte? If not, your dad could do it, or your mum. Or we could do it ourselves. Either way, we want to get something on the news this evening. It's vital to get the help of the public in this sort of situation.'

'No. I'll do it,' Charlie says, firmly. 'That will work best, won't it? And I need to do whatever will give us the best chance. Of finding her.'

Tears fill her eyes again and she brushes them away angrily. Her dad closes his hand over hers.

'Obviously we want to know if you'd made progress in finding my ex-wife.'

DI Stratton shoots him a sharp look, his eyes narrowing behind his glasses. It's DS Ross who speaks, with a distinct West Midlands twang. 'Right, so… I've been liaising with DC Khatri down in Brighton. They've not located her car via ANPR, and I'm afraid an extensive trawl through CCTV at both Brighton and Hove stations hasn't picked up anyone matching Mrs Glynn's description.'

Vanessa gives a little frown of displeasure as she puts the tray on the table. DS Ross flushes slightly. 'The former Mrs Glynn, I mean, obviously… And we have spoken to Angela Dixon and your friend' – she pulls out a notebook and checks it – 'Mrs Farzeen Coker.'

Tom raises an eyebrow. 'And?'

'Mrs Coker had a mobile number for Marian, but it's an old one, no longer in service. That leaves us at the mercy of all the mobile providers, trying to trace her phone via their records. Obviously we've flagged it as urgent, and we hope to get a result soon. Angela Dixon saw Mrs… Marian… fairly recently in Brighton, but said she seemed fine. There was nothing in Marian's demeanour that disturbed her, apart from one thing.'

'Which was?' demands Tom.

DS Ross glances in Vanessa's direction. 'She said she mentioned to Marian that you and Mrs Glynn had adopted two children together, assuming she knew, but apparently she didn't. And she seemed upset by it, cut their meeting short.'

'Well, there we are then.' Tom leans back in his chair, his tone grim. 'That sounds as though it could have triggered something.'

'We need to take another statement from you, Charlotte, with a full description of Marian's appearance, get it circulated. Maybe think of getting a composite sketch done. Someone may have seen her. You never know.'

'No,' agrees Tom heavily. 'You don't.'

The press conference is filmed that afternoon at the Metropolitan Police Communications Centre, with a strained but composed Charlie wearing a plain white shirt and clutching one of Bonnie's teddy bears. Tom and Vanessa flank her on either side, sitting at a temporary trestle table in front of a Metropolitan Police poster. DI Stratton is to Tom's right. Three plastic cups of water sit untouched in front of them.

'Yesterday morning, my life was changed forever,' Charlie begins, her voice trembling. 'Someone went into my flat while I was carrying something out to the car, and took my two-week-old baby daughter, Bonnie.' She stifles a sob. Vanessa reaches over and squeezes her hand. 'I'm asking, if anyone knows who did this, or has any information that could help, to please come forward. Thank you.'

'I know that was hard,' DC Sanchez says, as the family is led away to a waiting unmarked car. 'But witnessing Charlie's distress first hand will be by far the most compelling way to get people to think, and to act.'

'Let's hope so,' says Tom grimly. 'Let's bloody hope so.'

49

MARIAN

'Here we are, my angel.' Marian speaks in a soothing tone, even though the baby is fast asleep.

It's mid-afternoon, and the light is just starting to fade. She parks the car on the Hove promenade and sits in silence watching the horizon streak pink then purple over the dark sea. Saffron sleeps on, her perfect rosebud lips twitching slightly. *My girl is so good*, Marian thinks with profound satisfaction. Truly, this is the child she was meant to have.

Only when it is completely dark does she drive to her flat, leaving the hire car in a visitor parking space.

'Home!' Marian exclaims, as she carries Saffron over the threshold. Her neighbours are engrossed in their evening television viewing; there's nobody about. 'I'm afraid we can't stay here very long this time, but we will be able to come back eventually. This is our proper home.' She thinks suddenly of the little blue-painted villa in Brighton she had coveted so much. 'Until you're toddling around anyway, and then we'll have to find somewhere with a garden for you.'

Saffron is awake now, squirming and searching for milk. Marian hurries to make and heat a bottle before there's a full-blown attack of screaming. She knows, to her cost, that the crying of a new baby carries very effectively. Saffron seems unsure about the formula – having been breast fed – pursing her lips and frowning at the teat. But hunger overrides her reluctance and soon she is sucking vigorously.

Marian settles in the armchair listening to the little sounds she makes. Just for those few minutes, she experiences more contentment than she has ever felt in her life. When she first had the twins, all she wanted was to be part of the magical realm of mothers. To belong to that club. But that world had failed to open itself up to her. The other women around her bonded during their pregnancies, and she missed out on that stage. Cliques at mother and baby groups and the school gates would never have fully acknowledged her or absorbed her into their ranks. But now she realises that none of that matters. All that matters is right here: just her and her daughter. After the lonely, empty years since her divorce, she has finally come full circle.

Women who adopt babies can sometimes produce breast milk and feed them themselves, Marian remembers, as she strokes the down-soft cheek. She saw a leaflet about it during her social work career. When she believed that she and Tom were going to adopt, she was planning to try it herself. It's probably too late, at her age, for that to work now. But no matter, Saffron seems happy enough. She dozes off, the teat falling from the side of her mouth. Marian spreads the pink blanket on the sofa and lies her carefully down on it, before making herself a cup of tea and switching on the television.

'…morning, my life was changed forever. Someone went into my flat while I was carrying something out to the car, and took my two-week-old baby daughter, Bonnie.'

Marian sets down her mug slowly, staring at the screen. It's her: the foolish girl who went out and left Saffron unattended. With Tom on one side of her and her mother – that tart – on the other. 'I'm asking, if anyone knows who did this, or has any information that could help, to please come forward. Thank you.'

The screen cuts back to the newsreader. 'A spokesman for the Metropolitan Police this evening said that they urgently need to speak to the former wife of Tom Glynn, Charlotte Glynn's father.'

Marian jumps as a photo of herself appears on the screen. It must have been captured on a camera while she was out shopping. She's wearing the yellow coat, currently in her suitcase, and the blonde wig. Then another photo flashes up, the one used in her passport, her face devoid of make-up, her hair grey and frizzy.

The newsreader continues: *Marian Glynn, 57, has been missing from her home in Hove, East Sussex since Wednesday. The public are requested not to approach her, but to contact the police immediately.*

'Not to approach her!' Marian snorts loudly. How ridiculous. As if she's the one who would put an infant in danger. She stands up and switches off the television, looks down at the sleeping baby. She hadn't planned on staying here long anyway – that would have been risky – but moving on has just become even more urgent. Can she risk delaying her departure until the morning? Might the police make a raid on the flat in the middle of the night? But no, they just said she was missing from the flat. And she drove here in a car that as yet she has no proven connection with. That will change; they'll work it out eventually, but not before the insurance offices are open tomorrow. She has a few hours.

While Saffron sleeps on, she unpacks her suitcase, shoving the mustard yellow coat and the blonde wig into a bin bag and taking them out to the communal dumpster. Back in the flat, she digs around in the back of the bathroom cabinet until she finds a pack of hair dye. Several years ago, when the grey started to take over, she toyed with the idea of going a different colour, but decided she would look ridiculous. It would be too obvious.

The pack describes the colour as 'Ultra Vibrant Red'. Marian looks dubiously at the woman depicted on the pack: she's about twenty-five and has a luscious auburn mane. But there's no possibility of going to a chemist to shop for something more suitable;

this is all she has. She shampoos her hair over the side of the bath, leaves the dye on for forty minutes, then rinses it off.

The result is a rather alarming carrot colour. But there's no time to change it, and the most important benefit is that it looks completely different. Once it's dry, she finds her hairdressing scissors and cuts the shapeless bob into a close crop. At the back of a drawer in her bedroom is a pair of non-prescription reading glasses she sometimes uses for small print. She puts them on, and discovers that the combination of short red hair and the blue frames is almost flattering. It changes her look, at least.

After repacking her suitcase, she feeds and bathes Saffron then lies down on her bed, fully clothed, with the alarm on her phone set for 4 a.m. They will be gone, long before it's light and there's a possibility of them being found. Nothing's going to get in her way this time.

Whatever happens, she and Saffron won't be parted again.

50

PAULA

She's in the kitchen, tidying up the breakfast things before heading to work, when she hears it.

'*On Sunday morning, my life was changed forever. Someone went into my flat while I was carrying something out to the car, and took my two-week-old baby daughter, Bonnie. I'm asking, if anyone knows who did this, or has any information that could help, to please come forward. Thank you.*'

Paula stares transfixed at the chyron scrolling over the bottom of the news channel footage. 'TEENAGE MOTHER CHARLOTTE GLYNN APPEALS FOR SAFE RETURN OF NEWBORN DAUGHTER.' She drops the cloth she was holding and gropes wildly for the TV remote, turning up the volume.

'*A spokesman for the Metropolitan Police this evening said that they urgently need to speak to the former wife of Tom Glynn, Charlotte Glynn's father. Marian Glynn, 57, has been missing from her home in Hove, East Sussex since Wednesday The public are requested not to approach her, but to contact the police immediately.*'

The feed cuts to the weather forecast. Paula snatches her phone and scrolls through every news update she can find. There it is, the same story everywhere: 17-year-old Charlotte Glynn, whose two-week-old baby daughter Bonnie was snatched from her flat.

And the police are treating none other than Marian Glynn as a person of interest.

Paula has to sit down on a chair to take this in, reading and rereading. Twin babies taken, one buried, one abandoned then adopted. That adopted child's own daughter now taken. A baby who was Paula's own flesh and blood, just as Charlotte was. Lizzie's granddaughter. Her great-niece. Some of the news sites have a photo of the baby, a particularly pretty newborn with plump cheeks and a rosebud mouth.

Her first instinct is to text Johnny and ask if he has seen the news, but this is too important for a text. They need to talk, decide what to do next. Because today, they had already agreed, they were going to go to 35 Laurel Road and speak to Charlotte's parents about her real identity. And about the twin baby brother that they doubtless knew nothing about. She dials the number for her work.

'Jody, hi… it's Paula. Listen, can you tell Calum I'm not going to be in this morning? I'm running a bit of a temperature. I'll come in later if I feel better… okay, thanks.'

She switches off the TV, grabs her car keys and hurries out to the car.

Paula knows where Johnny's offices are, but she's never been inside the building. He rents two floors of space above a dry-cleaning business on Green Lanes. From the outside you would barely know it was there, and there's no lift from the ground floor, but once inside it's quiet, clean and freshly decorated. Paula taps on the door and a young, lanky youth comes to open it. This, Paula is pretty sure, is Brandon, one of Johnny's many nephews.

'Is Johnny Shepherd in?'

The boy jerks his head to a closed internal door. 'Over there.'

But the door has already been thrown open and Johnny is standing there, resplendent in a pin-striped suit and crimson tie. He'd already told her he had meetings with 'the money men' that day. 'Sweetheart!' He gathers Paula into his arms. 'Thought we weren't meeting till this evening?'

'Something's happened.' She closes the office door behind them, and takes out her phone. 'Have you seen this?'

Johnny frowns, starts to read. His expression morphs from one of mild interest to one of shock. 'Bloody hell, Paul! This is her – your niece? And someone's nicked her baby?'

'Not just someone… carry on reading.'

Johnny's hand goes to his forehead. 'Jesus Christ. Her? Marian Glynn? They reckon she's done this?' He hands Paula's phone back to her. 'Hard to fathom; talk about bloody coincidences. Well, I suppose that's the point: this *isn't* a coincidence.' He pulls Paula into a hug again. 'I'm sorry, babe.'

'Sorry? Why are you sorry?'

'Because it's obviously out of the question us going over to the Glynns' place now. Not now this is all kicking off.'

Paula pulls away from him, forcing him to meet her eye. 'But we've got to, Johnny. That was what all this time and effort was for. And money – you had to pay Big Tony, remember? It was to find Lizzie's baby. And now we have. We can't just leave it there. I have to—'

'Paula, Paula…' He pushes her down into the chair facing his desk. It's not done roughly but with a definite firmness, making her glare at him. 'Look at what's just happened to these poor people! A seventeen year old has had her kid taken, just a couple of weeks after giving birth. You can't just waltz in there, someone they don't know from Adam, and say, "Sorry you're going through some shit but by the way, I'm your alcoholic birth mother's kid sister: surprise! Oh, and by the way you had a twin brother you knew nothing about, who was probably murdered." Yeah, that would go down brilliantly, I'm sure…'

He's on a roll now, pacing to and fro and enhancing his argument with hand gestures. 'For all you know, Charlotte doesn't even want to know about her birth mother. And it's hardly going to make her parents feel any better.'

Paula narrows her eyes. 'I'm sorry, but I don't agree. This girl is my family. I've spent most of my adult life wondering what happened to her. Now is exactly the time I need to be there for her. To give her my support.'

Johnny makes a snorting sound and slaps his forehead. 'Come off it! That's just not realistic. They're just going to tell you to fuck off, however polite you are about it.'

Paula's on her feet again. 'How do you know that?' she rages. 'Because you're Johnny Shepherd, the big I-am? The one who knows everyone and everything and has a finger in every bloody pie!'

She snatches up her handbag, turns on her heel and stamps out of the room, running down the stairs and slamming the street door. Instantly, her phone buzzes: Johnny trying to call her. She cuts the call and then swears out loud as she reaches her car. She has a parking ticket.

Back at her house, she fills a glass from the half-empty bottle of red on the kitchen table. But the acidity of the wine catches in her throat and besides, red wine is something she now associates with Johnny. They always drink it together. She tips the wine down the sink and takes a can of Coke from the fridge, filling a glass and adding a pour of rum on top.

Once she has drunk it, she feels calmer. She's still angry with Johnny, but accepts that some of that anger is because she knows he's right. The abduction of baby Bonnie means that it's impossible for her to approach the Glynns. Not now. She should go into work, but she doesn't. Instead she walks the dog, then skulks around the house, unable to settle, with the TV news channel on a continuous loop. The police are apparently following up multiple leads on the baby Bonnie abduction after the public responded to her mother's appeal.

At the end of the afternoon she collects Ben and his friend Connor from school and drops them at the nearest cinema multiplex, before taking Jessica home and helping with her homework. At 9 p.m., just after Jessica has gone up to bed, the doorbell rings. Johnny stands there in his covert coat, holding a huge, gaudy bouquet of flowers.

'Paul, I'm sorry… Can I come in?'

She steps aside silently, and he stands awkwardly in the hallway. 'Can we talk?'

Paula sighs heavily, and waves him into the living room. Despite everything, her heart leaps when she sees him. He's still the dazzling Johnny Shepherd. Still her girlhood crush.

He wraps his arms around her and kisses her forehead. He smells of London rain and sandalwood. 'Paul, I really am sorry. I shouldn't have gone off on you like that. Not when you were so emotional.'

'It's okay.' Her shoulders drop with relief and she allows herself to lean into him. 'You were right. I was so fired up I just wasn't thinking straight.'

Johnny pats her back. 'I could murder a cuppa.'

She makes them tea and lights the fire, and they curl up on the sofa together.

'So what now?' Paula asks. 'Do we just do nothing?'

Before Johnny even speaks, she sees that light in his eye, a look she has come to know so well. 'No, we are bloody well not doing nothing. If we don't act, well, what has all this been for, eh?'

Paula clasps her mug, staring at him. 'So, what do we do?'

'We've already found a baby. Actually, two babies. The baby boy in the garden, and young Saffron. Charlotte Glynn. So what's to stop us finding a third?'

Her eyes widen. 'You mean little Bonnie?'

'Yes. That's exactly what I mean. We've done it before: we can do it again.'

It's her turn to scoff now. 'Come on, Johnny, the police are all over it! What can we possibly do that they can't? Best thing we can do is let the professionals get on with it. They're bound to find her eventually.'

'Will they though? With that nutter taking her? Who's to say she won't end up buried in some garden somewhere?'

Paula shudders and covers her ears. 'Don't, Johnny. I can't bear to even think about that.'

Johnny sets his tea mug down and puts an arm around her shoulders. 'Look, think about it as us trying to give the police a hand. Anything we manage to find out, we'll share with them straight away. How about that?'

Paula shrugs. 'I suppose so. So, what are we going to do first?'

Johnny grins. 'We're going have another chat with Big Tony.'

51

CHARLIE

Charlie watches the appeal go out on the ten o'clock news, covering her eyes with her fingers intermittently, and shaking her head. Despite her parents telling her she must go to bed, she paces the ground floor of the house, unable to settle. Her father is still up too, checking his phone constantly. At 10.45, it rings.

'Did it work?' she hears him asking. 'Has someone come forward?' Then:

'No, that's fine. It's not as though I'll be able to sleep anyway.'

'That was DI Stratton,' he tells Charlie as he hangs up. 'He wants to talk to us. I'll wait up for him, darling; you really need to try and get some rest.'

'No point,' says Charlie, stubbornly. 'I won't be able to sleep now anyway, will I?'

Stratton arrives fifteen minutes later, dressed in jeans and a tan bomber jacket, carrying a manila folder. His thin, sandy hair is slicked to his skull as though he recently got out of the shower. Tom leads him through into the sitting room and waves a bottle of Scotch in his direction, which Stratton declines. Charlie follows and sits silently on the sofa.

'A very thorough search of footage from all the live street cameras in the Tufnell Park area on Sunday gave us this.'

He produces a still of a thickset woman in an anorak pushing a baby's buggy along the pavement. Charlie's hand flies to her mouth. 'Oh my God! Is that Bonnie?'

'Our technical guys pieced together a trail of images of the same woman, following her all the way down from Highgate Road to Russell Square. It was early on Sunday, with hardly anyone on the street, which made it relatively easy to spot her. That and the new-looking buggy.'

He looks up at Charlie and her father, waiting for them to absorb this.

'Eventually she arrived at a two-star hotel just off Russell Square, the Briar Inn B&B. So I sent officers round there to question the staff and go through their security camera footage. And their cameras picked up this.'

He pushes another still across the table. It appears to be the same woman, only this time in a light-coloured coat, her blonde hair visible beneath a woollen hat. She's in the hotel reception area, pushing an identical baby buggy into the lift. Charlie stares intently at what can be seen of the woman's face, but her head is turned away.

'Obviously these images are in black and white, but when we questioned the receptionist she says she remembers the woman's coat, because it was quite a striking shade of yellow.'

'This has to be her: the woman who came to your flat. The one in the yellow coat.' Tom looks over at his daughter.

'I think so,' Charlie says slowly. 'It's hard to be a hundred per cent certain.'

'According to the statement, she paid for her room in cash, giving her name as Anne Webber. This morning she also told the receptionist that she was minding someone else's child.'

Charlie stares at her father, whose eyes have widened in shock. 'Marian's maiden name is Webber,' he says eventually. 'And Anne is her middle name. It's her. It's Marian. It has to be, surely.'

'It looks that way.'

'Have you managed to get a mobile number for her?'

'We've traced a contract phone issued to her by Vodaphone, but the number's out of service. Last used in or near her flat last Tuesday.'

Charlie is standing now, agitated. 'So where the fuck is she? She's got her! She's got Bonnie!'

Stratton takes off his glasses and rubs his eyes. 'There is CCTV footage of her wheeling the buggy out of the hotel again with her luggage, then we lose her. The receptionist says Marian asked her something about parking a car nearby. Now, we know her car wasn't at her flat in Hove, so that would tally. So we've currently got a special ANPR alert set up across all forces. As soon as it picks up her number plate – which it will – we'll be able to trace her. And we'll update the information on the appeal, using a photo of Marian, asking people to look out for her. Someone will see her.'

'Oh my God.' Charlie sinks down onto the sofa again, her legs suddenly giving way. 'Please hurry up. Hurry up and find her.'

'We'll get your daughter back, I promise.' Stratton echoes the words her father used to her on that Sunday. 'With any luck we'll have news in the morning.'

52

MARIAN

Despite only a few hours' sleep, Marian feels relaxed, even elated.

Vivaldi's *Four Seasons* is playing on the car radio, and Saffron is sleeping peacefully. She'll need feeding soon, so they can't drive to their final destination in one go. They'll need to stop, somewhere discreet where they can't be spotted by the public. Hence the 4 a.m. departure, to reduce the number of curious eyes.

She drives for an hour and a half before selecting a motel-style lodging on the edge of a dual carriageway. The single storey chalet-style rooms are separate from the building that houses reception, and she parks some distance from it so there is no need for anyone to see her taking the car seat from the back of the car.

She fills in the form with her maiden name and an invented car registration, and pays in cash for two nights. The man at the reception desk tells her he still needs to see ID. Her heart thumping, Marian rummages through her wallet until she finds an old university library card in the name of M. A. Webber. The man glances at it and nods, pushing the key across the desk to her.

'Room 104. It's back that way a bit.' He points to the far end of the car park.

Marian unloads Saffron and their belongings into the sparsely furnished, slightly grubby room. After feeding and settling the baby, she pulls her coat on again and heads out to the car park.

It's still dark, and very cold, and hers is only one of four vehicles. She stares at the number plate for some minutes, thinking. Before long, someone will discover that she has this car on loan, or the insurers will become suspicious. She is sure she has read somewhere that you can obscure a registration plate with a special spray, or even hair lacquer, neither of which she has access to.

Think, Marian, think.

She has a flash of memory, of driving along narrow country lanes on childhood summer holidays in Devon. Of her father, in his driving gloves, complaining about the tractors that obstructed their progress. 'So much mud on their plates, you can't even take a note of the number to make a complaint. Can't read them, they're so dirty, which is illegal.'

She squats down by the grassy verge and tugs at the turf with her fingers until she manages to dislodge a section. Beneath it is cold, sticky mud. She scoops up a generous handful and smears it thickly over the courtesy car's number plates, first the back and then the front. Once it has dried, she tells herself, there's a decent chance it will prevent a camera from identifying the car. Not a long-term solution, but it might just last until they reach their destination.

Which is little more than an hour away now. Almost there.

But Marian desperately needs to catch up on her sleep – she can barely focus on the road. She spends the rest of the day in the motel room napping while Saffron is quiet, and avoiding any source of news while she's awake.

Once it's dark, she loads up the car again and uses her phone to check the route, before powering it down and dropping it at the bottom of her bag. Saffron grizzles faintly from the carrycot on the back seat, as if disgruntled to be on the move again.

'It's okay, my angel, it's not very far. And once we're there, we'll be safe, I promise.'

*

The front door key is under the mat, just as it always used to be. The first thing that strikes her is how cold the place is. Of course it is; it's the beginning of December and there's no central heating. Yet the reality of it – of the chill damp air that pervades every inch of the place – is still a shock. That and the fact that there's no food at all, bar a dried-up jar of instant coffee, a bottle of English mustard and a tin of spaghetti hoops. Saffron, sensing the chill and the isolation, starts to wail forcibly for the first time in the last thirty-six hours. There's enough formula left for three more bottles, and only half a dozen nappies. Marian had forgotten how quickly a new baby can work through them.

Someone has left some wood in the log basket, but it's so damp that despite repeated attempts, she can't get it to light. In the end she abandons her efforts, and after feeding Saffron with unheated formula, takes her into her own bed. It's unaired, but there are plenty of quilts and blankets that she heaps in a deep pile over them, using her own body heat to keep the child warm. They stay like that until it grows light.

In the morning, Marian goes downstairs and makes a more thorough investigation of the kitchen. The fridge isn't working, but the kettle is, allowing her to make a black coffee from the dregs in the jar, and warm a bottle of formula. She finds a hot water bottle in the bedroom chest and fills it, placing it in Saffron's carrycot and tucking the baby in next to it. The sudden increase in warmth sends her into a contented doze. As soon as she's asleep, Marian tugs on coat, boots and hat and sets off on foot to the shop in the nearest village. Even if she weren't reluctant to draw attention to herself by pushing a buggy she wouldn't be able to propel it over this terrain: all swamp grass and rutted tracks. It makes her anxious leaving the baby unattended, but she has no choice.

It takes her nearly thirty minutes to reach the shop, where she buys basic food supplies like milk, bread, teabags and firewood. She still needs nappies and formula, but doesn't want to buy them here in a tiny general store, with the shopkeeper noting every single purchase, gossiping to the villagers. By the time she's walked back again, Saffron is just starting to stir, taking in her surroundings with her unfocussed gaze. Marian picks her up and holds her close, feeling the tiny lips move against her neck.

'It's okay, I'm here. You knew I wouldn't leave you for long.'

She lights the fire with the new, dry firewood, and soon warmth is permeating the air, along with an amount of smoke. Clearly the chimney flue has not been cleaned in years. After hoovering and sweeping, Marian makes herself a cheese sandwich and administers the last of the formula to Saffron. She's barely eaten in the last few days, and the waistband of her skirt is feeling loose. That's a good thing, she tells herself, especially since the weight loss has resulted from having someone other than herself to take care of.

This is the way it is supposed to be.

'Right, you're coming with me this time.'

Later that afternoon, Marian tucks the baby into the buggy and lugs it out to the car. She can no longer use her phone to access the internet, but she's sure she remembers passing a big supermarket on their way there the previous evening, just a few miles away. Sure enough she finds it, and it's big enough and busy enough for her to push Saffron around it in the buggy without looking conspicuous. Better that than risk her being spotted alone on the back seat of the car. She fills a trolley with ready meals and baby supplies, even adding a few pot plants, cushions and throws from the home goods department.

'We'll soon have our new home feeling and looking cosy,' she tells Saffron, putting more firewood into the trolley. So far their wood supplies are only what she could carry that morning, and they will need plenty more.

'What a lovely baby,' the cashier comments as she swipes the shopping through the till. 'Isn't she bonny?'

Bonnie. That name again. Marian grimaces and looks determinedly away from the woman, refusing to fall into conversation.

'That's £173.69,' the cashier says. 'Card?'

'Cash,' Marian tells her firmly, counting out the notes. She checks her wallet anxiously, trying to work out how much money she has left. Several hundred pounds still, enough for the time being, but she will have to watch her spending carefully. Using a cash machine is as good as planting a flag on a map these days.

Outside in the car park, a man from a mobile car washing service is wheeling his cart towards her car. 'Is dirty,' he says in broken English, grinning. 'You want I clean?' He takes the jet washing nozzle and points it at her mud-caked number plate.

'No!' Marian says, angrily. 'No, leave it alone. I don't want it cleaned.' She jabs the washer away with one hand.

He watches her, confused, as she stows the carrycot and dumps her shopping in the boot, before driving off at speed.

53

PAULA

Paula and Johnny meet Big Tony at a pub in Whitechapel called the Wheatsheaf.

It's a typical yellow-brick Victorian establishment with a piano for East End singalongs cheek by jowl with a pool table and Sky Sports on the TV over the bar. Big Tony is sitting at a small circular corner table, so small that he can't fit his huge legs underneath it and has to sit with them splayed wide.

Tuesday afternoons don't bring in much trade and the place is quiet. Paula phoned Calum that morning and told him she needed to take leave for personal reasons. He was less than pleased, especially after she has just been off sick.

'Jody can't manage the front of house, *and* help me, not for more than a few hours. We need notice if you're not going to be here, so I can get temporary cover.'

'I'm really sorry, Calum,' she had muttered, meaning it. 'I wouldn't do this unless it was extremely important.' She was about to tell him that her absence was related to the missing baby in the news, before checking herself. That would sound dodgy, and risk him asking questions, even calling the police. 'I'll explain it all to you eventually, I promise.'

So she's self-conscious and feels guilty about finding herself in this setting halfway through what should have been a work day.

Johnny, on the other hand, is quite relaxed, all back slaps and hand clasps. In his element.

'Tone, always a pleasure. What can I get you, mate?'

Big Tony, who is at the bottom of a packet of crisps, licks the salt from his fingers and holds up his empty glass. 'Pint of Truman's,' he says, grunting in Paula's direction, which she takes to be a greeting. Johnny comes back from the bar with the pint of stout, lager for himself and a gin and tonic for Paula, along with more crisps.

'So, what can I do for you?' Big Tony mumbles into his glass, ripping open one of the bags of crisps.

'Great work you did for us, last time, Tone.' Johnny rubs his hands. 'Really brilliant. Exactly what was needed. The things is, though, we need something a bit more... involved now. A bit more technical.'

'Such as?' Big Tony's sausage-like fingers rummage in the crisp packet.

'We need to try and track someone who's deliberately gone missing. Through whatever means we can. Phone records, financial activity: anything. Any way her location can be nailed down.'

'You're talking hardcore.' Big Tony sucks his teeth. 'Dark web stuff. Not the sort of thing my police contacts necessarily get into.'

'But you know someone? Come on, Tone, you always do.'

He's shaking his head slowly. 'There is someone I know of, yes. Someone who specialises in that stuff. It'll cost you, though.'

Paula glances nervously at Johnny, who remains unperturbed. 'Of course, whatever they need. But it's urgent. We need this person finding yesterday.'

Tony drains his glass and stands up, his bulk almost knocking the table over. 'Come on then. No time like the present.'

'Where are we going?' Paula asks. She's barely started her own drink.

'Taking you to meet Spider. He's the best there is.'

*

The three of them cross Whitechapel Road and head east towards Stepney.

After ten minutes they come to a drab block of flats built from soot-stained brick, with a dank stone stairwell and a lift so tiny that the three of them can't fit into it together; Johnny and Paula take the stairs to the fourth floor, leaving Big Tony to cram his huge frame into the lift. They are admitted, wordlessly, to a dark, airless flat whose windows are all obscured by lowered blinds. Several cats weave their way across the hall and between their legs, meowing for attention. At least the animals acknowledge their presence. Their owner says nothing.

Spider is as thin and emaciated as Big Tony is corpulent. His face – all hollows and shadows beneath the shaved head – resembles a skull. It's impossible to discern his age, which could be anywhere between twenty and forty. He leads them into the flat's cramped sitting room, which resembles an Aladdin's cave for the twenty-first century hacker. Every available surface is covered with micro-PCs, motherboards, filters, radio receivers and USB sticks. On a large table that takes up most of the room there are several laptops, satellite phones, mobile handsets and a huge tangle of Ethernet cables. Faint wisps of marijuana smoke hang in the chinks of light that escape around the edges of the window blinds.

Spider sits down at the table, resuming smoking the joint he abandoned in order to open the door. He still says nothing.

'These good people need your help, Spide,' Big Tony tells him.

Spider merely narrows his eyes, blowing smoke at the ceiling.

'They need you to find someone.' Big Tony nods at Paula. 'Tell him.'

'She's called Marian Glynn,' Paula starts. If Spider recognises the name from recent news bulletins, he gives no sign of it. 'She's fifty-seven years old, permanent residence is in Hove. Used to live at twenty-one Ranmoor Road, London N10.'

There's still no response. Paula shrugs helplessly at Johnny, who adds, 'She owns a car, but she's not driving it at the moment. Probably has another vehicle, though. We can show you a photo of her.'

He reaches into his coat, but Big Tony stops him. 'No need,' he says. 'Spider can access images of her before you can say "data breach".' He grins, pleased with his own joke.

'How much will it cost?' Paula asks anxiously. She scrapes by on her wages and the maintenance Dave pays her, but has nothing in the way of savings.

Spider speaks for the first time. 'That depends,' he says. His voice is surprisingly deep and resonant, in contrast with his slight frame, his accent educated. 'Depends how deep and how fast.'

Johnny reaches in his coat again, but this time it's Spider that stops him. 'Settle up afterwards. When I've got results.'

'And how will you tell us what you've found out?'

Spider reaches into the clutter on the table and extracts a basic mobile phone with a charger attached. 'Keep this charged and switched on. I'll send you real-time updates.'

Paula turns the phone over in her hand, as though it has magical powers. 'Do you think there's any chance you'll be able to find her?'

'Of course.' Spider's face forms something approaching a smile, his skin stretching tight across the bony contours of his face. 'I can find anyone.'

54

CHARLIE

'It's now four days since baby Bonnie Glynn was snatched from this block of flats, and so far her whereabouts are still a mystery, as are those of Marian Glynn, the woman who is believed to have taken her. The Metropolitan Police spokesman said this morning that they remain hopeful that the three week old is still alive, and they are following up leads following a huge response from the public. Even so—'

Vanessa reaches out and takes the remote from her daughter's hand, switching the TV off.

'Enough now, darling. Don't keep torturing yourself.'

'But I need to know. I can't *not* know.'

'Take a break at least. You're not doing yourself any good by focussing on Bonnie all the time.'

Her mother is right; Charlie knows it. Her physical health is starting to suffer. Her back aches, as does her neck and her jaw. The state of constant tension is affecting her physically as well as mentally. She sleeps, somehow, but relaxing is impossible. And now she has become a mother herself, albeit only for a brief time, she understands her own mother's instinct to fuss over her. To try and fix things, make things right for her.

'Is this my fault, Mum?' she asks, miserably. 'Because I was thinking of getting rid of her. Of having a termination. Am I being punished? Only I wasn't sure I wanted her, and now she's gone.'

Vanessa wraps her arms around her tightly. 'Of course not, Lottie. You mustn't think that way. Your dad and I are so impressed with what a great mum you are. It may not be what any of us had planned, but you're doing so well.'

'I *was*.' Fresh tears well up in Charlie's eyes. Just when she thinks she can't possibly produce any more of them, more arrive.

'Why not go for a walk? Or go over to Hannah's for a bit? She keeps messaging me to ask how you are.'

'Because the police might come round.'

Fifteen minutes later, when the doorbell rings, Charlie hurries into the hall, her expression once again wrestling with hope and fear.

'I'll get it, darling,' Vanessa tells her, bustling to the front door. 'You go and run yourself a bath. If there's any news, we'll come and tell you right away.' She opens the front door. Their family liaison officer, DC Teresa Sanchez, is standing there.

'No,' Charlie insists, her eyes widening. 'Whatever she's going to say, I want to hear it.' She follows her mother and Teresa Sanchez into the kitchen.

'Just a quick update,' Sanchez says, refusing the offer of a hot drink and remaining on her feet. 'Sussex Police have found Marian Glynn's car, parked near her flat. We've also heard from her insurers – some bright spark at their office recognised the name from a news report and had the sense to call the incident line.'

'That's good,' says Vanessa, managing a weak smile.

'Apparently she reported her car stolen on Sunday, and was provided with a courtesy car, which was delivered to her in central London.' She smiles at their uncertain expressions. 'Trust me, this is a good development. We've now got the details of the vehicle she's using.'

'So why can't you bloody find it?' Charlie demands hotly. 'If you've got the car's number then why can't you pick it up on your cameras?'

'Well, that's just it.' Sanchez pulls her bag tighter against her body as though protecting herself from Charlie's fury. 'The cameras can only pick up a vehicle that's mobile. It may be off the road somewhere. But we'll be giving out the details of the car to the press and as soon as it's public, someone will spot it. It's only a matter of time.'

'And in the meantime that madwoman has got our grand-daughter,' Vanessa snaps.

'I know this is hard, but in the case of women abducting newborns, it's highly unusual for the baby to be harmed in any way. Usually they take them because they have an overwhelming want – or need – for a child to care for. Chances are, Bonnie is perfectly safe.'

'You are kidding, aren't you?' Charlie stomps around the kitchen, pulling at her hair. 'Safe? Jesus Christ!'

Sanchez flushes. 'By that I mean she's probably being very well cared for. I know that's hard to hear, even so.'

Vanessa sighs heavily, and covers her face with her hands. 'We. Just. Want. Her. Back.'

'There is something else…' Sanchez hesitates and looks from Vanessa to Charlie, as though weighing up whether the information should be introduced into this fraught atmosphere.

'Go on.' Charlie stops pacing.

'Uniformed officers from Sussex Police returned to your dad's ex-wife's flat in the early hours of Tuesday morning.'

'And?'

Sanchez flushes. 'There was evidence she had been there very recently. The bed had been slept in and there were used nappies in the bin.'

'Dear God, and they missed her?' Vanessa shares a look of disbelief with her daughter, shaking her head. 'They should have been watching the place, waiting for her to go back there!'

'I can only assume they thought the chance of her returning home was non-existent. Since the appeal had gone out on TV, it would have been very risky behaviour. And at that point they didn't have intel on the car Mrs Glynn… the former Mrs Glynn… was driving. We found that out a few hours later.'

'But surely they can access footage that shows where she went next?' Vanessa reasons.

'Exactly.' Sanchez adopts a positive tone. 'Tech support are examining footage from all the routes out of Hove, and they will find something. And at least we know that she's stayed relatively local. I know it's disappointing that they just missed her, but it means she hasn't had the chance to go very far. That's a positive thing. We *are* getting closer. We're starting to build up a picture of Marian's recent movements.'

'If you say so,' Charlie mutters darkly, as her mother shows Sanchez to the front door.

She flicks on the TV news again, but her mother comes back into the kitchen and switches it off.

'I meant it: you need to take a break. I'm running you a bath and then I'm going to ask Hannah to come over.'

'They missed her, Mum,' Charlie says, bleakly. 'They almost found her, and then they missed her.'

'I know it's frustrating, but DC Sanchez is right, it's a good thing. They are getting closer.'

Charlie chews the side of her thumb. 'Do you really believe that, though?'

'I have to. And you have to, too. Otherwise you're going to completely fall apart.'

55

PAULA

Paula stares at what she now privately calls 'the Spider phone', but it doesn't ring.

She's carried it with her constantly since she and Johnny returned from Stepney. She slept with it on her pillow, switched on and volume turned up, but it remains inert. Taking leave of absence from work now feels like a waste of time, when all she's doing is staring at a cheap handset that, according to its label, was made in India.

Finally, at five thirty on Wednesday it buzzes into life. A text arrives, then another, then another. Paula sits on the edge of the bed squinting at the poor quality screen and trying to make sense of what she's reading. There's no preamble, no 'Hi, this is Spider.' Just information.

> *Vodaphone has contract phone registered to Mrs M. A. Glynn, 36 Cavendish Court, The Parade, Hove. Last used on Wednesday 27th November, then service discontinued.*

Paula scrolls to the second text.

> *Have checked distributors of SIM-only packages within one mile of Cavendish Court, Hove. Nearest one is PayRite*

convenience store. My local contact spoke to employee Abshir Mahad. Claims to know Marian Glynn by sight, as she popped in frequently. Last saw her in the shop on Wednesday 27th.

The text ends there. With shaking hands, Paula opens the next.

She used the in-store ATM to withdraw a large amount of cash, and bought a SIM card. Mahad says she'd changed her appearance and thought this sufficiently unusual to keep a note of the phone number associated with that SIM. Have tracked that number to London, back to Hove on Monday evening, then to the Happy Lodge Motel on the A259 near Folkestone on Tuesday morning. The SIM went out of service at that location later on Tuesday and has not been used since. Given the route Glynn used, my guess is that she is somewhere in Kent.

After reading and rereading the messages, Paula summons Johnny, who arrives at her house just after the children have returned from school.

'Bloody hell, he's good, isn't he, this Spider?' Johnny says, once he's read the texts. He's brought the obligatory bottle of red wine with him, and pours them both a glass. 'The Old Bill could do worse than to employ him.'

'Somehow I don't really think that's his style,' Paula says, drily. 'But do you think we should share this with the police? I was thinking I should call Detective Inspector Stratton.'

She walks over to the stove and stirs the beef chilli she started making to distract herself.

Johnny is shaking his head vehemently. 'No. Not right now. Apart from anything else, Spider doing what he's doing without authorisation and for financial gain is illegal. And by procuring his services, I reckon we could be charged with a crime too. Though, honestly, I doubt in the circumstances it would come to that.' He helps himself to some of the garlic bread Paula has just taken out of the oven. Biscuit hovers at his side, waiting to scoop up any crumbs. 'But I know I don't want to risk it. Do you?'

She shakes her head.

'Anyway, his guess that she's in Kent is just that: a guess. With her phone off, the only chance of tracking her is going to be picking up the car on ANPR. Which means the police still have the edge over us. They'll probably get to her first anyway.'

Paula sighs, pushing a hank of wavy hair off her face. 'It's not a race, Johnny. There's a baby's life at risk.'

She puts packets of instant rice in the microwave to heat and goes into the hall to shout upstairs to Ben and Jessica.

'Tea in ten minutes, kids!'

When she comes back into the kitchen, Johnny is holding up the Spider phone with a look of triumph. 'We just got another message!'

They read it together.

Marian Glynn background: parents both dead; one sister, Carolyn, emigrated to New Zealand 1992. Social media and networking sites show zero active accounts but have recovered a deleted Facebook account, used sporadically between 2007 and 2010. Very little online interaction, other than occasional messages between her and a Lilian Hadfield, born in 1954. In comments they address one another as 'cousin'. Search of GRO records proves they are first cousins: Lilian's mother was Priscilla Webber, Marian's paternal aunt, and she married a John Hadfield. Lilian Hadfield address: 9 Ashleigh Gardens, Woking, Surrey.

'Is that it?' Paula asks, disappointed. 'An address for a cousin she hasn't been in touch with for a decade? How's that going to help?'

'It's something, though, isn't it?' Johnny asks. 'A family member, someone who knows the woman. Surely it's worth trying to speak to her.'

Paula shakes her head firmly, sticking her head out into the hall again. 'Kids! Wash your hands, please!' She looks back at Johnny. 'Waste of time, if you ask me.'

'That's as may be, but right now it's all we've got.'

At ten thirty the following morning, Johnny's car turns off the M25 into Woking, with a sullen Paula sitting in the passenger seat.

'Ashleigh Gardens… can you find it on your phone? Paul?'

She squints at the screen reluctantly. 'Carry on down the A320 till you get to the common, then turn right and it's on your left.'

Ashleigh Gardens turns out to be the epitome of Home Counties respectability, with deep grassy verges, manicured hedges and off-street parking. They knock on the front door of number nine – a trim red-brick semi – but there's no reply.

'See, I told you this was a waste of time.' Paula sighs. She waits a few seconds and knocks again, as though this will prove her point. 'Come on, let's go.'

'No, wait a sec.' Johnny points up the street. 'Someone's coming.'

A tall woman is approaching on foot, carrying two shopping bags. She has highlighted blonde hair that doesn't quite disguise the grey underneath, and is dressed in tailored wool trousers, a camel coat and what Paula thinks of as 'sensible' shoes. A pair of glasses hangs on a cord around her neck.

'Hi.' Johnny steps into her path, flashing his most charming smile. 'Are you Lilian Hadfield?'

'Yes.' She seems flustered, and a little annoyed. 'Are you from the estate agents? Only I asked for an appointment this afternoon, and I was told—'

'No, we're not the estate agents.'

Her frown deepens. 'Good God, please don't tell me you're from the press. Because I've no comment to make.' She turns away abruptly and hurries up the path to the front door.

Of course, thinks Paula, *the poor woman's seeing her cousin all over the national news.* She's the type who would find the public shame deeply humiliating. She had mentally rehearsed a speech on the car journey, but it deserts her now.

'Please, please can we talk to you?' She reaches out and catches the hem of Lilian's coat sleeve. 'Please, this is really important.'

Lilian pulls away angrily, but Johnny has moved deftly around her, intercepting her before she can reach the front door. 'Just give us a few seconds of your time, that's all we ask. I swear we're not from the newspapers.'

'I'm not asking you in.' Lilian's tone is still wary, but she stops and turns to face them.

'I'm related to Bonnie Glynn,' Paula tells her, a sudden rush of emotion making her voice quiver slightly. It's so strange to be saying those words out loud to a stranger. 'The baby that's been taken by Marian. By your cousin. I'm her mum's aunt.'

'They don't know that for certain,' Lilian snaps. 'That Marian is responsible. That's just supposition.'

'I think it's a little more than that,' Johnny says, trying to keep his tone neutral.

'Well, I can't help you anyway, I'm sorry. I haven't been in contact with Marian for years, and I've barely seen her since we were children. And even then we weren't all that close. She's quite a bit younger than me. We saw each other for Christmas sometimes, that's all. And spent part of the summer together, at our grandparents' holiday place.'

'So you don't know where she might be now?' Paula presses.

'No, I'm sorry, I have no idea. And even if I did, it would be the police I would share that information with, not complete strangers.' She brushes Johnny aside and puts her key in the front door. 'Now, if you'll please excuse me…'

The door is slammed in their faces.

'Now what?' Paula asks Johnny. 'This is all we had to go on. Where do we go now?'

He shrugs. 'The way I see it, there's only one place we *can* go.'

The door to Spider's flat is inched open a crack. 'Hello?' The voice, unexpectedly, is high and female.

'Um, is Spider there?'

The door is opened a little further, admitting just enough light from the communal stairwell for Paula and Johnny to see who they're talking to. She's petite, of Korean or Japanese descent. Her hair hangs in a glossy dark bob and she's dressed only in a T-shirt. The cats snake between her bare legs.

'Are you his girlfriend?' Paula asks.

'His wife.'

'Well, well, well.' Johnny is amused. 'The bloke is full of surprises, I'll give him that.'

Behind her, a door opens and Spider emerges into the semi-darkness of the flat's hallway, wearing nothing but a pair of orange boxer shorts. Although it's now after midday, it's clear that Spider's day has yet to start. Nor is he happy at their arrival.

'Not much point you being here, unless it's to pay me. I've done all I can with the information that's out there on Marian Glynn.' His deep voice and middle-class vowels are at odds with the squalor and stale air of the flat.

'Please, Spider.' Having just driven for an hour and a half from Woking to Stepney, bickering with Johnny most of the way, Paula is quite prepared to beg. 'We spoke to Marian's cousin, but she hasn't seen her in a long time and knows nothing. She really only knew her when they were both children, and had summer holidays together.'

Spider's eyes glint in the darkness. 'Where?'

'Where what?'

'Where did they go on holiday?'

Johnny and Paula exchange a glance. 'She didn't say, mate,' Johnny tells him. 'Just that it was at their grandparents' place.'

Spider has already turned and is heading back to the bedroom, pulling his tiny wife by the wrist. 'Leave the phone on. I'll get back to you.'

Johnny has a business meeting in Watford that afternoon, and after a fractious and frustrating day, he and Paula mutually agree that they will not meet up that evening.

Instead, she takes the children bowling and buys them burgers for tea as a treat. They both go up to bed early, leaving Paula to a welcome hour alone with her thoughts.

'On the fifth day since baby Bonnie Glynn was snatched from a North London flat, police say an expanded task force is actively following up crucial leads…'

She has just switched off the TV in disgust when the Spider phone buzzes with a text.

Land Registry search shows a property called Wader's End, in Stodmarsh, Kent, belonged to Mr Ernest Webber between 1955 and 1983. Earnest Webber was father of Norman and Priscilla Webber, Marian Glynn's father and aunt. Ordnance Survey reference for the property is latitude 51.300553, longitude 1.1832079. It was compulsorily purchased to form part of the Stodmarsh National Nature Reserve, now unoccupied apart from occasional use for birdwatching.

A second text arrives, giving bank sort and account codes, and naming an eye-wateringly large fee for Spider's services. *I guess that means he's done*, Paula thinks.

She spends a couple of minutes reading and rereading the first text, then fetches her laptop from the kitchen and opens Google Earth, inputting the coordinates. She wasn't particularly good at geography at school, but from only a brief glance at the map she can see that there's a logical line east from Hove, to Folkestone to Stodmarsh. It makes sense as a journey. Paula's heart quickens. Could Wader's End be Marian Glynn's destination?

She copies and pastes the content of the text to Johnny. He replies with one word.

Bingo

56

MARIAN

On Friday, Marian has to drive to the nearest town again.

She has already run out of firewood, which has to be burned constantly day and night in an attempt to keep their accommodation heated. And this time she needs to visit a pharmacy too. Saffron has developed a snuffle and a slight temperature, so she urgently needs to buy some Calpol.

Her hat is pulled down and her scarf pulled up as she pushes the buggy along the high street but, even so, she is convinced that everyone is staring at her. They try to peep into the buggy too, usually beaming in that indulgent way people do when they see an angelic new baby, but Marian refuses to slow down or make eye contact. Sometimes she is convinced they stare after her and whisper, and that makes her fearful.

She has started to wonder how long they will be able to stay in this place. The constant battle against the cold is starting to wear her down, and she can't ignore the possibility that it's affecting Saffron's health. They need to be somewhere warmer, at least until the winter is over. The ideal would be to go abroad, to France perhaps, or even Spain. Using her passport is out of the question though, and she would have no idea how to obtain one in a different name. She's sure she read somewhere that if you take a ferry crossing to Ireland, you're not required to show a passport.

So perhaps Ireland is a possibility. Research is needed, and for that she will have to switch on her phone again. Trying to solve one problem always creates a new one.

Reluctant though she is to admit it, she's starting to grow tired. Being cold makes you tired. And although Saffron is a model baby, she's still very young and needs feeding during the night. And since she became ill, she's waking more frequently and is harder to settle.

The Calpol will help, she tells herself, after she has loaded her purchases and the carrycot into the car and driven 'home'. Maybe Saffron will sleep better once she's had a couple of doses, and Marian herself will feel better rested. Better able to cope. Because whatever happens, she and her baby are staying together. For the rest of their lives. For always.

Marian gives Saffron a dose of the medicine and walks around the kitchen with her over one shoulder, patting her back with one hand and unpacking her groceries with the other.

She wonders what sort of an evening meal she will be able to prepare with no cooker or microwave, just an old kettle that takes an eternity to boil. For something hot, she's limited to packet soup or instant noodles. Otherwise it's variations on a sandwich theme. There's no toaster, but she decides to try toasting a slice of bread over the open fire.

After a frustrating thirty minutes and a lot of choking wood smoke, she manages to revive the waning blaze in the grate. She feeds and settles Saffron, then sets about making toast over the flames. It singes at the edges and the fork gets so hot she can barely hold it, but eventually she has a couple of slices that she can smother with butter. The sensation of the melted butter on her tongue makes the struggle almost worthwhile.

But this situation will not be tenable for much longer, Marian is forced to accept that. With the baby still sleeping, she reaches into her bag for her phone. Switching it on long enough to do some online research is now a necessary evil. There's the issue of money to think about too. She was paid until the end of November, so her monthly salary recently cleared into her account, but she doubts she will still be paid any longer. The university will surely be aware of her… situation by now.

As she's waiting for the phone to boot up – wondering whether she will be able to get any signal – she hears a sound.

Instantly she freezes.

But there it is, and it's unmistakable. The sound of a car.

Somebody has driven down the track. Who would do that, given that from the road there's no indication whatsoever of the building's existence? Marian presses herself against the wall and squints sideways through the window. It's not a police car, she can see that at once. It's black, shiny and expensive-looking. Two people get out: a tall, handsome man and a woman.

The woman is instantly familiar. At first, panic rising, Marian thinks it's her: the girl who claimed to be Saffron's mother. But no, it's not her. As the woman walks towards the front door, the memory clicks into place and she realises who it is. It's Lizzie Armitage's little sister. Paula.

Adrenalin surges through her, and with it comes crystal clarity. She snatches up the car keys first, then the baby in her carrycot. She darts to the back door and runs out to the hire car, pressing the automatic door release on the key fob as soon as she's within reach.

'Oi!' the man shouts. 'Wait!'

Marian dumps the carrycot on the back seat and leaps into the driving seat, throwing the car into gear. Paula Armitage stares in shock, then starts pointing and shouting. The man says something to her and she takes out her phone and jabs at the keypad. The man, meanwhile, leaps into the path of her car and waves his arms to and fro across the front of his body, a flagging motion meant to indicate that she should stop.

She does not stop.

She squeezes the accelerator with her foot and lurches towards him. He only just has time to leap out of the path of her vehicle, stumbling to the ground as her nearside front wheel hits him on the leg. Still she doesn't stop. She drives faster, careering over the bumps on the track, the carrycot bouncing on the back seat as she does so. Saffron starts to scream but she keeps going.

Paula and the man are in their car now, with Paula at the wheel. But Marian knows this strip of land like the back of her hand, knows every twist and pothole, and despite their more powerful vehicle, she manages to out-drive them. As she turns right onto the main road she looks into her rear-view mirror, but they're no longer there. She's escaped.

57

PAULA

Wader's End turns out to be little more than a timber shack.

The former birdwatching hide perched on stilts at the edge of the marshes has been modified and extended to create a single storey house, of sorts.

'Is this it?' Paula asks, as they bump down the long rutted track.

'It has to be,' Johnny replies, glancing at the app on his phone. 'We put the grid reference into the map. There's someone in, anyway – look.' There's a white car parked outside, and smoke is coming from the chimney.

Paula instinctively presses her hand to her mouth and exhales hard through her fingers. 'Oh my God... this is it.' She reaches for her phone. 'We need to call the police, right?'

'In a minute. But let's just make sure it is Marian Glynn then try and talk to her. A police car showing up is bound to panic her, and someone who's panicked is more likely to do something stupid. Keep your phone at the ready though, okay?'

They get out of the car and start walking to the front door, but while they're still several yards away, a woman with short auburn hair shoots around the side of the building. She's carrying the top compartment of a baby's buggy, and before Paula and Johnny have had time to react, she slings it on to the back seat of the white car and opens the driver's door. The engine starts and the car moves forward.

'Call 999!' Johnny barks, stepping to his left to try and block the car's path.

The car drives straight at him, the roar of its acceleration audible. Johnny flings his body to the right. He just avoids being run over, but the front wheel clips his left leg.

'Oh, Christ!' Paula wails, 'Johnny, are you okay?'

'Never mind me.' He speaks through gritted teeth as he pulls himself to a standing position. 'Come on, get in the car!'

'Did you phone them? The police?'

Paula daren't turn to look in Johnny's direction. She's driving his car well above the speed limit, desperately trying to keep the white car in her sights.

'I was about to, but I didn't get through,' she tells him, keeping her eyes straight ahead. Her heart is hammering so hard that she can feel her torso shaking. 'I hung up when the car hit you. How's your leg now?'

'Reckon my ankle's broken.' She can hear the catch in his voice, even though he's trying to play it down. 'But that's going to have to wait. I'll call the cops now.'

He attempts to give a concise summary of the situation, but it still takes him a couple of tries to get the operator to understand where they are and why.

'On the A253 eastbound... heading for the A299... yes, we're following a vehicle driven by Marian Glynn... we're pretty sure she's got that baby girl who was abducted... a white Mitsubishi saloon with plate number C something... 18... J something. Can't read it properly. Okay, thanks.' He hangs up. 'She said they're sending "units". Reckon it'll be the flying squad.'

Ten minutes later, as they're nearing the coast, they finally hear the wail of police sirens. Paula pulls into the slow lane to allow the two marked cars to race past her then speeds up again. Ahead of them, the white Mitsubishi is driving at reckless speed, eventually careering off the main road and onto the path that leads to the white cliffs of Pegwell Bay.

'Oh dear God,' Paula says, braking instinctively. 'She's going to crash!'

The white car has been abandoned at a crazy angle, the bonnet steaming in the cold air, doors left open.

'Look!' Johnny points to a large stand of trees at the end of a sandy path. Marian Glynn is running along it with Bonnie clutched against her chest. The baby is screaming with distress. Three officers in flak jackets – two male and one female – are following her, one talking into an Airwave set.

An ambulance appears just as Johnny and Paula start to run too, Johnny limping and swearing.

'Oh, Christ, Paul, look!'

At the end of the wooded area there is a thin strip of chalky ground, and then nothing. A sheer hundred-foot drop off the cliffs to rocky ground and salt marshes.

Marian Glynn plants her feet deliberately at the very edge, the baby still clutched to her. 'Don't!' she shouts to the police officers. 'If you come any nearer, I swear, I'll jump.'

To make her point she slides her right foot backwards, sending a shower of gravel over the cliff edge.

They step back, but the female officer holds up a compact loud hailer. 'Marian, please just let me have Bonnie. We're happy to just talk, but to keep her safe, why don't you let me hold her.'

Marian shakes her head vigorously. 'She's called Saffron. And she's staying with me. Forever. If I jump, she's coming with me.'

Paula feels a ringing in her ears, as though she's going to faint. She glances at Johnny, who shares her look of alarm. 'See if she'll talk to you, Paul,' he hisses. 'It's got to be worth a try.'

Her heart thudding, Paula approaches one of the policemen. 'I know her,' she says. 'I've known her for ages, since I was a kid. Can I try talking to her?'

'Best leave it to the experts, love,' he tells her. 'Safest you stay back.'

But Marian is shaking her head. 'Let me talk to Paula,' she says. 'There's something I need to tell her.'

The policeman nods. 'Take it gently, okay? Very gently. Don't get too close.'

The bones in Paula's legs have turned to fluid and her mouth feels as though it's filled with sand. Her brain is commanding her feet to move, but nothing happens. Eventually she shuffles a few steps forward, until she's about ten feet away from Marian. The baby squirms in her arms, but she's calmer now.

'This is Saffron,' Marian says. 'She's one of Lizzie's twins.'

Paula senses it would be wrong to contradict her. 'I know,' she says, simply.

'Lizzie had a boy, too. I took care of them both. His name was Noah.'

Paula pictures the little blue blanket with its embroidered 'N', disinterred with his skeletal remains. Tears start in her eyes.

'Noah. That's a lovely name. Lizzie would have liked it.'

'Noah died. He died when he was ten days old.'

Paula nods. 'Yes, I know he did. They found him.'

'I gave him a proper burial. You do realise that, don't you?' Marian's voice is scratchy, her eyes wild. She presses Bonnie's head against her shoulder. 'It's important you know that I didn't harm him. He was poorly, and he died in his sleep. Of natural causes. I swear on Saffron's life, I didn't hurt him.'

There's an unnatural silence. Paula is aware of the four people behind her, all watching her. Further back, Airwave sets crackle as the other officers talk into them. Are they waiting for her to try and snatch Bonnie from Marian? She feels as though she should try, but is simultaneously terrified she'll mess it up and both of them will go over the edge. Or all three of them.

'Marian…'

The two women's eyes meet. Panic washes over Marian's face, and she takes a half-step back.

Oh God, please no. Please don't.

And then it happens, very fast.

Marian extends her arms forwards, holding out baby Bonnie towards Paula. Shocked, her vision blurring, Paula steps forward and reaches for the baby, sinking her fingers into the blanketed bundle and stumbling backwards. Her relief is so intense, so violent, that she's only aware of the bodies rushing up behind her, taking the baby from her, before she realises what has just happened.

Marian was there, and then a split second later she was gone. There is nothing in front of Paula now but the chalky cliff's edge, and the bleak winter sky.

EPILOGUE

DECEMBER 2019

The sky above the cemetery is a heavy grey-white, presaging snow.

Some of the plots are festooned with coloured lights or trimmed with tinsel; an attempt by visitors to involve the deceased in the approach of Christmas.

As the Armitage party arrange themselves at the graveside, Wendy Armitage starts crying. Paula can't remember the last time she saw her mother in tears. Possibly two decades ago, when Wendy's own mother died.

But now she is sobbing openly as the tiny white coffin is lowered into the square hole that has been dug at the foot of her daughter's grave. A temporary headstone is in place while the permanent one is re-engraved. It says simply:

> *Elizabeth Jane Armitage*
> *15th March 1979 – 22nd July 2003*
> *Noah Armitage*
> *18th July 2003 – 28th July 2003*

The funeral director stands at a tactful distance, gloved hands crossed in front of his body, giving the family some time to reflect before the grave is filled in. Dear old Uncle Alan is there, stalwart as ever. Paula scans Ben's and Jessica's faces, but although they're sombre, they're dry-eyed. Other than her concern for them, her overriding emotion at this moment is relief. Relief that Noah could be buried in his mother's plot without the need to dig up Lizzie's ashes. That would have been more than she could bear.

'It's my fault,' Wendy whispers. 'I shouldn't have been so hard on her. If I'd not pushed her away, then this wouldn't have happened. My grandson would be alive.'

'You can't be sure of that,' Paula points out. 'Anyway, it's just as much my fault. I should have tried harder to convince you about Lizzie being pregnant.'

'You were just a kid.' Her mother links arms with her. 'You couldn't be expected to make things right.' She takes a bunch of half a dozen white roses from her bag and hands one each to Alan, Ben, Jessica and Paula. She places her own rose on top of the small coffin, and stands back while the others take it in turn to lay theirs.

Paula finds her mind wandering to Marian Glynn, who was not killed immediately by her fall from the cliff, but sustained critical injuries and died in intensive care four days later. She tries to picture Marian's funeral. She hopes she was not alone, that there were friends and family there.

'That fella of yours not coming then?' Wendy asks.

'I told him he was welcome, but he felt it should just be family,' Paula says, staring down at the white blooms. They look fragile, ephemeral in the frosty ground, their petals already dusted with fresh snow, which has just started falling.

She and Johnny had disagreed about the Glynns, too. Johnny thought she had every right to go and visit them once baby Bonnie had been returned to the Glynns' house in Laurel Road, but Paula did not feel it would be right. All she had wanted on that awful day two weeks ago was to see Bonnie safely in the care of the ambulance crew, then to return straight home to her own children.

'It's almost Christmas,' she told Johnny. 'Not the time for a stranger to be turning up at their door, reminding them of the past. Especially when the past nearly cost them their precious granddaughter.'

'You're not a stranger,' Johnny had remonstrated, 'You're Charlotte's family. Her aunt.'

The fat snowflakes fall heavier and faster. The funeral director is giving a subtle signal to the gravedigger to get started when there's the distinctive sound of wheels rolling over gravel. A tall, pretty girl with golden skin stands there, her hands on the handle of a sporty-looking buggy. Underneath her pink bobble hat, her hair is exactly the same colour as Paula's.

'I'm Charlie,' she says, simply. 'I hope I'm not too late.'

Wendy smiles. 'I'm Lizzie's mum. Your granny.'

She hands Charlie the last remaining white rose and they watch while she bends to lay it in the grave. 'For my twin,' she says, with genuine sorrow, before straightening up and facing Paula. 'I really wanted to say thank you. For what you did. Honestly, I can't ever thank you enough.'

Paula reaches out and puts a hand on her arm. 'No need to. I did it for me.'

She looks back at the gravestone, now capped with snow as white as the roses. 'And for Lizzie.'

A LETTER FROM ALISON

I'm delighted you have chosen to read *Her Sister's Child*. If you would like to stay informed about future releases, then click the following link to sign up. Your email address will not be shared, and you can unsubscribe at any time:

www.bookouture.com/alison-james

There have been plenty of instances where fiction tackles babies being snatched, but in *Her Sister's Child*, I wanted to take things further and explore what would happen to someone who committed this drastic act but then changed their mind. If you've enjoyed reading it, then do please leave a review. It's always valuable to receive feedback, and it helps more readers to discover my books. I also love connecting with readers, and welcome you getting in touch via Facebook, Twitter or Goodreads.

Alison James

 17361567.Alison_James

@AlisonJbooks

Alison James books

ACKNOWLEDGEMENTS

With profound thanks to my wonderful and talented editor Lucy Dauman, who helped keeping me going when things got tough.

Printed in Great Britain
by Amazon

36499062R00182